As we sat by the fire tonight, listening to Cyrus and Jubal spin their yarns about searching for gold, I marveled at this Jonathan and David relationship, the likes of which one rarely sees. Never have I witnessed it between a white man and a Negro. I love to listen to their plans of adventure, but it brings so much sadness. It's clear only one of them knows Cyrus isn't likely to leave this house alive, and when word reaches Charleston, Jubal's freedom must be stolen, rather than earned.

Prudence Willard
Marietta, Ohio
October 16, 1858

Secrets of Wayfarers Inn

Family Secrets
River of Life
All that Remains
Greater than Gold
A Flame in the Night
Never the Twain Shall Meet
The Innkeepers' Conundrum
At Face Value
Moonlit Shadows
Picture This
Forget-Me-Nots
All the Inn's a Stage
Stolen Goodbyes
Red, White, and True
The Secret Ingredient
Submerged Surprises
Hushed October

Hushed October

BECKY MELBY

Guideposts
New York

Secrets of Wayfarers Inn is a trademark of Guideposts.

Published by Guideposts Books & Inspirational Media
110 William Street
New York, NY 10038
Guideposts.org

Cover and interior design by Müllerhaus
Cover illustration by Greg Copeland, represented by Deborah Wolfe, LTD.
Typeset by Aptara, Inc.

Printed and bound in the United States of America
10 9 8 7 6 5 4 3 2

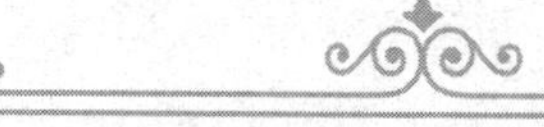

Chapter One

October 11, 1858
Marietta, Ohio

Prudence Willard set her mending down and rested against the back of her rocking chair. The days were getting chillier, and the warmth of the fire dancing in the hearth was welcome. She waited for her husband to look up from cleaning his rifle. When he did, he caught her staring at him and smiled.

"What is on thy mind, Wife?"

"Another letter from Catherine Fay."

Jason sighed. "What will she be wanting from thee this time?"

"No more than I have offered. I wish to help her raise funds." When Jason's smile began to pucker into a scowl she said, "I know thee finds her somewhat...overbearing, but it is just her way. Imagine the obstacles encountered by a woman in such an undertaking. She now has nine orphans in that two-room cottage out by Moss Run. All of them under ten years. And she is encountering problems at every turn. They have had threats against the children, their property has been vandalized, and now she needs to hire a tutor to come to the home because there are those who have blocked the children from attending school." She was aware her voice was rising right along with her renewed indignation, but she felt powerless to control it. "She may be a bit strong in her approach, but she is a lone woman advocating for helpless children in a world—"

"Dominated by men." Jason's eyes twinkled, and not only because they reflected the firelight. "I am only too aware of the strength needed to be a woman who is out to singlehandedly alter the future of humanity." He reached out and took her hand. "My concern is only for one woman whose tender heart I must protect." He squeezed her hand. "Thee can only do so much." He nodded toward the open Bible on the small table between them. "I have kept record. Does thee know how many desperate souls thee has led to freedom?"

"The numbers do not matter." In truth, she did know. Eighteen children and forty-three adults, plus three women heavy with child, two who gave birth while in hiding in the secret room at the Riverfront House. The numbers did not matter to those who were yet living in bondage on plantations south of the Ohio, nor to the orphans Catherine, known affectionately to those close to her as Katie, had rescued from unspeakable conditions in the county infirmary where they'd been hidden from public conscience, housed alongside alcoholics and mentally unstable adults.

Prudence considered her husband her greatest blessing. The dear man had only one flaw—his wish to protect her from giving overmuch to the work that fed her very soul.

With quick, efficient movements she folded her lap robe, set it on the basket next to her chair, and stood. Wrapping her shawl tighter across her shoulders, she stepped away from the hearth. "Would thee like more tea?"

Jason fingered a small square of powder-stained muslin as he stared at her. They had been together long enough for her to read an entire book in one of his stares. The slight upturn of the right side of his mouth said he would let the subject lie. For now. "I have had plenty of tea, but I would not refuse were thee to offer another piece of pie."

Prudence laughed, as usual, unable to remain disgruntled with this man for long, and picked up the knife to cut a slice of apple pie. "I am happy with our apples this year. They—"

Blue, Jason's old hound, howled from the front porch. A low voice and a knock at the door followed. Prudence swung toward the door, knife in hand.

"I do not believe that will make for a hospitable greeting, my love." Though Jason's tone was light, she heard the rapid click of his rifle snapping back together.

"I am afraid I am a bit nervous tonight." She set the knife down, wiped her hands on her apron, picked up a lamp, and went to the door, keeping her body shielded behind it as Jason had taught her.

She opened the door. Her shoulders lowered, and she breathed a sigh. "Ambrose. How good to see thee. Come in." She stopped short of a curtsy. She'd been taught the Quaker ways since she was taken in by her adoptive family when she was twelve—a hungry, terrified Melungeon girl running for her life. Still, the manners her mother had taught her, and the rules of conduct for a slave girl, were ingrained. A woman should curtsy and address a man by his title. Not so with the Society of Friends, who treated all as having equal standing. Were she still on the Fitzhugh Plantation in Virginia, her head would be bowed as she referred to this man as "Elder Morris" or "Sir."

"Don't get up, Jason." Ambrose strode to the fire. Turning his back to it, he glanced at Prudence and then back to Jason. "I have something to ask of thee. An imposition, in truth."

"Yes?" Jason leaned forward, hands clasped.

"There is a gentleman, a visitor to Marietta, who is in a"—Ambrose cleared his throat—"difficult position. The family he came to see has left town, and the man is not well. He and his servant need a safe place to stay."

"Safe?" Jason stood and laid his hunting rifle on the table.

Ambrose shifted from one foot to the other. "Truth is, someone's after them. They don't know who...and they don't know why."

"Too tight." Tess Wallace's strangled whisper matched the reddening of her face reflected in her antique vanity mirror.

Janice Eastman, one of her two best friends and business partners, tugged at the back of the vintage-styled dress. "Only one more button. Suck in."

"I am." Tess could only mouth the words as Janice forced the last button through its hole.

"There." Janice fingered a pagoda sleeve on the rust, brown, and sage-green plaid dress. "Perfect colors for your hair." She picked up the hairpiece Tess would pin to the back of her head to give the illusion of an 1850s hairstyle—long tresses braided and twisted into a bun. The swirl of faux hair glinted copper in a shaft of morning sun streaming through the fourth-floor window. "You'll look positively Scarlett O'Hara-ish."

"A sixty-four-year-old Scarlett would have gotten over herself and wouldn't be vain enough to wear something she couldn't breathe in." Tess gripped the side of her dresser. "Unbutton it before I pass out."

Thankfully, the tiny pearl buttons slid out much easier than they'd slid in. "I could let it out a bit," Janice said, but Tess heard the doubt in her voice. Tess had already checked the seams. Not much extra fabric for "letting out."

When she was finally set free, Tess gasped, "No more cinnamon rolls." She collapsed on the bed. "I have to drop a couple of pounds before the Heritage Tour."

"We can do that if we really put our minds to it."

"We?"

Janice nodded as she patted the space just above her waist. "Unless I want to spend the day strapped into a corset, I have to lose an inch or two." They'd ordered the dresses from an online seamstress two months ago, not taking into consideration the allure of the goodies produced by Wayfarers Inn Bed & Breakfast and Soup Café's extraordinary cook, Winnie Washington. Including the big-as-a-man's-hand pumpkin cinnamon roll Tess had devoured a few minutes ago.

"Bet LuAnn's dress fits perfect." Tess didn't bother disguising her envy. The third member of the Inn Crowd, as the owners of Wayfarers Inn called themselves, had been blessed with a naturally trim figure. Well, to be fair, LuAnn Sherill possessed something else neither Janice nor Tess excelled at when it came to healthy living…self-discipline.

"It probably does. And speaking of bet, wanna make one?"

Tess sat up. Holding the bodice of the plaid dress to her chest, she fanned her face with her other hand. "Why, Miz Eastman, what are you proposin'?" She gave her best Scarlett impression. "Fine-bred Christian ladies do not bet."

Janice feigned a look of remorse. "A contest then. Nothin' wrong with a little friendly competition. We agree on a goal, then whoever doesn't make it has to donate to the Moore House fund."

"I like it." Tess stood and scooped up her much more comfortable twenty-first century outfit—non-skinny jeans and a sweater with a pumpkin embroidered on the front. "How much?"

"It has to be painful enough to motivate us. How about—"

LuAnn's entrance interrupted whatever Janice was about to suggest.

"Are you guys talking about me again?" LuAnn tucked sleek silver hair behind one ear. Without waiting for an answer to her question, she beckoned with one hand toward the door that led to the hallway of their fourth-floor living quarters. "Come downstairs. Elliott wants to show us what he found out back."

"Elliott...the metal-detecting guy?" Tess asked. Five new guests had checked in this morning, and she hadn't had time to attach names to faces yet.

"Yep." LuAnn smiled. "You'll be proud of me. I restrained my history-loving self and said I couldn't look at any of it until you two are there." She took a step back and pivoted. "So you'd better hurry."

Janice followed LuAnn, leaving Tess alone to get dressed. As she ran fingers through her short spiky hair, she scanned a row of framed pictures hanging above her dresser. There were six of them, and they formed a timeline of the phases of her life. The first was taken when she was nine, on a weekend getaway with her parents the day Cedar Point amusement park opened Blue Streak, a seventy-eight-foot-high wooden roller coaster. Next, a wedding picture of her and Jeffrey standing on the church steps, oblivious to anyone in the world but each other. Number three was taken the day they adopted Lizzie. Five-year-old Jeff Jr. sat in the middle, grinning as he held his new baby sister. The next picture of her and Jeffrey alone never failed to tug at her heartstrings. Their re-honeymoon trip, he'd called it. California redwoods formed the backdrop. She leaned on his shoulder, his head rested on hers. Two years later a stroke took his life.

She'd thought, for a while, there would be no more smiling photographs, but the next two pictures were proof her joy had dimmed but not disappeared. One showed Tess with three giggly toddlers on her lap. *Three.* The thought still shocked her at times. She remembered the day Lizzie and Michael arrived at her house after the ultrasound. "Three, Mom. *Three,*" Lizzie had stammered over and over. Henry, Harper, and Liam had turned four in April. The last picture was only a few months old. Tess and LuAnn and Janice standing on the stairway, proud new owners of Wayfarers Inn. "Thank You, Lord," Tess whispered as she shut the door to her apartment then descended three flights of stairs to the café where LuAnn and Janice waited with Elliott MacIntosh.

It only took a moment for Tess to catalog Elliott as one of the inn's most colorful visitors to date. Larger than life in more ways than one. The many-pocketed Scotch-plaid vest he wore with equally pocketed cargo pants broke all the rules of clothing that camouflages an ample waistline. With a swoop of his arm, Elliott gestured toward a white cloth that covered one of the square tables. "Are you ready for the reveal, ladies?" Bushy red-streaked-with-white eyebrows wiggled, independent of each other.

Tess pointed at the drab-green zippered pouch Elliott held. "Tell me you found something that will pay off our mortgage."

"Sadly, no. But I guarantee you will be richer in historical knowledge." He winked then gave a jovial laugh, his belly jiggling like a Scotch-plaid Santa. He pulled out a rectangular object about two inches wide. "I'm guessing this belt buckle is Civil War era."

LuAnn gushed over the piece of tarnished metal. Having taught history for more than three decades, she had a genuine passion for rusty artifacts. Tess tried to appear interested but couldn't hide her disappointment as Elliott pulled out two wheat pennies, a suspender clasp, and a bent-up lamp sconce.

"And now"—Elliott tapped out a drum roll on the table—"the *pièce de résistance*." He reached into his bag. "This Art Deco piece is from the early twentieth century. You could probably get a hundred and fifty dollars for it, but I'm guessing you'll want it right over there on your front desk." Slowly, he pulled his hand out then carefully set something on the palm of his other hand, revealing a reception desk bell with a decorative brass base and "Wayfarers Inn" etched in the brass dome.

"Whoa..." Janice and LuAnn echoed each other, and Tess found herself mouthing the same word. They gave Elliott the honor of placing it on the front desk. The ornately carved desk had once been used as a bar and had sat below the massive mirror that still hung at the back of the café.

"The inn used to be called the Riverfront House," LuAnn said. "It was renamed Wayfarers Inn around the time of World War I."

Elliott lightly tapped the bell. "Maybe this was a grand reopening gift."

"Maybe..." LuAnn looked thoughtful, and Tess knew she was daydreaming back to a time when Woodrow Wilson was president and women's hemlines crept daringly above the ankle.

"Where to next?" Elliott looked at Tess. "I'm here on business, but I'm setting my own schedule. Today, I've got all the time in Ohio." He laughed. "Do you know anyone who wouldn't mind me detecting on their property? I'm meticulous about covering my tracks, and anything I find goes to the property owner. All I want is pictures and the right to share my finds online. Not in this to get rich…except in historical knowledge." He winked again, at no one in particular.

Tess didn't have to think long. She glanced at LuAnn. "Do you think Jerry and Amy would mind?"

LuAnn's eyes shot wide. "They put No Trespassing signs all over the property after that article came out, but we're friends, right?" She pulled out her phone. "I'll call." LuAnn stepped a few feet away.

"Article?" Elliott looked from LuAnn to Tess.

Tess drummed her fingers on the front desk. Where to start? "We found a journal belonging to a woman who once worked here at the inn back in the 1800s and was also a conductor on the Underground Railroad. The tract of land along the Muskingum River where she and her family lived belongs to the city, and the city council recently sold an acre of it to a foster family. The father is a paraplegic, and they want to take in children with disabilities. Right after they signed the deed, the *Marietta Times* came out with a story about a legend that says there was buried treasure on the property."

"Seriously?" Elliott rubbed his hands together.

“Probably not.” Tess laughed. “There are a lot of legends about this town. Anyway, they broke ground last week and found what they assume is part of a foundation wall for a barn.”

LuAnn turned around, slid her phone back into her pocket, and gave an uncharacteristic fist pump. “Jerry’s out there now. He said he doesn’t want just anybody hunting around on his land, but for us, absolutely.”

The gleam in Elliott’s eyes was almost comical. Tess stifled a laugh. “I need to be at our booth at the farmers market in about an hour. If we leave right away, you can follow me to the Moore House site, and I’ll introduce you to Jerry.”

“Perfect!” Elliott gave a three-finger salute. “Yesterday’s rain made the ground just right for digging. Lead the way!”

“...electricity flows through the coil, a magnetic field is created all around it. If you move the detector over a metal object, the moving magnetic field affects the atoms inside...” As they walked toward the spot where Jerry Moore sat in his wheelchair poring over a blueprint, Elliott gave Tess what he described as a “crash course in the science behind metal detecting.”

Tess did her best to pay attention, but Elliott had lost her at “the detector induces electrical activity in the metal, which creates magnetism...”

When he stopped for air, she asked, “How deep can it detect?” Hopefully the question would result in an answer she could understand.

"I have a couple of detectors. My two-box can produce findings more than a meter underground."

"That's incredible."

"Hey!" Jerry waved at them. It was good to see him smile.

"Almost a year ago, Jerry was injured on the job when a steel beam fell on him." Tess lowered her voice as they drew closer. "The doctors hoped the paralysis was temporary, but it wasn't. Jerry and his family adopted two kids and were fostering three more at the time of the accident. Several churches started raising funds to help them build an accessible home so they can continue fostering and take in kids with disabilities."

"Well then"—Elliott's apple cheeks rose in a grin—"we'll just have to find something they can sell for a hefty sum. I will give it my all." Again, the three-finger salute.

Tess introduced the two men, and Elliott spent a few minutes admiring the massive front loader parked behind Jerry like a long-necked yellow dinosaur before rattling off a well-rehearsed code of ethics.

Jerry laughed. "Have at it. *Mi tierra es tu tierra.*" Jerry swept his arm out to include the whole staked-out acre. "And don't bother filling your holes. You're only digging up weeds. This whole place will be sodded come spring…assuming we raise enough to pay for it."

Elliott stood at attention. "Mr. Moore, I intend to cover every inch of your property. If there's any bling or relics of value here, I will find them, and whatever I find is yours to do with as you please. If you're a praying man, now'd be a good time to ask for a little favor."

Jerry laughed again. "I am a praying man, sir, and we've been asking God for miracles since the day we first set eyes on this piece of land. So far, He hasn't disappointed."

Tess stood next to Jerry, looking over the blueprint while Elliott unpacked his gear, holding up each item and explaining its purpose. He extolled the wonders of his Fisher Gold Bug Pro detector, then went on to tell them about his digger, pinpointer, headphones, coil cover, extra coils, scoops, gloves, coin field guide, multi tool, batteries, and probes. There was even a whistle, "in case you scare up a bear." Something about his intensity struck Tess as funny, and she could tell Jerry was struggling to keep a straight face too.

They watched as Elliott put on headphones and began sweeping the ground, starting in the southwest corner and moving methodically to his right in uniform arcs, as if he had a grid drawn out in his head. He stopped several times. "Roundness!" he called out once, then "Silver!" and "Coinage!" He bent, stuck his probe in the ground, dug around the spot with a trowel, then lifted something that he gently brushed clean. "Whoot! '52 Rosie!" He held it up. "1952 S Roosevelt dime!"

"What's it worth?" Jerry called.

"Forty bucks, maybe."

Jerry smiled. "Find me about three hundred of those," he said, just loud enough for Tess to hear.

After depositing a smashed silver ring and a rusted toy car on Jerry's table, Elliott asked Tess if she'd like to give it a try.

"I have to get going, but maybe just for a minute."

Elliott explained the tones she'd hear if she ran across anything. "Junk finds like soda can pull tabs or 'can slaw'—that's shredded aluminum cans—will give a choppy, broken sound. A coin, or anything substantial, will give a distinctively solid tone. I'll set it to detect just about anything so you can have the fun of finding something, even if it's an old canning jar ring."

Tess put on the headphones and tried to copy Elliott's technique. She glanced out at the river with her second swipe, imagining Prudence Willard standing on this very spot, hanging clothes on the line or tending a garden. After reading Prudence's journal, Tess felt as if the woman who'd lived a hundred and fifty years ago had become a dear friend. Any connection to her was a treasure. A button or a hairpin that might have belonged to Prudence would make them, to quote Elliott, "richer in historical knowledge."

On her fifth arc, she heard something. "It wasn't very loud." She moved the detector slowly to her left until she heard it again.

Elliott looked at the screen. "Pretty strong. I'm guessing about five inches down. Let's try the pinpointer." With surprising agility, Elliott lowered to his knees and unholstered the orange instrument that reminded Tess of the toothbrush holder she used for travel. He pressed the pointer to the ground. A high-pitched beep sounded. "That's the spot." He pulled out a trowel and within seconds had a horseshoe-shaped cut. "Here." He handed her the trowel. "You do the honors of pulling the plug."

Tess knelt, slid the trowel under the grass, and lifted it like opening a can of cat food.

Elliott stuck the probe in the dirt and stopped when it began to vibrate. "If you don't want to get your hands dirty, I…"

Before he finished, she had shoved her fingers into the soft black earth. She let the dirt sift through her fingers, then tried again. "I feel something!" Her pulse picked up speed, a ridiculous response to what was likely a metal slug or bottle cap. But it was flat. And it wasn't round. She set the mud-caked square in the palm of her hand.

"Brush it off carefully," Elliott instructed, hovering over her shoulder.

Tess brushed until letters, and then numbers, appeared. When she held it like a diamond, so the words were readable, she noticed the hole in the top corner.

Elliott let out a long, low whistle. "I think I know what that is."

Tess ran her finger across the rusty, corroded surface then held it so the sunlight could hit it more directly. "CHARLESTON" arched over the other words.

CHARLESTON

1855

FIELD WORKER

2143

"That's a slave tag." Elliott's voice was hushed with reverence.

Tess nodded. She'd heard of them. When a plantation owner loaned out a slave to another property, the slave would be required to wear a tag.

"There've been a few found from other places, but Charleston's the only city that had a sophisticated system of recording slaves. Some of those records still exist. We might be able to find the name of the owner and the slave."

Tess stared at the dented piece of copper, imagining what it would have been like to be "loaned" to someone, to have no rights, no choice. Not a name, just a number. "How did it get here?"

Elliott shrugged. "Good question."

"I think we need to answer that question." She ran her finger across the number. "You had a name," she whispered. Hopes, dreams, maybe a family. As she started to hand it back to Elliott, she noticed scratches on the back. No. More letters and a date. She brushed off the loose dirt until she could make it out. Etched on the back in wobbly, uneven print, was the inscription:

1 Cor. 7:21

Oct. 20, 1858

Hopes, dreams…maybe they'd actually been realized. *Whoever you were, your story needs to be told.*

Chapter Two

River City Farmers Market, only a block from the Moore House site, was an explosion of color. Pumpkins, squash, and gourds piled high in the back of a pickup created a striking still life. Tess walked between tables laden with items that were "Handmade, homemade, or homegrown." Jars of jam, chunks of homemade soap, tomatoes, green peppers, zucchini, hand-stitched quilts, beaded bracelets, candles, cherry and apple pies, rows and rows of fresh baked bread, and a rainbow array of yellow, pink, and purple mums.

Tess stopped to talk to the woman sitting next to a hand-lettered sign for the Gospel Mission Food Pantry. Wayfarers Inn made regular donations of leftover baked goods to the worthy cause. As she carried a basket of pumpkin cinnamon rolls through the crowd, Tess greeted other familiar faces—friends from church and faithful patrons of the inn's soup café.

Brin McLoughlin waved as Tess approached the inn's booth. Brin, who'd transferred to Marietta College from Boston this semester, was, at least in the minds of Tess, LuAnn, and Janice, soon to become Janice's granddaughter. The relationship between Brin's mother and Janice's son Stuart had been blossoming since February when the two had reconnected after a twenty-year separation. Now that Brin was settled in her dorm and in the swing of the fall semester, she'd started working at the inn when she didn't have classes. Since Robin, one of their loyal employees, had taken two weeks off while her sister recovered from surgery, Brin's help was invaluable.

"Morning, Brin. How's business?" Tess set the basket on the ground and straightened the table tent sign that read, ALL PROFITS WILL BE DONATED TO THE MOORE HOUSE.

"Crazy busy." Brin retied her long, unruly curls in a hair band. "Good thing you brought more cinnamon rolls."

The farmers market booth was something new for the inn. If it turned out to be a success, they'd likely continue it in the spring. Good exposure, plus a way to give back to the community. Tess began arranging bags of individual rolls and boxes of four on the table. "Sorry I'm late. I have to show you what we found." She told Brin about Elliott, then pulled her phone out of her pocket to show her a picture of the tag.

"Seriously?" Behind her square-framed glasses, Brin's eyes widened. "This was actually worn by a slave before the Civil War?"

"What's that?" The voice seemed to appear from nowhere, but Tess didn't have to look up to know who lurked…*stood* in front of the table.

"*Maybelline.* Good morning." Tess almost had to laugh at the quizzical expression on the little woman's face. Maybelline ran the Marietta Underground Railroad Museum, known locally as simply the MURM. Though the woman had been the source of some stress for the Inn Crowd in the past, they'd come to realize she really had a good heart…a good heart that sometimes got overshadowed by her zeal for preserving the town's history.

"What's that you're looking at?" Maybelline ran slightly gnarled fingers with bright red fingernails through short hair that was her own unique shade of orangey-red. Tess guessed the gesture was an attempt to look relaxed when she was anything but. "Did you find something?"

To tell or not to tell, that was always the question when it came to Maybelline. The woman was a walking encyclopedia of facts on the Underground Railroad and the Civil War. She could be a wealth of information, or she could, as she'd done in the past, insist that anything relating to the Underground Railroad should be turned over to the MURM for safekeeping. Tess took a deep breath and decided to chance it. Without a word of explanation, she handed her phone across the table.

Maybelline lifted the glasses she wore on a cord around her neck. She squinted, then her eyes popped wide. "Do you know what this is? Did you find it at the inn? Where was it?"

Reluctant to give out any more information, Tess turned the questions back on the little woman who was nearly trembling with anticipation. "What can you tell us about it?"

"It's a slave tag! Do you have any idea how much this could be worth?"

"Worth?" The second Tess said it, she realized how dumb she sounded. It just hadn't crossed her mind that the tag could be of any value other than simply its historical significance.

Maybelline sighed like a teacher exasperated by students who weren't taking their lessons seriously. "I saw one sell for $20,000."

Brin gave a long, low whistle, and Tess almost choked as she involuntarily inhaled as if she'd been punched in the stomach. "Twen…ty…thou…sand?"

"Most wouldn't get anywhere near that, and you certainly aren't going to sell this."

We aren't? If Tess were the one to decide whether to hand a big fat check to the Moores or put the tag on display at the MURM, there was no question Maybelline would be disappointed in her decision.

"And, of course, you'd have to prove it wasn't a fake. Lots of fakes out there." Maybelline's eyes were still fixed on the phone now in Tess's hand.

"Who would bury a fake in—" She stopped. Jerry and his wife would have to decide if they wanted anyone to know about this. Legally, as Elliott had said before they'd started detecting, anything found on the Moores' property belonged to them. Tess pressed her lips together. She wouldn't say anything more about it to Maybelline. But she would say something to the Lord. *Father, the Moores could sure use twenty grand about now.*

When Maybelline realized she wasn't going to get any more information from Tess, she moved on but only after giving what sounded like a command. "Keep me in the loop on this, Tess."

As soon as Maybelline was safely out of earshot, Tess let out the breath she'd been holding. "Elliott says we might be able to find the name of the slave and the owner."

Brin reached for her purse then paused. "Do you want me to stay so you can go do research?"

"No. But thank you. I'm here to sell, not research. Present in the moment, not stuck in the past, you know." With a decisive nod, she shut off her phone's ringer. She gave Brin a quick hug, shrugging off the niggling thought that her offhanded remark about being present in the moment represented the exact thing God had been whispering in her ear for months. She turned to the woman who'd just approached the table.

"Mmm. Cinnamon rolls." A stark comparison to Maybelline, whose lips barely turned up when she smiled, this woman's round face seemed almost engulfed in merriment. "Don't suppose you have any with the carbs removed, huh?"

"I wish. I'm trying to take off a couple of pounds, and I promised myself this morning, right after I ate one, that I wouldn't touch another one all day." Tess grimaced. "Not a great sales pitch, is it?"

The woman grinned. "Actually, it is. You're saying they're hard to resist. Which is why I'm going to buy two. One for my husband and one for my son." She opened her wallet, pulled out a bill and a business card, and handed them to Tess.

"'God's Weigh'?" Tess somehow managed a straight face as she read the words on the card. "'Don't let the scale run your life, learn to live God's weigh.'" The card showed a meeting time and place. Was this for real?

"It's okay to laugh." The woman's eyes danced with mirth. "It's meant to be funny...but not." She extended her hand. "I'm Lynette Gibson. I'm the God's Weigh leader."

Taking the offered hand, Tess introduced herself.

"Oh, I've been to your café. Scrumptious. I always call ahead and make sure you have one of your broth-based soups before I come."

Note to self and Winnie: Make sure we always have lower carb and calorie options. "So this is a weight-loss group?"

"Yes. And no. It's a figure-out-who-God-made-you-to-be group. We talk about healthy choices—food, exercise, but also how we think about ourselves and about food. It's all about honoring God by taking care of what He's given us." Lynette's hand swept along her side. "We focus much more on the type of food we eat than counting calories. It's not one of those measure everything plans. I teach tips like looking at a restaurant meal as actually two. Divide it in half, and you have one meal to enjoy now and one for tomorrow. It's all positive, based on the things we can have, not the things we can't."

"I like your approach. Is it open to anyone?"

"Absolutely. Tuesday nights, seven o'clock, at Jeremiah's Coffee House." Lynette took the bag Tess handed her, opened it, and sniffed. "I'm learning to appreciate the beauty and smell of goodies like this without having to put it in my mouth. Maybe someday I'll learn how to take a couple of bites and save the rest for later. Until then..." She pulled an apple out of her purse. "Love to have you join us."

"I'd like that. Anything I need to bring?"

"Two dozen of these." Lynette pointed to the basket of cinnamon rolls, holding her deadpan expression just long enough for perfect comedic timing before bursting into an easy laugh. "Just yourself and your garbage." Lynette laughed again at the surprise that must have registered on Tess's face. "We all have it. The emotional junk we carry around contributes to us wanting to find solace in food. Don't you agree?"

Solace in food. She hadn't exactly thought of it that way, but maybe Lynette was right. "I'll have to think on that. I'll see you at the meeting."

Lynette held up her apple and flicked her wrist as if in toast. "Looking forward to it."

Janice would be at choir practice during the meeting time, so Tess wouldn't feel obliged to invite her. Maybe this was just "healthy competition" for a good cause—the Moore House and their waistlines—but it certainly wouldn't hurt to have a few secret weapons in her arsenal.

Lunch was in full swing when Tess returned to the inn. She set her empty basket and the wheeled cart holding the tablecloth, money box, and signs in the back entry and reached for her apron.

"How'd it go?" LuAnn asked, scurrying past her with a tray of empty soup bowls.

"Resounding success. I sold out by eleven thirty, then just stood around handing out brochures for the inn and telling everyone about the cinnamon rolls and snickerdoodles they missed out on. I really think this needs to be a regular thing next year. And…" Her pitch rose as she strung out the word. "I have to tell you all about metal detecting."

"Elliott told us. So exciting. I wish I could have been there. Wait till you see what's happening." With that, LuAnn deposited her tray by the sink, picked up a basket of muffins, and walked out the swinging door.

Janice walked in before the door stopped swinging. "Hey, it's the famous archeologist! How was the market?"

Tess filled her in while starting to empty the dishwasher. "LuAnn said something's happening. What did she mean?"

"I suppose she was talking about the comments Elliott is getting on his blog."

"Blog?" Tess slid a glass pitcher into the cupboard next to the sink, then turned to look at Janice.

"His metal detecting blog. Plus, he put your find on a couple of sites that have like a hundred thousand followers each. Wait till you hear what people are saying." Janice took two bowls of soup from Winnie, set them on a tray, and disappeared through the swinging door.

Tess set a stack of clean bowls on the back corner of Big Red, their vintage gas stove. Winnie looked up from ladling butternut soup into a bowl. "Sounds like my pumpkin rolls were a hit."

"People loved them. I probably sold a third of them to vendors who bought one, ate it, and then came back for a box or two. I know I shouldn't say this, but you really could open your own bakery."

"And leave this circus? No, ma'am, this place is way too fun. Being here with y'all is better than watching my favorite spy shows. What's this I'm hearin' about a slave tag? What is a slave tag anyway?"

Something your great-great-great-grandmother could have worn at one time. Winnie was a direct descendant of a woman Prudence had sheltered here. Tess explained what she knew, watching the lines between Winnie's brows deepen as she talked. Tess ended with a frustrated, "'Man's inhumanity to man.'"

"People do what they do out of fear, most times." Winnie stirred the soup then rested the ladle against the side of the pan. "No less true now than it was back then or back when Jesus was on earth. Gotta keep sayin' His words. 'Father, forgive them,' for they sure don't know what they're doing."

Tess put her arm around Winnie's shoulders. "You're a fount of wisdom, my friend."

"Life'll teach you things. Just gotta listen."

"Amen to that."

The door swung wide, and LuAnn walked in. "I told Elliott we'd pow wow in the parlor as soon as we're done. Does that work for you?"

"Sure." A tinge of resentment colored Tess's answer. She felt like a toddler stomping her feet and yelling "Mine!" She'd found the thing, after all, and now everyone else seemed to know more about it than she did. She breathed a repentant prayer-sigh and went back to emptying the dishwasher.

After the last table had been cleared and wiped down and the café floor swept, the Inn Crowd gathered in the parlor. Janice had started a fire. With clouds darkening over the river, the crackling flames were a welcome sight. Tess took one of the wingback chairs. Janice and LuAnn sat on the love seat.

LuAnn checked her watch. "I told Elliott we'd be ready by two thirty, so he should—" Footsteps on the wood stairs interrupted her.

Elliott, wearing a red-and-white plaid shirt with his many-pocketed pants, carried a laptop under one arm. "Thank you for convening, ladies. Jerry wanted to be here but didn't feel he could leave the work site. He's given us the green light to find out whatever we can. He wondered if you'd be willing to keep the tag in your safe, even though I did not"—he nodded toward Tess—"tell him I'd seen one sold for twenty grand."

Janice and LuAnn visibly straightened, as if their reaction to the dollar amount caused their spines to suddenly lengthen. Tess knew the feeling. Her two friends sat in stunned but rapt attention. "Twenty...*grand*?" Janice whispered.

"That's not the norm, but this is a specialty tag. Most simply say 'servant,' but the fact that this one says 'field worker' makes it unique. And the words on the back certainly lend a touch of mystery." He opened his laptop. "With Jerry's permission, I put a picture on a detectorist site that gets a lot of traffic, plus I wrote about our experience"—he smiled at Tess—"on my *Treasuretecting* blog. I just love sharing finds and seeing what other people uncover. I usually get a pretty decent response, but this one was interesting." He brought up the website then turned the screen around.

LuAnn and Janice scooted close to each other to make room for Tess on the love seat. Amid a long list of comments like "Awesome find!" "Good work!" and "Nice slice of history," was a long comment by someone who went by the name "Goldilocks."

Goldilocks: I may know something about this tag. Where, exactly, did you find it? Was it on public land? How far down was it? Did you find anything else at the same site? If so, please share. This could be significant. Very, very significant.

Tess looked up at Elliott. "What do you think 'significant' means?"

Elliott's caterpillar eyebrows wriggled. "It means...we need to get back out there and search for more."

Chapter Three

A steady drizzle had started the day before at four o'clock. Now, as Tess walked out of church just after eleven, gripping Henry's and Harper's hands while Lizzie carried an on-the-verge-of-a-meltdown Liam, the sun was finally showing its face. "Think it's too wet to go to the p-a-r-k?"

Lizzie shook her head. "I don't care if it's too wet. The kiddos need to run and jump for a bit, or I'll never get them down for naps."

Tess gave her daughter a smile she hoped conveyed all her admiration. "I'm glad you came this morning. I know it's not easy." Michael was out of town on business for the weekend, and she hadn't expected Lizzie to take her up on the invitation without an extra pair of hands at home.

"I've missed church. And hey, I have to get them fed and dressed every morning anyway, this just got us moving a little earlier and gave me an hour to focus on something other than who's stuffing the cat in the toilet."

Tess laughed. "Too bad the kids didn't hear the message this morning." Pastor Ben was doing a series on the fruits of the Spirit. Today he'd tackled self-control.

"Do you think Henry's too young to understand that hiding Mommy's keys under a pile of Daddy's shaving cream is not exercising self-control?"

Tess kissed the top of Henry's head as she helped him into the van. "You just have a creative mind, don't you?"

Henry nodded. "Daddy says I'm a *queative genus.*"

"That you are." She laughed again, slightly out of breath with the effort involved in corralling three four-year-old balls of energy into Lizzie's van and buckling them into car seats.

On the drive to the park, she told Lizzie about Elliott and the slave tag.

"Mom, you lead the most exciting life of anyone I know." Lizzie parked the van near Muskingum Park, and they began the unbuckling process.

It exhausted Tess just thinking about what her daughter dealt with every single day. "You certainly can't call your life dull, my dear."

"No, but it's the same thing day after day. Wake up, make breakfast, clean syrup off the walls, take the kids to school, come home, do laundry, dig Play-Doh out of the carpet. By the time I get the house in order, it's time to pick up the kids. Then the rest of my day is spent trying to keep the cat from being shoved in the crisper drawer, making supper, washing ketchup off the walls, then wrangling three balls of energy into the tub...Wash. Rinse. Repeat the next day. I love it, but it's...repetitive. You and LuAnn and Janice have adventures. And you have each other. I haven't done anything with my girlfriends without the kids in...I don't know when."

"Let's fix that. Pick a night next week, and I'll come and watch the energy balls." Tess remembered the card she'd stuck in her purse at the farmers market. "Any night but Tuesday."

"What's happening on Tuesday?"

"You'll laugh." She found the card and handed it to Lizzie, who laughed as expected.

"This is a real thing? 'God's Weigh'?"

"It's a real thing. Janice and I have a little friendly competition going. Whoever doesn't meet her weight-loss goal by the day of the Heritage Tour has to contribute to the Moore House fund." She pointed to the card. "I met the lady who runs this. I think it might help."

Lizzie scrunched her nose. "You're not fat, Mom."

"Thank you. I'm mainly doing this because my dress for the tour is a little snug, but I think it's smart to stay on top of it. I want to be healthy and have enough energy for these guys." She picked up her phone and took two pictures of Liam and Henry chasing Harper up the steps to the slide. "Self-control is one of the fruits of the Spirit, and mine is wavering in the face of pumpkin cinnamon rolls."

"I get that. Which reminds me, Michael asked me to pick some up. Were there any left over from breakfast?"

"Sometimes Winnie takes them to her church, but—" An incoming text from Janice caused Tess to look down at her phone, and she cringed.

"What's wrong?" Lizzie put a hand on her shoulder.

"Nothing...exactly." She showed the text to Lizzie.

Remember Tippi Coddlesworth? She's coming to the inn tomorrow. For an indefinite stay!

"Interesting name." Lizzie handed the phone back. "Who is she?"

"She was in our dorm in college. Her room was across the hall." Tess kept her voice even, void of emotion.

"You seem a bit dismayed. Not a fan of Tippi Coddlesworth?" Lizzie giggled. "Sorry, I just like saying her name."

So much for disguising her feelings. "Oh..." Tess racked her brain for a kind way to describe Tippi. The fact that she'd never mentioned Tippi to her daughter said a lot. "She's a... well...she played the lead in a lot of school plays."

"So she's a drama queen?"

"Well, she's...one of those people who lives life in technicolor and at full volume." Maybe Tippi had changed. Tess had to give her the benefit of the doubt, had to be hospitable, but memories of the caustic remarks Tippi had thought were funny made her shrink from what Janice, the pastor's wife, would call "a kindness opportunity." She'd known, back in college, that Tippi was one of those people who covered a poor self-image with sarcasm, but knowing that hadn't made her any easier to deal with. One comment in particular still stung. Standing in the doorway of the dorm room Tess shared with LuAnn and Janice, Tippi had declared, "Tess the Mess. Look at this place. And you're majoring in hospitality? How are you going to run a hotel if you can't even make your bed?"

Looking back, she couldn't say why it had bothered her so much. She'd never been one to obsess over what other people thought of her. But she'd never once left her bed unmade after that. Maybe she should be grateful to Tippi for starting her on a path toward self-discipline...at least in that area of her life.

Tess thought back to the time a pipe had broken in their dorm, and they'd had to evacuate their room and disperse. She, Janice, and LuAnn had drawn straws to see who'd bunk with Tippi. Not a proud moment. They could have been more gracious. Tess had gotten the short straw, and it had tested every shred of willpower she possessed to act civilly. As memories flooded her mind, she expanded on her last comment. "Full volume with no filter."

"This could be a very interesting indefinite stay." Lizzie smirked as she nudged Tess's arm. "You'll have to keep me posted."

Tess gave a wry smile. "I might be posted on your doorstep." She shook her head. "No. Clearly the Lord is nudging me to work on self-control in all areas of my life. I can do this." Her voice sounded firm, confident. Her outside voice anyway. Inside, the stubborn, sometimes defiant college girl screamed, "No way am I putting up with Tippi Coddlesworth for more than sixty seconds!"

Tess and Lizzie picked up pizza and brought it back to the inn. When the kids had their fill of Hawaiian pizza and chasing Tom and Huck, the inn's four-footed mascots, Lizzie announced it was time to head home for naps. Maybe they weren't tired, she said, but she was. As Tess buckled Harper in her seat, pudgy hands had framed her face. "Mimi, I *yuv* you more than the moon and the *pwanets* and the wide, wide *woord*."

After they left, Tess spent an hour in the tiny office behind the inn's front desk. In between checking out three of their weekend guests, she balanced the drawer for the café and made out a deposit slip for Monday morning, allowing for the right amount of change in the right denominations so they'd be ready for the lunch crowd. Then she did the same for the reception desk, tallying charge card receipts and counting out the money they'd taken in on Saturday. It always surprised her that there were still people who paid for their stay at the inn with cash.

When she finished, she went upstairs and settled in her comfy reading chair in the corner of her sitting room. Looking out at the sun peeking through thinning clouds in the western sky, she thanked God for a good day. She considered taking a nap but knew it might interfere with sound sleep tonight. Instead, she took out her phone and flipped to the picture of the slave tag. Then she opened a search page and typed in a few key words. *Slave tag Charleston 1855 field worker 2143.*

The list that came up led her to a site with a photocopy of an old record written in a spidery hand. The brownish ink was faded and smudged in spots. It took her a minute to realize they were listed by number. She scrolled to the bottom, but the numbers stopped long before 2143. There had to be another way. "Goldilocks" apparently knew something. Was the information public record?

The front door chime echoed through the speakers they'd installed on the fourth floor. LuAnn was out, and Janice was spending the day with her son Stuart and Brin's mom, Zelda. Tess got up and opened the fourth-floor door. She listened for the ding of their "new" front desk bell. LuAnn had put a sign next to it, telling guests to ring the bell if they needed anything. They also had the option of calling a number which was, for the afternoon, forwarded to Tess's phone. Neither her phone nor the bell rang, which meant it was probably a guest who was already checked in, but she decided to go down anyway. And not via the elevator. Stairs were good for her.

Elliott, wearing his plaid vest once again, stood next to the coffee bar pouring hot chocolate mix into a cup. He looked up and gave her a jovial grin. "Hope you've had a restful day," he said.

"I have. Spent time with grandkids at the park. How about you? Out detecting again?"

"No. Not on Sunday." He broke into song. "'Never, never on a Sunday...'"

Tess laughed and tapped her chin, then pointed at him. "The Chordettes, 1960."

Elliott's eyebrows tented. "Impressive! I know the song but not who sang it. That's some memory."

"My husband managed a golf course. The clubhouse hosted an oldies night with a DJ every week. After you've heard a song introduced about eighty-five times, the details stick."

Elliott laughed. "I imagine."

"Have you done any research on the tag?" Tess wasn't sure if she hoped for a yes or a no answer. Selfishly, she would have liked to find out something about the owners—of the tag and the person—on her own. "Any more comments on your blog?"

"Just a few more questions from Goldilocks and…what might be construed as a warning."

"What?" Tess felt her eyes open wide.

Elliott pulled out his phone and tapped on the screen. "What do you make of this?" He turned it toward Tess.

There could be a greater reward in this find. If you talk to the right people. Or greater trouble if you don't. Message me before it's too late.

"Too late?" Tess turned away from the words. "Too late for what? Did you private message her?"

"Not yet. I wanted to talk to you and Jerry first." Elliott rubbed a hand across his beard. "Could this have something to do with the *Marietta Times* article about buried treasure?"

"I suppose. If someone took it seriously. Just a minute." They'd kept the article, intending to frame it and hang it in the café since it mentioned Prudence. It took her a few minutes to find it. She set the paper on the desk. "It's not very long." She tapped on a headline near the bottom of the page. *City Sells Legendary Site.*

Elliott picked it up and read silently. "This really doesn't say anything at all. 'In a 1973 interview, Herbert Armstrong, 92 at the time, remembered seeing a letter addressed to his great-grandfather urging him to hunt for the treasure buried on Prudence and Jason Willard's land.'"

Tess had read it many times before. The rest of the piece was nothing more than a series of questions. What was the treasure? Who buried it? Was it ever found? "There's a social media site called Marietta Buzz that's really just a place for town gossip. After the article came out, people went crazy on there, posting stories about lost gold and somebody getting shot on the property. It eventually just died away because there weren't any facts to support it."

Elliott shrugged when he finished reading. "I was hoping for more detail. Not enough here to think Goldilocks is referring to the legend of the buried treasure."

"And if she is, that means Goldilocks knows where we found the tag." Why hadn't she read his blog? "What did you say about the location?"

Elliott grimaced. "I never thought to be secretive. I didn't give an exact address, but I did say it was in Marietta on a tract of land once owned by conductors on the Underground Railroad. I just never thought..."

"It's okay." Tess shook her head. "People are bound to figure it out. Do you use your real name on your blog?"

"No. I go by Mac. N. Tosh." Again, the cringe. "Not much of a disguise, is it?"

What else had he put on social media? "I just want to protect Jerry and his family. The first few days after that article came out in the *Times,* Jerry's brother had to camp out there to keep people off the lot. If that tag ends up being valuable..."

"You're right." Elliott nodded slowly, thoughtfully.

"Is there a way to find out how much the tag is worth without the information going public?"

"I know an antiques appraiser in Gettysburg. Dr. Felicity White. No clue if she could be sure it's the real deal without seeing it in person, but if she can, I know she'd give me an estimate and keep it quiet. Felicity keeps her ear to the ground. She might even know something about whatever Goldilocks was hinting at. I'll give her a call. Are you free all evening? Maybe we can set up a video call."

"No plans for the rest of the evening. I think LuAnn and Janice will be back soon. They'd love to be in on it if you can arrange it."

"I'll see what I can do." He slipped his phone in his pocket. "If Felicity says it's a fake or just not worth much, I'll ask her to post something. It'll be more credible coming from her."

"And if she says it's worth twenty grand?"

Elliott stood at attention and gave his trademark salute. "Then I'll do something to throw Goldilocks off the scent. I'll check out and find another place to stay and, if Jerry is okay with me still working on his land, I'll disguise myself"—the now familiar twinkle lit his eyes—"as a six-foot-four, hundred-and-fifty-pound guy with hair."

His laugh echoed in the stairway as he walked up to the second floor. When he reached the balcony overlooking the café, he looked down at her. "Tomorrow's going to be a perfect day for detecting. I'll bring out the big guns so we can search deeper. If you three would like to join a tall, dark, and handsome guy with a lot of hair, I'd enjoy the company."

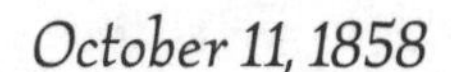

October 11, 1858

Supported by Ambrose on one side and a tall, muscular Negro on the other, the pale, shivering man was nearly carried to the bed. Prudence had swept the sheets with the bed warmer and left a heated, cloth-wrapped flat stone at the foot of the bed. She set Jason's heaviest flannel nightshirt on the dresser and then stepped out.

Prudence cut thick slices of the bread she'd made that morning then set her knife to the venison roast they'd had for dinner. "Broth," she muttered to herself, stepping into the larder to retrieve a crock of leftover stewed chicken. "What did they tell thee?" She spoke to Jason in hushed tones as she swung a full teakettle on its hook over the flames.

"Very little. They were prospecting for gold in California. Heading back home to South Carolina."

Prudence turned sharply. "If that man returns to a slave state..."

"He will gain his freedom." The deep voice came from the mountain of a man who'd entered the room making no sound at all.

She waited for the man to say more, but he didn't. "Please, come and eat." She gestured toward the table, then held out her hand. "I am Prudence."

"Jubal Hudson." He shook her hand firmly, his gaze meeting hers without wavering. "My friend in there is Cyrus Tuttle."

"Friend?" The word slipped out before she had the chance to catch it. Why had Jubal Hudson not referred to Cyrus Tuttle as his master? She'd seen the tag hanging from his neck, marking him as an owned man. She quickly added, "We have a bed for thee in the loft. Thee can rest easy. I will hear him if he wakes."

A slight smile spread across Jubal's face as he pulled out a chair. He evidently thought her impertinent question amusing. "I 'magine he'll sleep for a real long time. It's been a rough journey."

Jason and Ambrose joined them at the table. Ambrose bowed his head, and the others joined in a silent moment of thanksgiving.

"Thank you, ma'am." Jubal turned his attention to Jason. "May God bless you for your kindness."

"He has," Jason answered. "What is thy story, sir?"

"Well, sir, 'bout three years ago, Cyrus up and decided he wanted to try his hand at prospectin'. Had a college friend here in Marietta who'd gone out to California in '49, and he'd heard all the glory stories. Couple of 'em might even been true." Jubal's laugh broke the somberness that hovered over the room. "Cyrus was used to an easy life, if you know what I mean. His uncle didn't think he'd survive on his own, so he sent me with him. Promise was, if I protected Cyrus, brought him home safe, Master'd let me go free. I aim—"

Blue barked, much louder than before, his yowls turning to a low and fierce growl. Jubal leapt out of the chair and strode to the window. Grabbing the rifle he'd leaned by the door, he jerked the door open. Horse hooves pounded in front of the cabin, and Jubal reached for his coat. "I'll draw him away."

"No." Jason stood. "Thee will sleep. I will stand guard tonight."

Chapter Four

Elliott set his laptop on the coffee table in the parlor. "Jerry had church commitments, but he said we should call him later and let him know what we learn." Elliott wiggled his fingers, then typed in a number.

A face flashed on the screen. Dr. White was blond, probably in her fifties. Thick leather-bound books lined shelves behind her. She smiled. "Nice to see you again, Elliott."

Elliott introduced LuAnn, Janice, and Tess.

"What do you have to show me, Elliott?"

"Tess here found this about six inches down. It was on a piece of land once owned by UR conductors." He held the tag up. "Can you see it okay? Enough light?"

"Yes." She squinted, then wrote something down. "Copper?"

"Yep."

"The date is raised?"

"Yes. And the serial number looks hand stamped."

Dr. White gave a slow nod. "It certainly appears genuine, though I can't be certain until I can actually feel it. It looks in good condition, and the 'field hand' notation definitely raises the value. I'd say you're looking at the possibility of a couple grand if you found the right buyer."

Again, the wave of disappointment. Not the five-figure amount Tess had hoped for. Still, it was something.

"There's something on the back." Elliott turned the tag so Dr. White could read the back.

Her eyes opened wide. "Hmm...A Bible verse? What is it?"

Elliott turned to Tess, who picked up her phone. "I looked it up in the King James they would have had back then." She found the screenshot. "It would read 'Art thou called being a servant? Care not for it: but if thou mayest be made free, use it rather.'"

Dr. White tilted her head to one side. "Very interesting. Tags were generally worn by slaves who were loaned out. Renting out their workforce was one way slave owners maximized their ownership. They'd hire out their slaves for twelve to fifteen percent of their value. That was income for the owners, especially during times when work was slow, and a savings to the renter. Makes you wonder if the inscription was written by someone who was set free, or someone longing to be."

"Any way we can find out the owner's or slave's name?" Tess asked. "I did find a list online, but the numbers stopped in the hundreds."

"Most of the records were lost—probably destroyed after the war. Hold back on posting any more details, Elliott. Keep the location quiet. In fact, you might want to take down your blog post."

"I can do that," Elliott said.

"I'm going to make a few calls," Dr. White said. "See if we can uncover some details."

"Thank you for your help."

After goodbyes, the screen went dark. Tess looked at Elliott. "You've met her in person?"

"Yes."

"So you knew she was blond."

"I did. Thought it might help to see her facial expressions." He shrugged. "She didn't tip her hand, but it's still possible Dr. White is our Goldilocks."

Monday morning dawned cloudless and warm. Tess stared out her sitting room window, savoring the peach-toned, rain-washed sky reflected in the still river. Mondays at the inn were busy behind the scenes. Beds to strip, bathrooms to clean, and a ton of laundry. It would be a hectic morning, but Tess felt only excited anticipation. Brin didn't have classes this afternoon, so when the last lunch guest left, the Inn Crowd was going metal detecting. Though she'd only tried it once, she was hooked. "Tess the Detectorist" had a nice ring to it.

The café's breakfast options included stuffed French toast and a ham and cheese skillet served with warm-from-the-oven cinnamon rolls. "Unfair," Tess declared, as she carried her fifth tray of French toast through the swinging doors. Thick Texas toast stuffed with sweetened cream cheese and cherry pie filling, soaked in Winnie's secret egg and cream mixture, then browned and dusted with powdered sugar and served with a mini pitcher of warmed maple syrup. Her stomach growled as she set plates on table five. Back in the kitchen, she sipped plain black coffee and nibbled on a slice of fresh pineapple. Would tomorrow night's meeting teach her some tricks for losing weight without going hungry? It wasn't likely eating God's "weigh" included starting her morning with anything labeled "stuffed."

When the breakfast crowd dwindled, Tess headed upstairs to start cleaning. She had a system, always working clockwise. The Honeymoon Suite was still occupied by the sweetest young couple. Gail and Todd Baxter met on the mission field while serving in Nigeria and had come home on furlough to get married near family. Friends had pitched in and given them a week at Wayfarers Inn as a wedding gift. The Inn Crowd had enjoyed adding extra touches—Putnam Chocolates, fresh flowers, and candlelight greeted the couple when they'd arrived on Saturday.

The two other rooms on the second floor had been occupied for the weekend by two sisters and their husbands. Their laughter had spilled down from the balcony, and Tess had fought twinges of envy at their easygoing relationship. She and Jeffrey had enjoyed that kind of camaraderie with several couples.

Shaking off the blues, she unlocked the door to Maple and Mum, one of her favorite rooms. As LuAnn had pointed out when they'd first started decorating it, the room was done in "Tess colors." The warm, bronzy tones of the antique maple bed and dresser nearly matched the color of Tess's hair, so it was only logical they'd accessorized with the colors Tess naturally gravitated to. The wedding ring quilt with its patches of deep green, scarlet, and several shades of orange always reminded Tess of walking through the woods on a fall day.

She put clean sheets on the bed, cleaned the bathroom, vacuumed, and moved on to Lily and Lace. This room, with its calming color pallet of sage green, cream, and yellow always made her slow down a bit, stare out the window overlooking the patio, and just breathe. "I Surrender," the song drifting from her phone, was the perfect accompaniment.

She'd learned long ago she could worship anywhere, even while scrubbing dried dabs of toothpaste from a sink. A bathtub in need of a wipe-down meant time on her knees, time she could also use to pray. She was standing in the doorway of the peaceful room, double-checking her list, when the ding of the front door chime followed by a too-loud voice shattered her tranquility.

"Hey, groovy girls, I'm here!" Tippi Coddlesworth's voice ricocheted off the pressed-tin ceiling and clattered up the stairs. "Let's party!"

Tess closed her eyes, took a deep breath, and shut the door on peace and calm. Mustering a brightness she did not feel, she descended the stairs.

Tippi, already engulfing LuAnn and Janice in an enthusiastic group hug, wore a multicolored faux-fur jacket over black leggings and slouchy red-leather boots. A black beanie sat on top of her head. A streak of red that matched her boots stood out in sharp contrast to the rest of her dyed-black hair, worn chin length with straight bangs.

At the sound of Tess's steps on the stairs, Tippi looked up. "Tess the Mess! Look at you! Girl, you don't look a day over sixty-four!"

Tippi's laugh jangled every nerve fiber in Tess's body, yet she managed to step forward for Tippi's enthusiastic squeeze. The faux-fur-covered arms gave new meaning to "bear hug." Tess managed a civil, "How are you, Tippi?"

"I'm good. Amazing, actually. Living the good life in New York City. Still working, but otherwise footloose and fancy free, as they say." LuAnn's and Tess's questioning looks prompted her to say, "Divorced. Again." She stepped back. "Look at us. Back together after forty years, and all single." Tippi whipped off her hat and tossed it onto the front desk. "Show me what you do for fun in Marietta, Ohio. I'm staying until you all get sick of me." Another laugh vibrated the air molecules.

And Tess sank her teeth into the tip of her tongue.

Chapter Five

"*This* is your idea of fun?" Tippi lifted one red boot and glared at the mud clinging to the bottom. "I knew you three didn't drink or party the way most of the free world does, but I thought maybe we'd do something like shop for antiques. Not dig in the dirt for them!" Tippi perched on a boulder and took out her phone.

Tess didn't dare look at LuAnn or Janice for fear of losing it. They'd offered Tippi articles of practical clothing—work boots, a quilted flannel shirt, worn jeans—but she'd declined. "I'm only going to watch," she'd said. Tess had told her the ground might be muddy after yesterday's rain, but that hadn't been enough to convince Tippi to leave her designer boots at the inn.

Elliott pulled his "best" metal detector out of a hard-sided, foam-lined carrying case.

"You guys have been to *Chez Francois,* right, Lu?" Tippi gushed the name with reverence. "It's one of my fave restaurants. Vermilion's only like three hours from here, right? We absolutely need to go."

Of the three of them, LuAnn had spent the most time with Tippi back in college, since they'd both majored in history. LuAnn nodded graciously as she tied her hair back. "That sounds like fun. Unfortunately, being innkeepers means we need to be here."

Tippi pouted. "Well, what fun is that? Here you were all retired and fancy free like me, and then you go and saddle yourselves to that old building?"

LuAnn appeared to be trapping her tongue between her teeth. Tess imagined they'd all need time for taste-bud-trauma recovery after Tippi left…when they all got sick of her. Would that be tomorrow…or yet today? *Lord, I'm sorry. Help me respond with grace.*

"You're still working." LuAnn pulled a pair of work gloves out of the back pocket of her jeans.

"True. If you can call it work. I've been with Legacy Quest for thirty-five years and don't really feel like I've worked a day. I travel, I set my own hours…the best of everything."

Elliott handed his pinpointer to Tess. "You know how to use this when we're ready for it." He looked at Tippi. "Legacy Quest. I've heard of them. It's like Ancestry.com, only way more expensive." He winked and laughed.

Tippi's chin rose a good inch. "That's apples and oranges. Legacy was the first of its kind, started before the internet. We *are* more expensive, because we're far more thorough. We give every client our full attention. If finding out who a client's great-great-grandmother was involves a trip to China, we travel to China. If it means spending days, or weeks, combing through genealogy records in an ancient basilica in Rome, we go to Rome. I'm here now because I'm meeting with a client across the river in Ritchie County."

Janice's eyebrows rose, and she looked at LuAnn. "So you two got the same degree, and you chose being locked in a classroom with a bunch of teenage hoodlums, and she chose hanging out in a Roman basilica. Hmm..."

Tess knew LuAnn wouldn't miss the admiration in Janice's gaze. They were all proud of LuAnn's years of teaching in an inner-city high school. With an exaggerated sigh LuAnn said, "Yep. Guess I was the dumb one."

"I'll say." Tippi smirked. "Couldn't have paid me enough to do what you did. Don't forget, I invited you to come join me. You could have seen the world, made a boatload of money, and had it all."

Tess couldn't let that one go. "Not all rewards are tangible."

Tippi shook her head. "Give me the tangibles any day." She pointed to the metal detector. "Can that thing find diamonds?"

"Good question," Elliott answered.

His patience was admirable. Tess tried to squelch the next snarky thought. *What part of metal don't you understand?* It sounded like something Brin would say.

"It can't detect nonmetal items, but what it can do is lead us to indicator minerals, which are used by prospectors to locate gems. Now, if we were to find chromium garnets, glassy green olivine, black picroilmenite, or magnetite, we might just find a diamond rock nearby." Elliott's eyes sparkled.

Tippi yawned.

Elliott pointed to the small orange stake he'd stuck in the ground where Tess had found the slave tag. "I think we should start here and widen our search around it. After we've thoroughly checked this area, we'll move up to the next row." He explained the grid he'd mapped out in his head. "Jerry said the foundation blocks they found were over there." He pointed north. "I'm eager to look around in that area. Remember"—he shot a glance at Tippi—"we're hoping to find things of historical significance. If a detectorist's goal is to strike it rich, he—or she—is most likely going to be sorely disappointed." He brushed a gloved hand along his beard. "Though I sure would like to see the Moores get something out of this."

"The Moores?" Tippi asked.

"They own the land," Tess explained. "Anything we find here belongs to them."

Tippi's red lips parted. "That's not fair. What about finders keepers? Or what if you find something that can be traced to someone else? If I lose one of my rings in your yard and you find it, I think I have a right to it, don't I?"

"Whoa." Elliott held up a hand. "We have to have laws about these things to prevent disputes, but most people are decent human beings. Besides, what we're looking for is stuff that belonged to people who are long gone. Hopefully nobody's coming back from the dead to claim their shoe buckles or hairpins."

Janice laughed. "Don't be too sure. Remember Fruma-Sarah in *Fiddler on the Roof*." She put her hands up, claw-like. "'I'll come to you by night…'" She gave a wicked laugh.

As Elliott gave instructions on how to use the metal detector, Tess studied Tippi out of the corner of her eye. Janice's silly beyond-the-grave act had seemed to disturb her. What was going on in her head?

"...use the pinpointer"—Elliott was pointing at the toothbrush carrier thing in Tess's hand—"to get a more accurate read if we get a good solid *ping* on something. Who wants to go first?"

LuAnn's hand shot up a split second before Janice's, so Elliott handed her the headphones. After she'd adjusted them, he showed her how to hold the detector, and she made her first arc. On the fourth swing across the area near the orange stake, she stopped. "I hear something, but it's not very loud."

Elliott looked at the meter. "No harm in digging it up." He gave LuAnn instructions. She didn't have to dig far to find two soda can tabs. She laughed and gave the headphones to Janice.

After a few minutes, Janice got a loud "hit" that turned out to be the handle from a Westinghouse refrigerator. Janice grinned as she brushed it off. "This is so fun. It may not be worth anything, but it's a trip down memory lane. We had a refrigerator with a handle like this when I was a kid. It wasn't much taller than me."

The sun was low over the river by the time they'd covered a full row of Elliott's invisible square-yard plots. The find bag clipped to Elliott's belt now held a bottle opener, bent clock hands, a fork that looked like it had been chewed up and spit out by a garbage disposal, half of a Zippo lighter, and a square nail that LuAnn said could have been used to shoe Prudence and Jason's horses. Tippi, sitting on a flat rock with her knees drawn to her chest, was sighing louder by the minute. Elliott nodded in her direction. "Time to call it a day?"

Tess stared back at the little orange stake marking the spot where they'd found the slave tag. "What about going to the edge of the woods?" Every place they'd looked so far had probably been plowed or mowed over the years. Had the line of trees existed in the 1800s? "I just have a feeling..."

"I never underestimate the power of gut feelings," Elliott said. "Sometimes they're as strong as the signals from the best detectors." When they reached the stake, he handed the detector to Tess. "Follow your gut."

Tess put on the headphones and began sweeping across the area, about six feet south of where they'd found the tag. She ignored the softer sounds. By now she was coming to recognize the "can slaw" sounds. After half a dozen sweeps, and an equal number of yawns from Tippi, a *ping* startled her. It wasn't like anything she'd heard yet.

When she determined the spot with the loudest, clearest sound, Elliott dug a U-shaped cut in the sod. Tess knelt and held out her hand like a doctor requesting surgical instruments. Elliott handed her the pinpointer and then the trowel. About six inches down, she hit something. Abandoning the trowel, she sank her gloves into the hole and pulled out a dirt-encrusted object about the same size as the slave tag. But even before she cleared the dirt away, she could tell by the weight of it that this was different.

LuAnn sucked in a breath. "It's gold."

Elliott's low whistle levitated Tippi from her rock. "What is it?"

As she cleared the dirt away, Tess swiveled to catch a shaft of light lasering between two pine trees. The light glinted off the convex surface of the round piece of metal she held in her hand. "I think it's the top of a pocket watch."

Elliott handed her a spray bottle and a soft cloth. As she squirted then rubbed, the metal gleamed. And Tess gasped. A déjà vu moment. Scratched in uneven letters and numbers was a Bible reference. *Romans 6:22.*

"Just like on the tag," LuAnn whispered. "It's carved by hand."

"Anyone know the verse?" Tess asked.

Janice was the first to find it on her phone. "'But now that you have been set free from sin and have become slaves of God, the benefit you reap leads to holiness, and the result is eternal life.'"

"What does that mean?" Tess matched LuAnn's low, hushed tone. "I mean, what did it mean to the person who owned this?" She turned the disk over and rubbed the other side. An inscription in beautiful flowing script read:

Cyrus V. Tuttle
Nephew of Vernon H. Tuttle
Camellia River Plantation
Wadmalaw Island, S. Car.

Tess stared down at the artifact in her hand. *Prudence, did you know this man? Did he have something to do with the slave tag?* So many questions that would probably never be answered. They'd found clues that represented entire lives of real people. She looked at LuAnn. "You know how you always say you want a time machine?"

LuAnn nodded. "Now would be a good time." She rubbed the small of her back. "Well, let's go back and do some research."

"No!"

All eyes turned to the most unlikely source of a protest. Tippi. Picking up the gloves LuAnn had just shed, she reached for the handle of the detector. "There's more here. I mean, there could be more, right? We need to keep looking."

Chapter Six

Tess set a bowl of popcorn on the coffee table in their fourth-floor sitting room. Janice was already settled with a blanket on her lap and cup of tea in hand. LuAnn sat at their small kitchen table with her laptop open. She held up one finger. "I'll be there in a sec."

After collapsing onto an easy chair, Tess propped her stocking feet next to the popcorn bowl. She tucked her tablet and copy of Prudence Willard's journal next to her leg. Though eager to plunge into researching Cyrus Tuttle, she needed a few minutes to decompress. "What a day, huh?"

Janice nodded. "Something strange is going on."

Elliott had handled Tippi's unexpected request with aplomb. "Let's save something for tomorrow," he'd said as he gently tugged the detector from her hand and set it back in its case. He'd straightened and patted his belly. "As with a smorgasbord, it's best to exercise some restraint. We don't want to risk burnout…or addiction."

That was the end of it, but it was clear Tippi wasn't in agreement. On the way home she asked him, "Do you share all of your finds with the metal detecting community?"

"Never had a reason not to."

"Is that wise?"

He'd given her a pointed stare. "Of course, I'll talk to Jerry, the property owner, first." He patted his find bag. "This may be gold, but it's not worth that much."

After they returned to the inn, Elliott headed out to meet a friend, and Tippi suggested the women all dress up, and she'd treat for dinner at Buckley House. Tess could tell by the tight smiles surrounding LuAnn's and Janice's thank-yous that she wasn't alone in feeling too tired to think about getting cleaned up and dressed up, but they'd all agreed…maybe partly in hopes of trying to figure out what caused Tippi's sudden interest in metal detecting. It hadn't worked. Over exquisite presentations of chicken Dijonnaise, salmon with peaches, Romano-crusted chicken, and eggplant parmigiana, Tippi regaled them with stories of her trips abroad. When LuAnn brought up the pocket watch, Tippi seemed disinterested. At one point she excused herself to take a call, and they watched her walking up and down the sidewalk in front of the window, using her hands to punctuate an animated conversation. When she came back, she didn't say a word about the call.

LuAnn closed her laptop and brought it with her, setting it on the coffee table as she stretched out on the love seat. She patted her belly. "Why didn't I listen to Elliott's warning about self-restraint? That was way too much food this late at night."

Tess agreed, though half of her salmon and peaches, along with half of her potatoes and vegetable medley, sat in a container in the fridge. It hadn't been as hard as she'd thought to picture her plate as two meals—one for now, one for tomorrow. She yawned and took a handful of popcorn—air popped with a light spritz of butter. "Am I the only one who thought Tippi was acting mysterious?"

"At dinner or out at the Moore property?" Janice asked.

"Both."

LuAnn nodded. "I agree. What's up with her?"

"I think she figured where there was a little gold, there might be a whole lot of it." This from Janice, who was scrolling on her phone. "Have you two done any checking on her?"

LuAnn picked up her laptop. "I read a lot of her social media posts. I haven't noticed any red flags. Did you find something?"

"She just sold her beach house." Janice showed them a picture of a pale blue, three-level clapboard house with white trim. White sand surrounded the house, and teal water shimmered in the background. "Maybe she's in financial trouble."

LuAnn looked at the screen. "Not unusual for someone our age. We're in the downsizing season." She arched one brow as she chuckled. Though they'd each downsized their possessions, they'd definitely *up*sized when they bought the inn.

"But in all her posts she doesn't say why she sold or where she's moving. Listen to this. It's under the picture with the Sold sign." Janice began to read. "'Life does not always lead us along the paths we plan. I had hoped to grow old here, but it seems that is not to be. Saying goodbye to this view will not be easy.'"

Tess tapped her chin. "Maybe she and her ex had to sell it as part of the settlement."

"One way to find out." LuAnn thumbed a message.

Tess looked at the time—just after nine thirty, not rudely late—but she still stared at her friend in disbelief. This wasn't like LuAnn. "You seriously just asked her if she's selling because she's hard up or because her marriage failed?"

LuAnn laughed. "Give me some credit for tact, girlfriend. I thanked her again for dinner, and then said I saw her For Sale picture and apologized that we kept her talking about her travels tonight and didn't get to ask what else was going on in her life."

Before Tess had a chance to respond, LuAnn received a reply. She read it out loud. "'No prob. Just moving beyond the memories in that house. It's all good.'"

Janice smacked her lips. "That really doesn't tell us anything. If the house was in foreclosure she might say the same thing."

A *ping* announced another text. LuAnn read it. "'Are we on for another round of metal detecting tomorrow? That was so much fun. I can see why Elliott calls it addicting. I'm going to go buy some outdoorsy clothes in the morning. You'll all be done working about three o'clock, right? Can't wait!'"

"Too weird." Tess shifted to a more comfortable position, and her folder of copied pages of Prudence's journal almost slipped to the floor. She grabbed it before the pages went flying. "Let's do some research before we're all too tired to think." She opened the folder. "Did the name 'Cyrus' sound familiar to either of you?"

Janice and LuAnn shook their heads.

"My grandmother was born in Cyrus, Missouri," Tess said. "I don't even think it exists anymore, but I remember her telling stories of her childhood, and they all started with 'Back in

Cyrus...,' so the name jumped out at me when we read it in Prudence's journal."

In what looked like a rehearsed move, Janice and LuAnn both sat up straight. Eyes wide, LuAnn said, "Prudence wrote about the guy who owned the pocket watch?"

"I think so." Tess turned a couple of pages. "I don't know where to start looking."

In another seemingly choreographed dance, both of her friends jumped up and strode out of the room. Tess laughed. "I showered today. Really. Twice, actually."

In minutes they were back, journal copies in hand. The sound of rustling papers filled the air. "I wish we could just click Control F and search for Cyrus," Tess muttered as she leafed through eight years of Prudence's thoughts and recorded life events. Many of the pages were dog-eared from past searches. She thought back to some of the things they'd learned about Prudence. Her husband had been wounded, shot in the leg while helping runaways escape to freedom. They'd lost a child, a baby girl who'd lived only long enough to take two breaths. They'd named her Hope. Years passed before Prudence gave birth again, a baby boy they named Moses—a fitting name for the child of two Underground Railroad conductors who sacrificed so much to lead others to freedom. "Come on Pru, tell me it wasn't just my imagination."

She scanned page after page of Prudence's neat, feathery script, recognizing names. Elswyth, the woman whose husband had been shot behind the inn. Ira Fitzhugh, spy for the Union... and son of the man who had put Prudence and her parents in bondage. Winnie's great-great-great-grandmother, heavy with child when she arrived. Prudence had "taken tea" with a woman named Katie whom she had labeled "sometimes obstinate." Tess loved to read the passages that spoke of Prudence's daily life, things like "Put up six jars of pie plant today," or "Finished two quilts for the orphans this week."

"Found it!" LuAnn stabbed a page with her fingertip. "October 16, 1858." As Tess and Janice leafed to the page, LuAnn read, "'As we sat by the fire tonight, listening to Cyrus and Jubal spin their yarns about searching for gold, I marveled at this Jonathan and David relationship, the likes of which one rarely sees. Never have I witnessed it between a white man and a Negro. I love to listen to their plans of adventure, but it brings so much sadness. It's clear only one of them knows Cyrus isn't likely to leave this house alive, and when word reaches Charleston, Jubal's freedom must be stolen, rather than earned.'"

Janice sighed. "So our Cyrus died right there in Prudence's house?"

"Maybe he was buried where we found the watch." Tess took out her phone and found the pictures she'd taken of the watch cover. "The inscription is strange. 'Nephew of Vernon H. Tuttle' is an odd thing to inscribe. If it was a gift from his uncle, why wouldn't it say 'With love, Uncle Vernon,' or something like that?"

LuAnn stabbed her stack of papers again. "A white man and a Negro."

Tess felt goose bumps skitter along her arms. "Jubal could have been the man who wore the slave tag. So maybe they both died here." She said the last words softly, in a funeral home whisper. It seemed fitting. "I'm looking up Cyrus." She picked up her tablet and typed in "Cyrus V. Tuttle, Vernon H. Tuttle, Camellia River Plantation, Wadmalaw Island, South Carolina."

Two ads for real estate on Wadmalaw Island popped up. She scrolled past them and stopped on the third option. "There's a Tuttle Plantation on Wadmalaw Island." She clicked on it and was sent to a site with a featured image of a classic plantation house—two stories, wide porch with white columns, surrounded by live oaks and a plethora of flowers.

"Ooh," Tess said. "I think we need a research trip." The plantation was open to the public. Pictures of rooms staged to look the way the plantation would have pre-Civil War caused her pulse to quicken. "'The historic Tuttle plantation, originally known as the Camellia River Plantation, was built in 1823–26 by Calvin James Tuttle, a direct descendant of one of the one hundred forty-eight colonists who arrived and settled on the west bank of the Ashley (Kiawah) River in 1670. The Plantation stayed in the Tuttle family until 1958 when the estate was donated to the Preservation Society of Charleston.'"

Tess turned the tablet to show LuAnn and Janice several of the pictures and then continued reading. "'Visitors are first greeted by two-hundred-year-old moss-draped live oaks arching over the quarter-mile drive. Then the house appears in all its majesty. Massive fluted Corinthian columns support the sixteen-foot ceiling on the wraparound porch that shades floor-to-ceiling windows. The porch ceiling is painted in the traditional "haint" blue, a pale blue-green shade used on Southern ceiling porches to protect the home's occupants from "haints"—restless spirits of the dead who have not moved on from this world.'"

"Creepy." LuAnn sat up. "Anything about Cyrus?"

Tess scanned the page. "No. Wait. Vernon is mentioned." She read silently then found a paragraph worth reading out loud. "'When his father died in 1848, Vernon took over running the plantation. His first order of business was to purchase an additional thirty slaves and start growing tobacco. The venture proved extremely profitable for a decade. In 1859, after a family crisis, Vernon became severely distraught and unable to run the business. The plantation was on the brink of financial disaster until Vernon's niece, Genevieve, took over the operation—not a small accomplishment for a woman in the 1800s.'" Tess looked up. "1859."

"The year after Cyrus and Jubal stayed with Prudence. And Cyrus probably died." Janice ran her fingertip down the page on her lap. "There's another entry. Three days after the last one we read." She held up the page. "'I wish now I had contacted the sheriff after my surprise visit outside RH. I have grown so accustomed to not trusting that I find it hard to turn to others for help. The man claimed to be sent by Cyrus's family. If that be true, what grounds would there be to hold him? Cyrus has urged Jubal to run, but he will not leave. Loyalty can be a beautiful thing. It can also be a fatal mistake.'"

Silence filled the room for several minutes, then was replaced by the sound of pages turning. "I don't see their names mentioned again," Tess said. "Though our Pru was good at writing in code. Maybe if we read everything from this point on, we'll uncover more."

"Elliott just posted about the watch cover," LuAnn said.

Janice and Tess found the blog page on their own devices. They read in silence. Once again, Elliott had been careful not to mention the location of their find, but he did say he'd found it in the same vicinity as the slave tag. He'd posted pictures of both sides of the watch cover. A third picture was taken from an angle that showed both orange markers indicating the spots where they'd found the tag and the watch cover. In the background, a slightly blurred image of the Putnam Bridge.

"Someone who knows Marietta might recognize—" Tess jumped as the type shifted and a comment appeared. "Goldilocks!"

I have tried to contact you privately, but you have not returned my messages. It is of the utmost importance that I speak with you ASAP. Until then, it is in your best interest to remove this post immediately.

October 15, 1858

The Ohio River glowed orange and gold, reflecting the sinking sun, as Prudence walked home from the Riverfront House. Her feet ached and her hands felt raw from hours of laundry, but her soul sang.

It had been four nights since Jubal had spotted the man who was following him and Cyrus. They hadn't heard nor seen anyone on the property since. Cyrus had risen from his bed this morning, joining them for breakfast at the table. Jubal was in high spirits, talking of the next leg of their journey. Prudence had exchanged looks with Jason. No one had spoken the name of Cyrus's illness out loud yet, but Jason recognized the symptoms. He'd worked on the Marietta & Cincinnati Railroad before they were married, worked alongside a man who'd come from the California goldfields—a man who died from a recurrence of malaria. Cyrus's skin was ashen and tinged with yellow. Still, they would not squelch hope. She and Jason prayed nightly with Jubal.

Lost in thought, she was startled by a sudden squawk. Her pet goose flapped out of the tall grass. "Patience! Where was thee hiding?"

Patience waddled close, turning her beak toward home as she reached Prudence. The goose had an uncanny ability to know when Prudence was done with work and heading home. "What spooked thee?"

She felt the approaching horse shaking the ground before she saw it break through the trees at the side of the road. Its rider pulled back on the reins then tipped his hat. "Evenin', ma'am."

Prudence tried to hide the tension that coursed through her. "Good evening." There was no good reason for someone to be riding in the woods past dusk. Too late for hunting. Prudence looked up, ready to whistle for Blue.

"Wondering if you could help me. I'm lookin' for a man, Cyrus Tuttle be his name. He's been missin' for some time, and his family's concerned. Hired me to find him."

The steely glint in the man's eyes belied his friendly tone. Prudence shook her head. Untruths came easy for her after years of protecting runaway slaves, lying to save lives. "Can't say as I have heard that name. Where can I reach thee if I do?"

A grin that made Prudence shudder accompanied an evil laugh. "I'll find you." He walked his horse several paces down the road. "Oh, I forgot to mention that the"—he used a word that made bile rise in Prudence's throat—"he's traveling with is a cold-blooded murderer." Another laugh and the man kicked his horse and thundered away.

Chapter Seven

On Tuesday morning, Tess reheated her salmon and peaches before heading down to the café, so the sausage-and-cheese-laden egg bake Winnie pulled out of the oven didn't tempt her. Too much. As she stacked plates next to Winnie, Tess spoke to everyone in the kitchen. "We need to talk about having at least one healthy, low-cal option at every meal."

Janice, leaning against the counter as she sipped a cup of tea, gave a vigorous nod. "Hear, hear."

"Good idea." LuAnn looked up from mixing pancake batter. "I've had people just order a bowl of fruit because they needed something without dairy, sugar, or grains."

Winnie drew back from Big Red as if it had bitten her. She turned slowly, looking from LuAnn to Janice and finally latching her gaze on to Tess. Her hands landed on her hips in a no-nonsense stance. "Say what now?" She grabbed a measuring cup filled with softened butter and held it out. "You see this? You go out there to the front window and look outside. I haven't looked, but I don't have to. I know there's a crowd out there just waitin' for that door to open. And I know there are guests who've already grabbed a table so they can be first. And you know why?" She moved the measuring cup in a circle. "Because of this. Butter." She sighed, a sound like steam escaping a pressure cooker. "I'm all good with organic and getting our vegetables locally, and I don't want any artificial anything in my cookin', but people come here for the butter. They want skinny food, they go to All Pro. They want comfort food that sticks to your ribs and puts a smile on your face, they come to Winnie." She smacked the cup back on the counter. "Case closed."

Silence reigned in the Wayfarers Inn kitchen. Repressing a smile, Tess glanced at her buddies then walked quietly through the swinging door.

The café almost glowed with autumn color. Maple leaves surrounded flickering electric candles set in Mason jars. Arrangements of dried cornstalks, pumpkins, and gourds filled corners, and the tree branches Janice had stripped and whitewashed back in February were lit with tiny orange lights. Cinnamon spice potpourri simmered in a hot pot hidden behind the front desk. The atmosphere invited lingering over a cup of hot cider.

As Winnie had predicted, three tables were occupied. Tess greeted Elliott, the newlyweds, and two "besties" who were checking out today after what they'd labeled "A no-kids-no-hubbies" getaway. Tonya and Carol wore matching I HEART MARIETTA T-shirts. Tippi was the only guest who hadn't claimed a table.

As Tess approached the front door, a glance at the front windows proved Winnie right once again. A small crowd gathered. Tess smiled to herself. They'd hired Winnie for her knowledge of down-home Southern cooking. Wayfarers Inn Café was building a reputation on recipes passed down for generations in Winnie's family. Once Winnie calmed a bit, Tess would explain that no one intended to change that. Adding a few more healthful options wasn't going to diminish the crowd. With a flourish, she opened the double doors. "Welcome to Wayfarers Inn!" She stepped aside to allow their patrons to enter, then sped back to the kitchen for her order pad.

"Guess what, Winnie?" Tess tucked a pen in her apron pocket as she grinned at their still-huffing cook.

"What?" Winnie's flat tone said she wasn't bending to the smile in Tess's voice.

"Most of our guests are waiting in the café, and there is a huge crowd outside. All waiting for your buttery delights." She gave Winnie a one-armed hug and received another huff in return. It made her think of one of Jeffrey's favorite replies when she was in a snit about something. Why had the man thought it would help to say, "You're so cute when you're mad"?

Tess waited on the newlyweds and the BFFs. After serving them, she turned to a middle-aged couple. He had a full beard and shoulder-length gray hair. Her blond hair was pulled up in a ponytail. They both wore plaid flannel shirts. "Nice place," the man said. "Lotta history here."

Tess gave them her one-minute spiel on how they came to own the inn.

The woman tilted her head to look up at the pressed-tin ceiling. "I'm so glad you restored it. I can't stand to see old buildings demolished. It feels irreverent or unpatriotic, doesn't it?" The way she drew out her vowels suggested she was from somewhere farther south than Marietta.

"We're history nuts," the man said. "Travel the country visiting museums and"—he nodded toward the woman—"collecting vintage children's books. And we just took part in a Civil War reenactment near Cincinnati."

"I've always wanted to do that," Tess said. "Where are you from?"

"Texas," the woman answered. She picked up her phone and showed Tess the wallpaper on her lock screen. A couple in Civil War-era dress. It took a second for Tess to realize she was looking at the same people who sat in front of her. The woman wore a dress with tight sleeves and a hoop skirt. The man was dressed in a Union blue uniform. Tess turned to the bearded man. "Doesn't that go against your Confederate roots?"

The man laughed. "My pappy always said you learn a lot when you walk a mile in your enemy's boots."

"Sage advice."

As the woman picked up her coffee cup, a heavy-looking charm bracelet on her wrist jangled.

"Love your bracelet," Tess said. "I had one when I was a kid." She leaned closer, admiring the charms. Ballet slippers, a Christmas tree, the St. Louis Gateway Arch, cowboy boots…there had to be at least two dozen charms.

"Thank you. There's a story with each one."

Tess would have loved to chat longer but had to quickly take their orders when the group of Red Hat Society ladies who'd reserved a table for seven came in the door. Janice poured coffee for the women while Tess took their orders. After she and Janice served them, Tess headed back toward the kitchen. Elliott, who'd finished his breakfast and was sitting with his laptop open, sipping coffee, stopped her.

"When you've got a minute, I've got some things to show you. I found out something about Cyrus Tuttle."

As soon as the Red Hatters were served, Tess turned her attention to the next group—Maybelline Rector, Axel Barrett, and their granddaughter, Belle Archer. Tess had never seen the three of them together. A few months earlier the Inn Crowd had learned about the child Maybelline and Axel had had together—Belle's mother, something Belle had learned about not long before the Inn Crowd. Back in February, Maybelline and Axel were anything but civil to each other. Tess approached the table with a bit of trepidation.

"Good morning." She didn't need to drum up false delight at seeing Belle. Single mom of three and an accomplished harp player, Belle was a joy to be around. Tess asked about the kids, but Maybelline interrupted her questions.

"I've been doing some research on slave tags, and I found that man's *Treasuretecting* blog." She peered over her glasses. "I see you found something else."

No point in trying to keep it quiet now. "Yes."

"The man who owned that watch was mentioned in Prudence's journal." Maybelline stated it like an accusation.

"We just read about him last night."

"That tag probably belonged to his slave." Maybelline touched the chain hanging from her neck, as if wondering what it would feel like to be forced to wear a tag marking you as someone's property. "Bet they both died at the Willard place."

"That's what we were thinking."

"The Willards could have hidden a lot of runaways out there in their barn before they started bringing them here to the inn." Maybelline looked around, as if imagining the place in the 1800s. "Have you looked up Cyrus Tuttle or the name of the plantation?"

Tess sighed mentally. "A little."

"Then you know about the—"

"Sorry to interrupt." LuAnn tapped Tess on the shoulder. "Clint wants to talk to you about the trolley." She winked. "Or at least that's his excuse. I'll take over here."

Tess turned away as her cheeks warmed. Clint Lowery owned Butterfly Farms Bed and Breakfast. He was a single man, not by choice. His wife had left him. When Clint had first opened his B&B, they'd looked at him as competition but came to realize he was an ally. Though they didn't see him often, LuAnn and Janice had, for some reason, hinted that his interest in Tess might be based on more than their shared business experience. In spite of what her friends might want to believe, Clint was just a friend. A nice neighbor. Nothing more. She cringed inwardly as she heard LuAnn's voice in her head. *Me thinks she doth protest too much.*

Tess entered the lobby and held out her hand to Clint, who would be their trolley car driver for the Heritage Tour. Since the tour was a fundraiser for the Moore House, Clint had volunteered his services as driver and guide. They would only need to pay for the trolley rental.

Clint's large hand engulfed hers. He did plan on letting go at some point, didn't he? She stuttered something about going into the office then motioned to a chair when they entered the tiny room. She left the door partially open and sat at her desk. "I have the deposit. So far we have thirty-two people signed up."

"Great. A full crew. So you're planning on talking when they first get on and before we get out at the Moore House site, and you want me to do my spiel about early Marietta while I'm driving, right?"

"Yes. We're focusing our part on the 1850s and '60s, the time the inn was used as an Underground Railroad station." She handed him the check.

"Thanks. I'll don a half-bow silk tie with my brocade vest. My daughter says I look like Tom Sawyer all slicked up for church when I wear it." He nodded toward the café. "Are you planning on including Maybelline's museum as one of the stops?"

"It's one of the options." The tour would start in the historic downtown and expand to encompass the residential area. Then they'd head across the Putnam Street bridge for a tour of historic Harmar Village and end up at the Moore property where Jerry and Amy Moore would talk about Prudence's involvement with the Washington County Children's Home and how they were honored and grateful to be following in that great Marietta tradition. LuAnn, English and history teacher extraordinaire, had helped the Moores write their speech, encouraging them to go a little heavy on stories that would tug heartstrings. This was, after all, a fundraiser.

Clint folded the check. "You might want to consider asking Maybelline to come along on the trolley. She's a pretty good speaker. Kind of eccentric, but she knows her stuff."

Tess took a bracing breath. "Well, I guess that's a possibility."

"I was at the MURM yesterday when one of your guests stopped by. Dark hair, wearing a coat of many colors. She kind of reminded me of Imogene Coca."

Tess tempered the laugh that surfaced so it came out as a small chuckle. She'd never made that connection, but now that he'd said it, she could easily see Tippi as a doppelganger for the feisty little comedian she'd seen on TV as a child. "She's an old college…acquaintance." Tippi would have been hurt that she hadn't said friend, but could you really use that label for someone who seemed to go out of her way to make your life miserable?

"Sure had a lot of questions. She wanted to know all about Prudence Willard." Clint pointed at the floor, a gesture Tess assumed referred to the secret room below the basement that had once been used to hide runaway slaves.

"Really?" Tippi had asked Maybelline questions she could have asked them? Why? And when was she there? It had to have been before they'd found the watch cover. "What time was she there?"

"A little after five. Maybelline was locking up when the lady got there, but she let her in."

Seriously? While Tess and LuAnn and Janice had been upstairs showering and dressing for dinner, Tippi had slipped out and paid a visit to the Underground Railroad Museum?

"What kind of questions was she asking? Did she mention any names?"

Clint rubbed his chin. "She did, but I can't remember. Old names, reminded me of some I've seen on tombstones at the cemetery. I didn't hang around long after she got there. Sorry."

"That's okay. Just curious."

"She said she'd gone metal detecting with you."

Great. Maybelline knew, now Clint. Was anyone else listening in on their conversation at the museum? "It's a hobby of one of our guests. We found something interesting yesterday, and we're just a little concerned about too many people finding out. We don't want a ton of history buffs with metal detectors bugging the Moores."

Clint's lips pursed. "You should have told Maybelline to keep it quiet."

Tess grimaced. "Why?"

"Somebody called while I was there, wanting to know where the slave tag was found."

"And Maybelline told them." Tess didn't say it as a question. She already knew the answer.

"Maybelline gave the caller Jerry's number." Clint stood, shook her hand again for a long moment and said they'd talk again before the Heritage Tour.

As they said goodbye, Tess wondered what the meeting had really been about. She could have stuck the trolley deposit in the mail. She shook her head. She and Clint were just friends.

Janice gave Tess a panicky look as she walked out of the office. Two tables needed bussing, and there were still people walking in the door. After twelve more orders of egg bake and nine plates of pumpkin pancakes with cinnamon whipped cream—and the three bowls of fresh fruit she hadn't mentioned to Winnie—Tess leaned against the counter, broom in hand. Janice wiped down tables with disinfectant while LuAnn filled condiments. Tess put the broom in motion, sweeping up crumbs, skirting around syrup drips that would have to be mopped. "Can't wait to do the numbers. I think this is the biggest breakfast crowd we've had yet."

"I wouldn't be surprised." Janice yawned. "Crazy for a Tuesday."

"All the retired people who waited to take vacations until after school started are out in force. I think—" Something shiny rolled out from under Tess's broom. She bent and picked up a miniature bottle. "Look at this." She stepped over to LuAnn and held up the tiniest bottle she had ever seen. It had a cork stopper and was filled with gold flakes floating in liquid.

Janice came close. "Stacy had one of those years ago. She got it on our Alaska trip."

"There's a spot on top." Tess held it under a light. "Looks like glue."

"Stacy's was on a chain," Janice said. "I bet there was a loop glued to it."

LuAnn agreed with a nod. "Where did you find it?"

"Under table three." Tess tried to remember the people who'd sat at or near the table, but the morning was a blur. She squinted to read minuscule letters stamped on the side. "Buckeye Rovers Gold. Any idea what that means?"

"No clue," Janice and LuAnn said in unison.

"I'll put it in the basket behind the desk." Tess leaned the broom on the back of a chair. "I doubt anyone's going to be distraught over losing it. Probably a kid's souvenir."

Tess's phone rang. Jerry. Tess answered.

"Hi, Tess. Hey, I just got the strangest call. Somebody named Misty. She said she knew Elliott MacIntosh had found a slave tag on our property and asked for permission to come and look for something that belonged to someone she works for. She wouldn't tell me what it was. She seemed, I don't know...angry maybe. Kind of frantic, like it was a life-or-death thing. What's going on? Elliott said Dr. White didn't think the tag was all that unique. Was she telling the truth?" Worry filled Jerry's voice. "If it's really worth something, let's get it appraised and sell the thing. I'll split the money with you. I just don't need any more drama in my life."

"No, you don't," Tess agreed. "You need to get this behind you. I'll see what I can find out. If you sell it, somebody else can deal with the drama."

"About that..."

Tess closed her eyes. "Something you're not telling me, Jerry?"

"Yeah. I might have given her your number."

Chapter Eight

Another perfect afternoon for metal detecting. But this time, it was only Tess and Elliott…and Tippi. LuAnn had a nail appointment, and Janice was taking Larry, her grandson, to an apple orchard.

Tess swept the detector across a swath of crabgrass about a yard from where they'd found the watch cover. They were hoping to find the rest of the watch or the chain that had likely once been attached to it. So far, they'd amassed a respectable pile of pennies and pop tops.

A loud ping startled her. "This sounds different." Tess took off the earphones and let Elliott listen.

A broad smile crossed Elliott's face, and he told Tippi to hand Tess the pinpointer she held. Tess knelt and jabbed the pointer into the sod. A clear, loud *ding* rang out. She cut a U-shaped flap out of the sod and gently lifted the hinged piece. With her gloved hands, she began carefully sifting through the dirt.

"I feel something!" She realized her voice sounded like a kid on Christmas morning. She dug deeper. "It's big."

"What is it?" Tippi lowered to the ground, crouching next to Tess's shoulder.

"Let's widen the hole," Elliott said. He made another cut in the sod. Then he handed Tess a longer, more pointed trowel.

"This will help you dig deeper. Try not to hit the object with the shovel."

Tess dug, scooped dirt away with her hands, then dug again. Finally, she was able to loop her finger under something and tug.

A knife, half of the handle missing, the rusted and pitted blade at least eight inches long, slid from the dirt. As Tess began lightly brushing dirt away from the knife, Tippi held out her hand, palm out, in a gesture that told Tess to stop what she was doing. "Wait. Couldn't there still be DNA evidence on the blade?"

Tess stopped. And stared. Elliott cleared his throat. "This kind of a knife, and the condition of it and how deep it was, tells me it's been here for a very long time. Likely more than a century. Pretty sure it wasn't used in any present-day crime."

"But…" Tippi appeared to be struggling to find the right words. "What if there was an old, unsolved crime that could be solved by matching DNA on this with someone alive today—maybe a descendant of the person who was killed right here on this spot?"

"Killed?" Tess felt her eyes bugging. "Why would you think someone was killed here?"

Tippi brushed dirt from the toe of her new boots. "Think about it. You found things that belonged to two people who were traveling together. Wouldn't it—"

Tess's interrogating gaze interrupted Tippi.

"I. Well…" Tippi stuttered. She looked around, appearing to be engrossed in the swoop of a red-tailed hawk above them. "I talked to the lady who runs the Underground Railroad

Museum. She said you found a journal written by the woman who lived on this land, and she said the man who owned the watch was traveling with a black man. It's not a stretch to assume that man was his slave." Tippi's chin elevated in the way that had always irritated Tess. "It seems very likely this was a double murder. If we keep digging, I bet we'll find another weapon. Can't you picture it...one guy stabs the other, then the stabbed guy pulls out his gun and shoots at point-blank range. That story would be a great draw for tourists, wouldn't it?"

The possibility both intrigued Tess and made her queasy. "Isn't that a bit far-fetched?" *Even for you?* "Maybe one person was carrying both, and they fell out of his pocket or his backpack. And the knife was the one Prudence used to cut rhubarb. If they killed each other in the Willards' backyard, Prudence and Jason would have given them proper burials. And not with their weapons."

"Unless this was all woods at the time. Maybe the Willards thought they'd left, but they only made it into the trees before getting into a heated argument and then *kapowy*!" Tippi used her index finger as a gun barrel.

Though she knew it was irrational, Tess felt the need to defend the long-dead men. Prudence's comment about their Jonathan-David relationship felt to her like a stamp of approval. If Prudence deemed them loyal and trustworthy, she would trust her word rather than Tippi's wild ideas. "I don't think—"

"Or maybe they didn't die at all. Maybe they buried things to make people think they died." Tippi's eyes lit up. "Or to mark the spot where they buried a treasure. What if"—she gestured to the heavens and back to the ground—"there was a giant oak tree right here, and they nailed the tag and the watch to it so they could find their treasure again when they returned from the war."

Buried treasure? Maybelline must have told Tippi about the legend.

"See?" Tippi continued. "We have to do a DNA test. Or we have to keep digging until we find their bones and whatever got buried with them."

And I thought LuAnn had a vivid imagination. Tess turned to Elliott, waiting for him to answer the DNA question.

Elliott ran his palm against his beard. "Theoretically, if there is still residue on the knife, we could figure out what happened here. I've heard of thirty-year-old cold cases that were solved by DNA testing, and archaeologists were able to use it on two Egyptian mummies to discover they were half-brothers. If we uncovered bones here, there's a chance a forensic specialist could determine whether or not this was a murder weapon." Elliott took out a zipper bag and carefully placed the knife inside. "What makes this so interesting to you?" His quizzical stare appeared to be making Tippi uncomfortable.

"Maybe I just have a flare for the dramatic, but in my line of work I hear all kinds of stories. One of my clients is a direct descendant of John Wilkes Booth. Things like that have happened since Cain killed Abel, right?" Tippi's look said she was expecting confirmation. "When you find what could be a murder weapon alongside evidence that two people could be buried here, I say we need to search for more clues." She turned to Tess. "Don't you want to know what happened to those men?"

Tess looked toward the middle of the property, at the tractor digging the basement and the pallets of cement blocks waiting to become walls. Of course she was curious, but she wouldn't ignore Jerry's comment about not wanting more drama. "This is all way too speculative. Just because there's a knife doesn't mean there was a murder, and the Moores certainly don't need that word bantered about. Maybe there are other ways of finding out more about them." Tess was ready to be done. What started out as a fun quest had taken a dark turn. "I need to get ready for a meeting. Maybe we should call it a day."

Elliott agreed. Tippi stared at the knife in the bag. "Where are you taking that?"

Jerry drove up in his wheelchair van and Elliott pointed toward it. "At the moment, I'm taking it right over there."

"We'll go with you," Tippi said.

Tess and Tippi had met Elliott here, so Tess had her own car. She was tempted to tell Tippi she'd see her back at the inn, but that wouldn't have been fair to Elliott. She followed the two of them to the van and waited while Jerry unhooked his wheelchair, and his lift lowered him to the ground. The van—a necessity for transporting not just Jerry but the children they would foster—had been bought with the accident settlement money.

When Jerry shut the van doors, Elliott showed him the evidence bag and explained where they'd found the knife. Tippi jumped in with, "We think the slave tried to kill his master and then the master stabbed him or shot him, and they both died right here on your property. Your land could be a very important historical landmark." She pointed to the place they'd found the knife. "Can't you just see a granite monument over there? Maybe even a statue depicting the fight?"

Jerry's eyes widened. Tess could only imagine what Jerry, with his ethnically diverse family of adopted and foster children, was thinking about now. Not that he needed to worry. There wasn't a chance the town council would approve a statue of master and slave brawling with unsheathed weapons.

"It's history," Tippi insisted. "We should never cover up the past just because it makes us uncomfortable."

After a slow, controlled nod, Jerry said, "Neither should we make assumptions about things we can neither prove nor disprove." He looked up at Elliott. "If you want to take this and find out what you can about it, have at it. I trust you will respect my family's need to build this house without trying to work around a media circus or a bunch of overzealous"—he glanced at Tippi—"sensationalists."

Tippi turned and walked toward Tess's car. Elliott shook Jerry's hand and said he'd look into it and talk to him before he did anything. "Pretty sure forensic testing is way too expensive, and right now we sure don't have any reason to pursue it." He nodded at the tractor. "You guys dig up some bones, we'll talk."

The God's Weigh meeting was a reprieve from drama. Tess instantly felt the stress fall from her shoulders. People stood, chatting and laughing, beside a table laden with healthful snacks—apples with yogurt dip, skewers of grapes, sweet potato chips with guacamole. All in all, a party atmosphere.

Tess recognized two women from church. They turned and welcomed her with a hug. Lynette Gibson walked into the room carrying a pitcher of water with slices of lemon and cucumber. "Tess! I'm so glad you're here." She set the pitcher on the table and began introducing her to everyone. Tess tried to etch the names in her brain using pneumonic devices she'd taught in her hotel management classes. Patty Paisley—the redhead wearing a pastel paisley scarf. Donna Donut—for the shirt that read "I Ate a Donut without Sprinkles—Diets are Hard." Fuzzy Fred—for the tuft of beard just below his bottom lip. "Have you met Evelyn?" Lynette put her hand on the shoulder of a dark-eyed woman with salt-and-pepper hair and café au lait skin.

"Not yet." Tess extended her hand.

"Evelyn was a professor of Art History at Marietta College. She just retired." Lynette then explained to Evelyn that Tess was also a retired teacher. Looking at Tess, Lynette gave a sheepish-looking grin. "I didn't stalk you. Maybelline Rector saw me talking to you at the farmers market and gave me all sorts of juicy details about you and your friends." She winked, then told Evelyn about the inn.

"Ooh! I've always wanted to get over there." Evelyn spoke with just the hint of an exotic accent Tess couldn't place. Jamaica, maybe. "Up until this year I was teaching during the hours your café is open. Isn't it hard to wrap your head around the idea that you don't have to be somewhere at a certain time?

I was in Haiti all summer and came back after classes started in August. I just feel out of step. I wake up in a panic every morning thinking I've overslept."

Tess knew that feeling. "It took me about six months to get beyond that." At some point during the conversation about retirement, Lynette excused herself. Tess and Evelyn walked around the table, chatting as they filled plates, then found chairs next to each other in the circle. "Were you in Haiti on vacation?"

"Partly. I took my mother to visit her sister, but I was also there as part of an art history study trip."

"Sounds fascinating. Were you there teaching or as a student?"

"Both." Evelyn's laugh was musical. "We spent a lot of time at the Musée d'Art in Port-au-Prince, studying the history of Haitian art styles. And we worked on an archaeological site, learning how to piece pottery found at the Sans-Souci Palace in Milot. I've done similar trips in other countries, but this was different. It gave me a sense of my own heritage."

"That had to have been rewarding. Did your mother grow up in Haiti?" As Tess listened, genuinely interested, she couldn't ignore the voice in her head telling her she'd just met someone who knew people who just might be able to help them find answers. She asked a few more questions about Evelyn's family history, then said, "So you've worked at other archaeological sites?"

"Yes. It's kind of a passion. But Mom's needing more help these days so—"

"Welcome!" Lynette sat across from Tess in the circle that had somehow filled while Tess was engrossed in conversation. "Let's start out our evening by thanking God." She clasped her hands around her knees and gave a short and simple from-the-heart prayer. "We have a couple of new faces, so we'll do introductions before anything else. Tell us your first name and why you're here. For those of you who are new, I need to explain that, in spite of our name, we don't focus on a weight loss goal. We each develop a personal reason for eating and moving healthfully. It'll make sense in a minute."

She put her hand against her chest. "I'm Lynette, and I started God's Weigh because my knees were so bad I couldn't walk, but my doctor said she wouldn't dare administer anesthesia at my weight. So I started changing the way I eat and move and, more importantly, think, out of desperation. That was five and half years ago." She grinned, making eye contact around the group. "A year into this I went back to my doctor almost pain-free, and she said she still wouldn't consider doing the surgery. Because I no longer needed it." Her eyes shimmered as the group applauded.

As each person in turn shared their goals—lowering blood pressure, training for a 5K, wanting more energy—Tess had time to think of reasons that went beyond "being comfortable in my dress for our Heritage Tour." She did start with that, feeling just a tiny stab of guilt for the shameless promotion, but then went on to say, "I have three four-year-old grandchildren. Triplets." A collective gasp rose from the group. "I want to have the stamina to thoroughly enjoy them." Her goal warranted another round of applause.

Tess took notes as Lynette and the others shared tips for eating right without feeling deprived. "Always order salad dressing on the side," Patty said. "Dip your fork into the dressing, then stab your greens. You get all the flavor but less than half the dressing."

Donna nodded. "If I order coleslaw when we're out, I use my straw to syphon some ice water from my glass and squirt it on the coleslaw. It thins the dressing so it doesn't cling to the cabbage, and you still get all the flavor."

Before Lizzie's wedding, Tess had joined a weight loss group that involved eating certain foods at certain times of the day, which meant carrying zipper bags of raw veggies, hard-boiled eggs, and an ice pack in her purse wherever she went. She'd lasted eight days. At the close of the meeting, she looked at Evelyn. "This seems doable."

"It's actually fun." Evelyn picked up her purse then angled in her chair. "I need to get home to Mom, but I would love to chat with you more. Would you like to come for dinner some night? I want to hear more about your Heritage Tour. Since I won't be traveling for a while, I'm volunteering at the historical society and learning everything I can about local history."

Tess rubbed her arms as a series of prickly bumps rose on her skin. Janice called them "Holy Spirit bumps." Meeting Evelyn was no coincidence. Tess smiled at her new friend. "I would love to come for dinner."

Chapter Nine

You can't catch me, Mimi!" Harper ran from the swing to the slide.

Tess had picked up the triplets from school so Lizzie could have the much-needed retail therapy with her two friends that Tess had promised her. When Thursday's forecast proclaimed a blue-sky afternoon, Tess had suggested that she and Janice take grandkids for a picnic in the park after school.

"Here I come!" Tess ran after Harper, only to be tackled by Henry and Liam and almost brought to her knees. "Go easy, boys. Mimi's getting—" No, she wouldn't use the *O* word. Reading the God's Weigh manual was starting to change her thinking on healthy aging. "Mimi's getting stronger every day, and I just might tackle you back!" She got on her knees and pulled them both into a hug. Harper plowed into her back yelling "*Gwoup* hug! *Lawee*!" Tess laughed at Harper's attempt at saying Larry. "Auntie Janice, Auntie *LuNan, gwoup* hug!"

In the middle of the mass of arms and legs and giggles, Tess stilled the commotion with a single word. "Food!" When the triplets had calmed, she led the way to a picnic table, and she and Janice pulled out bags of chips, a package of string cheese, and a bowl of red grapes from a basket while LuAnn filled cups with apple cider. "Snickerdoodles for dessert!" Tess said, and the kids cheered. She glanced at Janice. "Or apple slices and yogurt dip." She caught herself before making it sound like a less-than dessert. "Caramel yogurt dip." Her phone buzzed in her pocket, and she stepped away from the noise to answer it.

A strange number. From Charleston, South Carolina. She didn't need to think twice.

"Ms. Wallace? I am connected with the Tuttle Plantation in Charleston. Is this a good time to talk?" The woman spoke with a thick drawl.

"Yes." Tess walked farther away from the picnic table. "Is this Misty?"

"That's the name I gave Mr. Moore, yes. Ms. Wallace, I've been following things up there in Marietta, and I've done some background checks on you and Ms. Eastman and Ms. Sherrill. I needed to know your...level of interest."

Tess felt the skin on her forehead ripple into furrows. Why the air of mystery? "Level of interest? In what?"

"In the truth about Cyrus Tuttle and Jubal Hudson."

"Oh." What should she give away? Should she tell "Misty" about Prudence's journal? Or should she keep quiet until she found out what Misty knew? Best not to say too much to someone who wasn't even using her real name. "I guess you'd say our level of interest is curiosity. We're always interested in learning more about the history of our area." Maybe it was time for her to ask a question. "What is your connection with their story?"

A pause answered her. "I'd really like to talk to you in person, Ms. Wallace. I have some understanding of what it takes to run a bed-and-breakfast, so I know your time is not your own, but I'd like to invite you to Charleston so we can share information and maybe get to the bottom of this."

"Bottom of...what?"

Another pause. "I thought you would have..." Misty took an audible breath followed by a forceful exhale. "There are legends, and some things in our archives, that indicate Cyrus may have come into some money, quite a fortune, actually, and there is the possibility, a very strong possibility considering what you've just found, that your information combined with ours might lead us to the truth of all this."

It was Tess's turn to not respond right away. Was Misty trying to use what she knew to get her hands on the fortune? Was she even telling the truth? Why in the world would Tess go to Charleston to talk to a complete stranger? Why didn't Misty offer to come to Marietta? What if—

"I know this is a lot to take in, and I apologize for sounding so vague, but I just feel it would be safest for both of us if we spoke in person. I have been authorized by the Tuttle family to extend an invitation for you—all four of you, including Mr. MacIntosh—to stay at the Tuttle Plantation on Wadmalaw Island for three nights, all expenses paid, including airfare, next week."

Tess felt her jaw muscles slacken. None of them had taken a real vacation since buying the inn sixteen months ago. All expenses paid? Was this a scam? Some kind of a trap? "I...thank you...I'll...have to talk to my business partners and get back to you. Can I reach you at this number?"

"Would it be all right if I called you about this time tomorrow? I apologize for sounding so clandestine, but one never knows who might be listening on either end."

Right. One never knows. Tess turned in a slow circle. It didn't take Tippi's imagination to picture microphones hanging from every branch. "Tomorrow at this time will be fine."

Tess chopped kale at the counter in the fourth-floor kitchen while Janice stirred up her mother's famous lemon poppyseed dressing. LuAnn had gone downstairs to get a container of leftover pumpkin soup and a maple walnut muffin for herself. Using self-restraint she didn't really feel, Tess had asked her not to bring one up for her, and Janice had dittoed the request.

Tess's fingers weren't cooperating. She hadn't had a chance to talk to Janice and LuAnn about Misty's offer since taking the grandkids home. She felt strangely nervous, unsure what answer she hoped to get.

LuAnn came in with a covered pan. "I warmed the soup downstairs while I was talking to Tippi."

Tippi was in the café kitchen? It wasn't like they never allowed anyone in, but it was against health codes, and it was something they were all very careful about.

"Hope it's okay I invited her up to eat with us." LuAnn set the pan on the stove then opened the cupboard above it to get bowls. Four bowls.

It is not okay. Not at all okay. Tess stopped chopping and closed her eyes for the space of a breath. A breath of surrender. And then she began chopping again. Fast. "I need to talk to you two about something." Her words kept time with her knife as she told them about the call from "Misty" and the invitation. When neither Janice nor LuAnn said anything, she turned around.

Tippi stood in the doorway, a grin on her face. "That sounds fabulous! Can I come with you? Pleeease? A road trip with you three would be just like old times, like our chorus trip to New York. I've seen *Man of La Mancha* three times since then, and I always think of the four of us sitting there in our matching skirts. Best memory ever."

When Tess realized her face was scrunched in a grimace that might leave permanent lines, she ordered her muscles to relax. She remembered those skirts and didn't dare make eye contact with Janice, who'd made them. At the time, Tess, Janice, and LuAnn were singing together as a trio. They called themselves the In Crowd—only one *n* back then. They sang at Christian coffeehouses and the student union and toyed with dreams of making it big someday. Janice, majoring in home economics, had made each of them corduroy skirts with wide loops for their white belts. Tess's skirt was rust-colored, LuAnn's was purple, and Janice's was a dark teal blue. They'd worn them for their shows and planned to wear them when they went to see their first Broadway musical together. And then along came Tippi and her "Make me one too! Please, please, please?" and Janice, who'd found it even harder to say no to people back then than she did now, had reluctantly agreed. And that was when Tippi, in her gold corduroy skirt, decided she was the fourth member of the In Crowd.

Tess looked at Janice and then LuAnn with a look she hoped conveyed "Why didn't you tell me to be quiet?" Neither of them seemed to catch her meaning.

"That could be fun," LuAnn said, motioning to Tippi to set the plate of two—*two*—muffins on the table. "But we can't all get away."

"Maybe we should draw straws." Janice, ever the peacemaker, smiled sweetly.

It was all Tess could do to not to bare her teeth and growl.

"Great idea!" Tippi grabbed four toothpicks from the cut-glass container on the counter and snapped the end off one.

"Wait a minute!" Tess gripped the knife handle. "The invitation was for us. And Elliott." That came out nothing short of rude. "The woman was very…secretive. She did background checks on all of us. I don't think we have the…freedom to invite anyone else. And I'm not at all sure any of us should go. We don't even know this woman's real name. What if it's some kind of trap to kidnap us and hold us for ransom or…" She slowed to a stop when she noticed the incredulous expressions around her.

LuAnn filled a bowl with soup, and then another. She'd always claimed that methodical work helped her sort her thoughts. "Let's sit down and pray, and then we can look at all of the pros and cons."

Without a word, Tess dumped chopped kale, dried cranberries, and pumpkin seeds into a bowl and shoved it over to Janice, who poured the dressing and mixed it. They sat at the table. Tess pressed her lips together. *How convenient to have four chairs.* She glared at the two muffins, wanting nothing more than to swallow one whole. LuAnn prayed, thanking God for food and lifetime friendships. Tess's fingernails bit into her palms as LuAnn calmly prayed for wisdom.

After they all chimed in on "Amen," Janice passed the salad to Tess. "You should definitely go. You're the one who found the slave tag."

Tess shrugged. "*If* I go, and that's a gigantic *if*, I won't go alone. And I won't go alone with Elliott."

"Elliott mentioned having back-to-back meetings next week anyway," LuAnn said.

"So that leaves the three of us." Tippi pointed to Janice and LuAnn before her finger aimed at herself. "There's nothing in my background that would make the woman not want me to come. In fact, my experience might be useful."

Not happening. Tess noshed on her tongue. "There's no reason I can't just ask Misty to tell us what she knows over the phone. We don't—"

"Unless there is." LuAnn stared at her, her expression not giving away what she was thinking.

"Unless there is what?" Tess was in no mood for twenty questions.

"A reason. I doubt this Misty person was just being dramatic. There's probably a really good reason why she's afraid someone wants to know what she wants to tell you." LuAnn broke her muffin in half and slathered butter on it.

"Fine. I'll go. As long as one of you goes with me." She stared at LuAnn.

"I would absolutely love to go. But I'm subbing at the high school three afternoons next week. This is the first time I've done this, so I don't dare get out of it."

Tess turned to Janice, whom she was sure had no prior commitments she couldn't break.

"I can't." Janice pouted. "Belle asked if I'd be interested in playing piano with their strings group. Their pianist's granddaughter is getting married in Italy and their next rehearsal is—"

"See?" Tess didn't bother apologizing for interrupting. "We're not meant to go. If we were, you guys would be available and—"

"I'm free." Tippi sat across from Tess, hand in the air like the donkey in the *Shrek* movies the triplets loved. The look on her face screamed, "Pick me! Pick me!"

No. No-no-no! Lord, You wouldn't…would You? It wasn't just that she'd never gotten along with Tippi, though that alone should be reason enough to not take a trip with someone, there was also Tippi's sudden, strange interest in what they'd found on the Moore property and her off-the-wall murder-scenario imagination. Tess was sure it wasn't a good idea to meet up with someone who called herself Misty—straight out of a thriller movie from the seventies—accompanied by a person who invented diabolical crimes in her head.

"I'm so jealous," LuAnn said. "I spent a month in Charleston about ten years ago. It was like being steeped in history. And beauty. Just like the description you read about the Tuttle plantation with its live oaks dripping with moss, and the flowers that are beyond gorgeous. This time of year there will be bougainvillea, hibiscus, impatiens..."

"Ooh, and canna lilies." Janice matched the envy in LuAnn's voice. "Lawrence and I spent our thirtieth anniversary there. The hydrangeas were gigantic and the—"

"Okay, I get it. It's beautiful." Resignation showed in Tess's voice before it settled in her mind. She knew this feeling—the inner-child-temper-tantrum—and had long ago decided it was never really worth it. If God had a lesson waiting for her, she was going to go through it one way or another.

But, Lord...Tippi Coddlesworth? Really?

Chapter Ten

Between breakfast and lunch on Friday, the Inn Crowd scurried to make beds and tidy rooms. Janice headed to the cabinet at the end of the hall on the third floor to gather fresh towels while LuAnn took a plastic tote of cleaning supplies into Woodsmoke and Pine, Elliott's room. Tess decided to start with Tippi's.

Lilac and Sage was the most feminine of all their rooms, or maybe a close second to Lilies and Lace. The color palette of soft greens and several shades of lavender and purple always made Tess feel like she was standing in an English country garden. Janice had painted the mirror above the dresser antique white then sanded the scrolled frame in spots. She'd used a similar technique on the shelf over the bed. On the shelf sat several old black-and-white framed portraits, lavender candles in pewter holders, and a green Depression glass vase filled with silk lilacs. In the bathroom, a diffuser wicked the scent of Lilies of the Valley into the air.

She'd just finished smoothing the sheets, pulling up the flowered quilt, and fluffing and arranging pillows when LuAnn walked in, tote in hand, followed by Janice with a stack of folded towels.

"We're kind of a well-oiled machine, aren't we?" Tess stepped to the open door, admiring the room and the way she and her friends of forty-plus years worked together. "Who would have imagined we'd—"

"Be taking a trip together again!"

Tess jumped at the voice and the hand on her shoulder. Tippi's stealthy approach had spooked her like she was a skittish horse. She grabbed the doorframe and tried to smile.

"We probably need to go shopping, right? I didn't pack clothes that would be right for Charleston. It'll be much warmer there. And who knows what we'll be doing? We'll have to pack for every possibility. We have to go to FIG, this adorable Southern bistro, and then there's Slightly North of Broad and Circa 1886. Do you like raw oysters? I know this place where—"

"Maybe we need to find out what 'Misty'"—Tess accompanied the name with air quotes—"has planned for us."

"Absolutely. Good idea. I'm going to go do some research and come up with an itinerary for our free time." Tippi giggled. "This is going to be so much fun!" She waved and sprinted out of the room.

Tess didn't want to be the person she was at the moment. She'd always struggled to remember her filter—the one on her thoughts, not just her words. The Apostle Paul's admonition to "take every thought captive" gave her a mental picture of a spring-loaded trap set in the jungle, activated by the paw of a stalking tiger. If only a heavy rope net would drop onto her thoughts the second they stepped out of line. At the moment, she was struggling with whether or not to tell her best friends about her dread of spending time with Tippi.

"I know she's not your favorite person." Standing in front of her with an armful of rumpled towels she'd scooped from the bathroom floor, Janice spoke in a quiet voice coated with empathy.

The words released the tension in Tess's shoulders, and she slumped against the doorframe.

LuAnn stepped out of the bathroom. "You can say no, you know."

To the trip? Or to Tippi? As much as Tippi annoyed her, Tess had always felt a bit sorry for her. A snippet of her conversation with the Civil War reenactment couple surfaced. What had the man said? *You learn a lot when you walk a mile in your enemy's boots.* Maybe there was a reason she was supposed to spend time with Tippi. "I can't shake the feeling this is something I'm supposed to do."

"A Holy Spirit nudge?" Janice asked.

"I think so. I just can't tell if the nudge is for talking to Misty or taking the trip with Tippi."

LuAnn peeled off a pair of disposable gloves. "I'm guessing both." She tossed the gloves in the trash bag she'd brought out of the bathroom, then reached for her back pocket. She pulled out her phone and made a failed attempt at hiding her smile. Without a word, she walked into the hallway.

Tess looked at Janice, and they exchanged a knowing look. "Brad," they said together. Bradley Grimes, the Realtor who'd first showed them Wayfarers, had become a regular visitor at the inn. Though Tess and Janice had backed off their teasing, it was hard not to laugh whenever LuAnn caught them smiling and gave some version of "we're just friends." The two had known each other for sixteen months and, as Winnie would often whisper behind their backs, "They aren't getting any younger." The comment was usually followed by, "What're they waiting for?"

After a shorter conversation than usual, LuAnn came back in, a look of confusion on her face. "I've been telling Brad about the things we found out at the Moores'." Her lips pressed together. "I hope that's okay."

"Of course," Janice said. "He's an honorary member of the Inn Crowd."

"You know we don't have a problem with that," Tess added. "What did he say?"

LuAnn slipped her phone back in her pocket. "Did you two know Maybelline is selling her house?"

Tess and Janice shook their heads.

"She just listed with him. When they did the first walk-through a few days ago, she showed him a spare bedroom she used for her home office. He said it was like the MURM overflow room—shelves crammed with labeled boxes of Underground Railroad files and artifacts, and the walls are covered with maps and old pictures. He showed a client through the house today." LuAnn tucked her hair behind her ears. "There was a box labeled 'Charleston' with a question mark."

"What?" Tess wasn't sure if she or Janice said it first. "Did he see anything in it?"

LuAnn nodded. “A pair of shackles.”

“The ones she had on display at the MURM or a different pair?” The rusty metal circles connected by a heavy chain had made Tess’s stomach turn. How was it possible for people to treat fellow humans with such contempt?

“Brad thought they looked like the same ones. He couldn’t be sure, but there was a symbol on one, he said it reminded him of a cattle brand. It was rusty and corroded, but he figures it had to have been molded or stamped in when they were being made.” LuAnn folded her hands. “He made out a circle with a *C* in it and thought it might stand for Cyrus, but then he was able to see the second letter was an *R*.”

“CR.” It took Tess’s brain a moment to fire on all cylinders and make the connection. “Camellia River.”

After lunch, Tess was counting the money in the drawer when Brad walked in. He stopped about four feet from the door and looked up. LuAnn, wearing a long burnt-orange sweater she’d just bought, walked down the stairs. Brad grinned at her, and Tess had to look away to keep from laughing. Could LuAnn not see the tenderness radiating from those blue eyes? Surely it wasn’t possible Brad was unaware of his own feelings.

“Nice décor,” he said then swept his hand out toward the whitewashed tree covered in orange lights and glued-on fall leaves. “‘O hushed October morning mild, thy leaves have ripened to the fall; tomorrow’s wind, if it be wild, should waste them all.' Robert Frost." He took a bow as LuAnn clapped.

Tess smiled, but the words of the poem only intensified the sense of foreboding that had started when she opened the drawer of the antique gold cash register. They were operating in the black, and that fact should make her thankful, but what would happen after the beauty of fall faded, and the stream of tourists dwindled to a trickle? Last year at this time they'd only been open a month. Business was good because they were new, and the locals, along with tourists, wanted to check out the inn and café. *Tomorrow's wind, if it be wild, should waste them all.* She zipped her fleece jacket and continued counting.

"The shackles I saw in the box are the ones that were on the wall at the MURM," Brad said.

LuAnn met him in front of the desk. "You're sure?"

Brad nodded. "I stopped in to give Maybelline the spec sheets I had made. The shadow box is still up, but there's a copy of a page from Prudence's diary mounted in it now."

"Hmm." LuAnn nibbled on her bottom lip. "Would it be breaking client confidentiality for you to tell us why she's moving?"

"I'm not sure I know. She's not looking for another house. Something she said made me assume she was moving in with her granddaughter, but I can't say for sure."

"Odd," Tess thought out loud, setting aside a stack of twenties. "The last we knew, Belle was living in a tiny upstairs apartment with three kids. Seems like it would make more sense for her to move in with Maybelline."

"Unless she was talking about her other granddaughter." LuAnn raised an eyebrow.

"The one who stole the ruby pin?" Brad asked. "Isn't she in jail?"

Tess felt a pinch in her heart at the thought of Natalie. Back in February, she'd stolen a leather bag owned by one of their guests, then later she'd taken a ruby-crusted Civil War decoder that had been hidden in the inn back in 1863. She'd done it to keep her grandfather, Axel Barrett, from stealing it. With a previous record for theft, his sentence would have been much worse. Though she'd done the wrong thing, the Inn Crowd had been touched by her protection of a man most people would say didn't deserve it.

"Natalie got a hundred and eighty days. They classified it as a misdemeanor because she hadn't taken it out of the building. She got out last month." Tess knew that because Natalie had stopped in two weeks ago to apologize once again and tell them her time in jail had changed her. Tess would never forget Natalie's tear-streaked face as she'd hugged Janice and then LuAnn and Tess. *"Thank you all. I took to heart every word you wrote in your letters. Because of Jesus and the three of you, I'm not the same person I was in February."*

"Natalie lives up in Columbus," LuAnn said. "I can't imagine Maybelline ever leaving Marietta."

Why had Maybelline put her house on the market, and why wouldn't she have told Brad where she was moving? If she had financial problems, all she'd need to do was sell her Porsche.

"Well, we should be going." Brad held out his arm for LuAnn. "I'm treating for a wild night on the town. Starting with a walk along the river, then moving on to the new nineteenth-century weaponry exhibit at the Campus Martius Museum, then on to ribs at the Boat House."

"What a guy." Tess laughed and watched them walk out. She fought a surge of envy. Strange how she could feel such joy for her friend, yet sometimes need to tamp down a wave of self-pity. She'd had decades of togetherness with Jeffrey. Why couldn't she rejoice in LuAnn's happiness without turning the focus on herself? *Another thing I need to work on, Lord.* The list seemed to be growing, but, as Janice had once pointed out, after years of being a disciple of Jesus Christ, the rocks they needed God to help them haul out of their spiritual gardens were much smaller than the ones they'd struggled with in the beginning. "We're getting down to the gravel now," she'd said. "Still numerous, but not so big."

She was in the middle of recounting the money when Elliott walked in.

"So...a couple of things." Elliott rested his forearms on the front desk. "Felicity wants to come and see our finds in person. And...I answered Goldilocks."

Her attention broken once again, Tess set the stack of twenties down and let his statement sink in. "Did you get an answer?"

"Just a word-for-word repeat of the warning: 'It is in your best interest to remove this post immediately.' She did add that she'd give me more details as soon as I took it down."

A tiny light bulb flicked on in the back of Tess's brain. Were Misty and Goldilocks the same person? "And did you?"

"Yes," he said. "Took it down this morning and gave her my phone number. What do I have to lose, right?"

"I hope you're right." She told him about Misty. "She knows exactly where we found the tag."

Elliott grimaced. "I'm so sorry. I've never used my real name on detecting sites, but that's just because I want anonymity. I don't need all of my business associates knowing what I do in my free time. People have figured out the site is mine, but it's never mattered much. This is different. If there's anything to these warnings and I've put any of you in danger, I'll..." His jaw clenched, his eyes turned steely. One thick-palmed hand smacked the counter. "I'll fix this. Now." Without another word, he turned and stomped up the stairs.

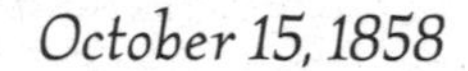

"She was only twenty when she became a missionary to the Choctaws." Prudence tried to steady her hand, but her needle trembled in her fingers. She smiled at Cyrus who, at her insistence, sat closest to the fire. She'd covered him with so many quilts he'd told Jason his wife was out to smother him.

It warmed her heart to hear the hint of teasing in his voice and to see him sitting up. It was the first time she and Jason and Jubal and Cyrus had all gathered by the fire. To keep their minds off all the troubles that weighed them down, and to keep her mind from straying to her distressing encounter with the man who'd startled her earlier, she told them about Catherine Fay. She would wait until Cyrus and Jubal went to bed to tell Jason about the man on horseback.

"While she was there, she got word of an orphan child who'd died from abuse. It made her heartsick and never left her. She moved to Kentucky and took up raising money to open her own home for orphans, which she has just this year accomplished, but not without coming up against much opposition."

"People can be heartless." Cyrus's voice was so low it was almost covered by the crackle of the fire. "I myself was one of them."

Prudence tucked her needle into the shirt she was mending. Folding her hands on her lap, she leaned toward

Cyrus. "We would love to hear more of thy story if thee is strong enough."

Jubal lifted his tin cup toward Cyrus. "I've told these folks 'bout some of our adventures, but I waited till you was up to tell 'em most of it. You tell it best, and that way I don't get in trouble for makin' you look bad as you was."

Cyrus laughed, glanced at Jason and Prudence, then turned his gaze toward the fire. "You know the story of the Prodigal Son. Well, that story could have been written about me." His voice seemed to strengthen as he spoke. "My folks died when I was a boy, and my uncle took my little sister and brother and me in. Uncle Vern never married, and the only children he'd ever been around belonged to his slaves. He didn't set down any rules. We had a nanny, of course, but she didn't much care what we did. We got what we wanted and, when I got older, I did what I wanted. I have a friend here in Marietta. Met him at Princeton. Do you know James Armstrong?"

Jason nodded. "Heard of him. Went west with the Buckeye Rovers in '49, didn't he?"

"Yep. I heard all the stories of gold nuggets as big as your fist lying on the ground just waiting to be scooped up. Jimmy said he'd loan me the maps he created, so I told my uncle I wanted the money in trust for me from the sale of my parents' estate. He gave it to me, along with this terrifying mass of a man to protect me." He nodded toward Jubal. "Uncle Vern said if Jubal got me home safe, he'd get his freedom. So we headed up here to Ohio. Promised to bring some gold back to Jimmy for the use of his maps."

Cyrus smiled at Jubal. "Anyways, there we were, two greenhorns on our way to California. We didn't much like each other in the beginning. Might be because of my gambling habit. Or my foul mouth, or the way I treated women. Or how much I drank. Didn't mix well with this Bible-spoutin' do-gooder." Cyrus waved his hand toward Jubal. "I was spoiled and ornery and needed a good whoopin'."

"California whooped him good," Jubal said. "Imagine him—never done a lick of work in his entire life, not a callous on them lily-white hands, and he gonna dig in the gravel from sunup to sundown. He was just about broken in two when somebody up and held us at gunpoint and stole all his money."

Cyrus yawned. His eyes appeared too heavy to hold open. "And that was just the beginning..." Within minutes he was snoring.

Jubal laughed. "Guess y'all have to wait for the bad part."

Prudence smiled back at the man who radiated kindness. No need to worry him more than he already was. She would tell Jason what the man she met on the road had said about Jubal. But she would not believe it.

Chapter Eleven

As soon as the Saturday breakfast crowd began to thin, Tess headed for the stairs to change for the farmers market. She met the newlyweds on the landing, suitcases in hand. They set their bags down, and Gail reached out and hugged Tess. "Thank you, thank you, thank you. You've all been so kind."

Todd slipped his arm comfortably around Gail's shoulders. "How am I going to drag her back to a mud hut and no running water after you've pampered her like this? She's going to expect mints on her pillow every morning."

Gail laughed. "The rats would eat them." Her brave smile hid one of the fears she'd asked Tess to pray about. Rats in Nigeria were abundant and a source of Lassa fever. "If we have children…" Gail had said, not needing to finish her sentence.

"We will miss you." Tess hugged Todd. "You have us on your mailing list now, right?"

"Absolutely." Gail patted her laptop case. "I have the next newsletter half done, and it's going to have pictures of the inn and a huge shout-out to you three wonderful ladies."

"Thank you. We're grateful for any and all promotion. Remember us if you're ever back in the States around your anniversary."

"We will." Todd picked up his bag then set it down again. "Is Mr. MacIntosh still here? I tried to catch him last night. Maybe I should have called the police...Last night, when we got home from dinner, there was someone by his truck. It was dark, so we couldn't make out any details, but the person tried every door handle. It was locked, and they just ran off. I thought he should know."

"Thank you." Tess smiled with an ease she didn't feel. "Did they try any other vehicles?"

"No, just his."

"Okay. I'll tell him. If we call the police, they might need to talk to you."

"Of course. You have my number."

They said goodbye, and Tess continued up to her room.

Standing in front of her closet, she tried to shake the same sense of impending *something* she'd had the day before. Was someone trying to steal the truck, or were they after what they thought was in it? Someone looking for the slave tag or the watch cover? Or something more? What had Misty been implying when she said information Tess had might help the Tuttle estate uncover the truth about the fortune? Was Elliott in real danger? Were they? And what had he meant yesterday when he said he'd "fix it"?

And why hadn't Misty called yesterday? Tess had checked her phone every few minutes between noon and bedtime, wondering if her phone had somehow failed to notify her of an incoming call. There were so many logical reasons for a person not to call—unexpected busyness, a dead phone, being out of cell tower range—but Misty seemed like a no-nonsense person.

The kind of person who would find a way to follow through on an agreement. Of course, it wouldn't be the first time Tess had read someone totally wrong.

As she reached for her sweater, her hand brushed her Heritage Day dress. Would trying it on be encouraging or discouraging? She put her hand on her waist. After a week, she could feel a change. Her pants were more comfortable than they'd been a week ago. She probably hadn't lost much, and she wasn't about to get on the scale to find out, but seven days of healthy choices could help the dress fit better. At the moment, she could use some good news. She slipped out of her work clothes and took the dress off the hanger. She held her breath as she stepped into it. Though she couldn't fasten the buttons without help, she could tell just by holding it together that it fit better. She exhaled. One good thing going right. Maybe it was the beginning of a great day.

Or maybe not. A buzz drew her attention to her phone. The name on the screen caused a quick inhale. Misty.

Tess answered with a cheery greeting.

"This is Misty." The edgy voice on the other end didn't come close to matching Tess's upbeat opening to the conversation. "My apologies for not getting in touch yesterday. Are any of you interested in our offer?"

Not when you say it like that. Misty was matter-of-fact and seemed impatient.

"Yes. Thank you. I will be coming with an old college friend who is visiting, if that's all right."

"Who is it?"

Misty reminded Tess of a librarian who'd chastised her for an overdue book back in elementary school. She suddenly felt like she'd done something wrong. "Her name is…" Tess racked her brain to come up with Tippi's real name. She was named after her father. A royal name. Andrew? Henry? Phillip. "Phillipa Coddlesworth. She's from New York."

"What is her interest in coming with you?" Tess heard a car door slam and the engine start. "I'm sorry to sound like I'm interrogating you, but it's vital that the information I share with you not get to the wrong people."

What *was* Tippi's interest? Tess wasn't sure enough herself to give an answer. "She's just an old friend who thought a trip together would be interesting. She works for Legacy Quest, a genealogy research company."

"That could be a problem. We don't know what she knows or who she's working with."

Why hadn't Tess made that connection before? She thought of Tippi's job as dry and boring—days on end of sifting through birth and death records in musty old buildings. "She wouldn't need to be in on our talks. And I promise I won't share anything with her. I'm very invested in not turning this, whatever it is, into anything that brings undue attention to the people who own the property where we found the artifacts."

"I will do some checking on her and the company. If all seems to be in order, are you free to come Wednesday through Friday?"

"That would work well."

"Good. I'll need full names, addresses, and birthdates. Send them to the email on our website. I'll call on Monday with your flight times. Goodbye."

Tess stared at the phone. The call had ended before she'd had a chance to say goodbye. *Lord, stop me if this is a crazy move. If I'm walking into something dangerous, or if I shouldn't be going with Tippi, please make it clear.* She looked up at the re-honeymoon picture. What would Jeffrey have told her to do? In truth, she probably didn't want to know. He'd warned her, on more than one occasion, that the adventures she and LuAnn and Janice planned could land them in serious trouble. Like the time the three went backpacking in the Smokies without training for the hike…A few blisters, some very sore muscles, a whole lot of beauty, laughter, relaxation—and only one encounter with a very small bear—later, they were very glad they hadn't listened to his warning.

After dressing in jeans, heavy socks, hiking boots, and a cable knit sweater over a flannel shirt, she was ready for a few hours outdoors. Winnie had filled two large baskets with pumpkin cinnamon rolls and chubby little loaves of cranberry bread.

"Just got a call from Brin. She's wondering when you're coming, because she's almost sold out." Winnie filled a third basket with small bags of snickerdoodles tied with orange curling ribbon.

"That's great news. And these are gorgeous. I'll get pictures for our website."

"LuAnn added all the froufrou. I just bake." Winnie helped Tess loop the baskets on her arms. The smile she was trying to hold back broadcast her pride. "Say, your friend—Tipper? Tipsy?—sure asks a boatload of questions, doesn't she?"

Tess glanced up as LuAnn walked in the door. "Has Tippi been in the kitchen a lot?" She kept her voice low.

Winnie nodded. "She got up early this morning and asked LuAnn if she needed help, so she was unloading the dishwasher and talkin' my ear off near as much as Brin did when she first came. I suppose she's just one of those curious people, but I always get a little uneasy around someone who wants to know all about a person's business. She asked me if I know Maybelline and how well and if I'd read Prudence's journal. When I made the mistake of telling her I was descended from a woman Prudence brought across the river and that my great-great-great-grandma was born right here in one of those little rooms downstairs, she was nearly beside herself. That just spurred way more questions about slaves and what I knew about that man Jubal, who y'all think wore that slave tag you found. Like just because I come way, way back from a slave, I'm supposed to know all about all the people Miss Prudence brought to freedom?" Winnie took a deep breath, as if coming up for air. "I just don't trust her, is all."

Tess nodded, not wanting to add fuel to Winnie's fire by expressing her own concerns. "She really shouldn't be in the kitchen. I'll talk to LuAnn." She tried to reassure Winnie with a smile she didn't really feel, then walked out the back door, baskets on her arms like Little Red Riding Hood. There was a wolf out there. If only she could figure out what disguise he—or she—was wearing.

The colors and scents of the farmers market helped Tess leave fear behind and focus on the beauty around her. After catching up with Brin, she added the things she'd brought to the table, tweaked the display a bit, then stepped out in front to take pictures for the inn's website. She set the lens on "portrait" and zeroed in on the snickerdoodles. The pops of orange ribbon stood out against the sage-green background of the table cover. A fuzzy blur of leaf-covered grass framed two sides of the picture. Perfect.

"Yum."

Tess startled at the voice. Southern drawl, slightly familiar. She turned around to see the reenactment woman. "Hello!"

"Hi. I think I might need to stock up on these for the drive home." She pointed to the basket then picked up a flyer about the Heritage Tour. "This looks fascinating."

"This is a first for us. We're doing it as a fundraiser for a foster family that's building an accessible home for children with disabilities." That information was on the back of the flyer but pointing it out gave her the opportunity to draw attention to the donation jar. "All of the profit from our booth goes to the Moore House fund also."

The woman stared at the jar half-filled with coins and bills. "Children with disabilities?" Her voice sounded hollow.

"Yes." What had triggered the woman's thinly veiled emotional reaction? "Jerry Moore, the father, is unable to walk because of a work accident, so they need an accessible home for him and the children. They've been foster parents for years, but taking in kids with special needs will be new for them. The community is rallying around them to help."

"They must be..." The woman fingered a stray strand of blond hair. It seemed to be a gesture to fill time while she thought of the words she wanted to use. "Very giving people."

"That would describe the Moores."

With a nod, the woman walked away. Without buying anything. Tess's heart went out to her. Did she have a child or a sibling with a disability? Something had made the Moores' story hit a tender spot. Tess prayed for comfort as the woman walked away, not stopping at any of the booths along the way.

The next two hours sped by. Wispy clouds drifted lazily across an intensely blue sky. Once again, Tess was struck by the kaleidoscope of color laid out before her. The sun, dipping toward the western horizon, glinted off a row of jelly jars filled with every shade of red imaginable. Hand-stitched quilts hung on a clothesline. Tess recognized a few of the patterns. Log cabin, wedding ring, and one that appeared to be a copy of the River of Life quilt Prudence had helped stitch. Fat pumpkins, strange-shaped yellow gourds, red apples. And over all, the heavenly smells of caramel corn, fresh-pressed cider, and barbecue. She'd eaten a Honey Crisp apple and a small bag of freshly roasted almonds for lunch. Her stomach growled just as she spotted a new friend. "Evelyn!"

A wave and a smile greeted her. Evelyn walked over to the table.

"No wonder you needed to join the group." Evelyn picked up a bag of cookies, set it down, then turned her attention to the pumpkin cinnamon rolls. "I do believe you need a bit more than accountability, Tess. Have you considered getting your jaws wired shut?"

Tess laughed. Much-needed therapy. "Every morning I wake up to the smell of cinnamon rolls in the oven. It's my reminder to pray for self-control."

"I get that. I dropped five pounds the month after I retired. No more doughnuts calling my name in the staff room." Evelyn turned her back to the table and closed her eyes, taking in a deep breath. "Tantalizing smells here. Speaking of which, I'm going to make a Haitian chicken dish for you tonight. Do you have any allergies? Anything you don't eat?"

Tess shook her head. "I wish. If only I—" A blur of blue in her peripheral vision made her turn. Amy Moore ran toward her. She stopped three feet away to catch her breath. "I called the inn. They said you were here. One of the workers f-found something." She pressed a hand to her chest.

Tess stepped around the table. "What did they find?" Her pulse galloped as she put her arm across Amy's shoulders.

"A grave." Her eyes were wide with fear.

They'd found Cyrus's or Jubal's grave. It hardly seemed reason for such intense emotion. "Bones? Or a tombstone?"

"N-no." The color drained from Amy's face, and she appeared ready to faint. "A fresh grave."

CHAPTER TWELVE

All the questions she'd asked Amy—"*Are you sure someone wasn't just out there digging for more artifacts? What makes you think it's a grave and not just a hole somebody covered up?*"—evaporated as she stood next to Chief Mayfield behind the police tape, looking down at the carefully mounded pile of fresh dirt roughly three feet wide and six long.

At one end, a wooden stake was shoved into the ground, three letters printed on it.

R.I.P.

Chief Mayfield took a few more pictures, zeroing in on footprints, the stake, and a broken branch. In spite of the chill in the air, he wiped his brow with his sleeve. Glancing at Tess, he said, "I called Dr. Eastman and a couple guys we've trained for this...possibility."

A swirl of emotion roiled in Tess. The last time she'd stood graveside, she and Janice had stood shoulder to shoulder with LuAnn as she said her final goodbyes to her mother. Three years ago, she'd held Janice's hand, whispering prayers for comfort, and the time before that, her children and two best friends had taken turns holding her hands. This time there were no whispered prayers, no offered support, only questions.

"No missing person reports," the chief said. "Your crew all accounted for?" He directed the question at Jerry, who sat with Amy standing behind him, her hands on his shoulders.

"My crew leader contacted everyone. They're all here." He nodded to the cluster of men standing several yards away. All work on the basement had ceased the moment one of the men spotted the fresh dirt at the corner of the property.

The mound connected the spots where Elliott had left his orange markers.

Tess looked at Jerry. "You're sure it wasn't here yesterday?"

"Dead sure. Sorry. Sick humor. I took pictures of the property from the road yesterday afternoon. They're on our website. You can see this corner clearly. There's just enough of a slope here that we didn't notice it pulling into the drive. A couple of the guys were throwing a football during a break and one of them literally stumbled into this."

Elliott's car pulled up and he, LuAnn, and Janice got out. Brad was right behind them. Tess glanced back at Jerry and Amy but couldn't think of anything that would ease the worry etched on their faces. And it was all Tess's fault.

There were so many other places Elliott could have taken his metal detector. Or she could have asked him to simply give the tag and watch cover to Jerry and Amy. They would have made nice conversation pieces in a shadow box on the wall of their new home. A great way to introduce the children to the history of the property they lived on.

Tess shuddered and pulled her hood down over her forehead, trying to hold the full impact of her actions at bay. It was a losing battle. Reality was starting to take hold. *Someone could have been killed right here in this spot because of our—*my*—find.* But why?

The tag and watch cover were locked in the office safe at the inn where Brin now watched the front desk. Alone. She motioned to Janice and took her aside where no one else could hear. "I don't think Brin should be alone. If this happened because of what we found here…"

Janice nodded. "I didn't think of that. I'll call her mom and see if she can go over." Janice hugged her arms to her belly. "Was there any…blood? Or signs of anything?"

Tess shook her head. "Nothing. Chief Mayfield says there aren't any local missing person alerts."

"Yet."

"We don't need any more doom and gloom, Mary Sunshine."

Janice shrugged. "It's just the truth. If there's no sign of foul play, and the person is over twenty-one and mentally stable, they might not issue an alert for days."

"I can't…" Tess turned and walked away. She needed a quiet moment to think and pray. She nodded to the men who now sat on concrete blocks, talking in low tones as they gestured toward the grave, and walked up to the edge of the partially finished basement. The footings were in now, and they'd begun laying block. Five rows high. Decades ago, when they'd built a new clubhouse at the golf course in Stow, Jeffrey had explained each stage, step by step. She knew about leads and plumb lines and sealing and curing concrete.

She tried to imagine it as it would look when the job was complete. The basement would be mainly storage, and that only minimal as, at least at first, they wouldn't be able to afford a chair lift. The laundry room would be on the first floor. Jerry had explained that even though the lot was above the BFE, Base Flood Elevation, Amy was worried about flooding. Her parents' house had suffered severe damage in the flood that had covered Marietta's downtown a year and a half earlier. Tess pictured the floorplan Jerry had showed her. Four bedrooms, three baths. Walk-in tubs, lower vanities, a section of kitchen counter that would adjust from thirty-six to twenty-eight inches. Tess had watched Amy as she adapted to Jerry's limitations and admired how she managed to balance helping him and stepping back so he could relearn a daily task. The children who lived in this house would not be coddled but would always be praised and encouraged.

The yard sloped away from the foundation, giving a view of the river the Moores would enjoy through large windows across the back of the house. Was this the same view Prudence woke to every morning? Did Patience, her pet goose, waddle around behind her as she picked apples or milked cows? As a child, Tess had loved the Little House on the Prairie books, spending hours dreaming of living a simple life close to nature. Having read Prudence's journal, she knew the reality of life in the 1800s was anything but easy, yet she still felt a longing for the simplicity and slower pace. Still, Prudence was no stranger to drama. "What happened here, Pru? What is it about the things we found that has so many people curious? Did Cyrus die here? Did Jubal—"

Her phone buzzed before she had to reconstruct the grizzly scene Tippi had so graphically described.

Misty. She wasn't supposed to call until Monday. This could only mean one thing...she'd found out something about Tippi that made her not want her to come to Charleston. "Hello?" Tess answered.

"Just wanted you to know I booked your flights. Okay if I send the information to the email on the inn's website?"

"That will be fine. Um..." What, if anything, should she tell Misty about the grave?

"Yes?"

"Can you tell me anything at all over the phone? We've had some...developments here, and I would really appreciate knowing something, anything. Why are you, and others, so interested in what happened here?"

Silence greeted her. And then a sigh. "When Cyrus Tuttle and Jubal Hudson arrived in Marietta, we believe they were in possession of up to"—another sigh—"thirty pounds of raw gold."

Half an hour later, Tess returned to the grave. After talking to Misty, she'd texted LuAnn and Janice. Not about the gold. *I need to walk after standing all day. Be back in a few.* Thankfully, neither of them had offered to go with her.

She needed to walk fast and not think. But she couldn't stop the flood of thoughts.

Thirty pounds of gold. Thirty *pounds* of gold. Thirty pounds of *gold*. Four words swirled through her brain like debris caught in a whirlwind.

She couldn't, wouldn't, do the math. She didn't know how raw gold translated into sellable gold, but not long ago she'd heard gold was selling for over a thousand dollars an ounce...

Worth killing for.

The words strung together. *Thirty pounds of gold...worth killing for.*

As she walked as fast as she could along River Trail, the words were joined by three more. *All my fault.*

Tippi's fantasy of two men wrestling, one stabbing the other and being shot in return, had been disturbing. Not something she wanted to picture, but it was distant. Even if they'd learned that things between Cyrus and Jubal had played out exactly the way Tippi imagined it, Tess would have felt far more curiosity than shock or sadness. It was history.

This was real. She climbed the rise from the trail to the Moore property just as a car drove up and stopped. Could she handle watching as the men dug? She stood at the top of the hill, wanting to turn away yet unable to.

But it was not the men Chief Mayfield had called that got out of the car. It was a woman. Black leather coat, blond hair.

Dr. White.

She'd come out of curiosity about the tag and the watch cover. Marietta would not disappoint.

If the police were involved, this place would become a frenzied feeding ground for gawkers, reporters, and photographers. She could see the area around the foundation crawling like an ant hill, people shouting, asking questions, making accusations. Pointing at her.

And no work getting done.

A city truck pulled up, and two men jumped out. Janice's son Stuart was right behind them. Tess followed Jerry's crew, listening in on their banter as they walked toward the grave.

"...should have told them."

"Not me. Not getting questioned by Mayfield over a stupid—"

"Hush."

As she stepped around the men to stand next to Chief Mayfield, the crew grew silent. Funeral quiet as the men wearing reflective vests stuck their shovels into the ground, one at each end. Horror movie images flashed through Tess's mind. They had no idea how deep the body was. What if the shovels...She couldn't go there. LuAnn came up behind her and put an arm around her shoulder. Too reminiscent. Her eyes stung with tears she knew she'd shed in moments.

"Shallow," Chief Mayfield said, and the men began using their shovels as scoops, taking no more than two inches of dirt at a time. The chief looked at Jerry. "When we're done, we'll sift through all the dirt for evidence."

Tess tried to hide her impatience. At this rate it would take hours to dig down—how far? Strange that she'd been thinking it would be a vault-deep hole. No murderer, hiding a body in the middle of the night, would dig down six feet. A hurried grave might only be two feet deep. She cringed when one of the men hit something.

"Just a rock." The man bent, picked it up, and tossed it aside.

Because she'd added a widget to the inn's website linking to a site with statistics on Marietta, Tess knew the number of murders committed in their city in the past fifteen years. Zero. Not one.

Thirty pounds of gold…worth killing for. All my fault.

To stop the noise in her head, she looked around, studying the people in the group. Elliott first. Had he gone out during the night? Not likely. They locked the doors at eleven and set the alarm system. Anyone needing to leave would have to call the emergency number they gave their guests. Unless…did Elliott know about the secret ladder leading to the basement? The only exit not connected to the alarm system was the door to the tunnel that led under the river.

Not possible. The key to that door was in the safe in the office. Besides, Elliott's Santa Claus physique would have a hard time fitting into the ladder shaft.

Who had Todd Baxter seen checking the doors of Elliott's truck last night? Someone with blood on his…or her…hands? She needed to tell Chief Mayfield about it, should have done it this morning when Todd told her about the stranger trying the door handles. There might be prints.

Her gaze turned to Dr. White. Strange timing. She'd known about the tag and watch cover for days. Why show up today? Tess stared at the doctor's hands. She was a sturdy woman who looked like she could wield a shovel. Was there dirt under the fingernails beneath the leather gloves?

Gloves. Other than the men who were digging, Dr. White was the only person wearing gloves. The air was chilly, but still in the fifties.

Next, Tess looked at Dr. White's feet. Boots. Fashionable, but designed more for function than looks. A dab of dried mud on the side of one. From last night? What scenario would Tippi's wild imagination create to explain how and why Dr. White was here during the night…and with whom? Had she come with someone or had a surprise encounter after arriving? Someone lurking in the shadows, waiting…for what? That was still the part that didn't make sense. If, in fact, the victim and killer had been searching for gold, how would they hope to find it at night? Were they using a metal detector? She looked around for any signs of fresh divots but couldn't find any.

Anyone who'd read the article in the *Marietta Times* would know that there was a treasure rumored to be buried out here, but how many people knew that treasure might be gold? Misty, any number of people who worked at the Tuttle Plantation and…Goldilocks. She stared at Dr. White's fluffy blond hair then back at her boots. Something caught her attention.

"Wait." Tess held up her hand. She was sure she'd seen a flash of something blue in a clod of dirt dumped from one of the shovels right in front of her feet. She picked up a clump of dirt and turned it over. Bright blue. She brushed at the dirt the way Elliott had taught her.

LuAnn leaned over her shoulder. "Looks like a piece of a magazine cover."

Tess held the triangle-shaped paper lightly between her thumb and forefinger. "It's too thick to be from a magazine."

LuAnn touched it. "Maybe an advertising flyer."

Chief Mayfield cleared his throat and held out an evidence bag just as Tess turned the paper over and saw something printed on the back. She pretended she hadn't heard Mayfield. She needed a moment more to study it. Straight top edge, about two inches long, rough, torn edges on the other two sides that converged at a point. Dark blue glossy paper, four large red letters above four rows of small white ones. Not enough to make sense.

VERS
he company began
who traveled
eposits
mini

The "eposits" had to be *deposits.* A bank brochure maybe? Was it actually a clue or something that had just blown here? It was crumpled but didn't look like it had been out in the elements long.

"Mrs. Wallace." The chief's voice indicated that he had lost his patience. He held the bag open in front of her. "It could be evidence."

He did not add, "And you're tampering with it," but Tess heard it anyway. She deposited it carefully in the bag.

"What do you think it is?" Janice stepped into the gap between Tess and Mayfield. She cupped her hand next to her mouth and spoke so quietly Tess almost couldn't hear her. "Did you know *she* was coming today?" One finger of the hand that shielded her mouth straightened, pointing almost imperceptibly at Dr. White.

"No," Tess whispered. "Do you think she could be—"

"Hit something." The man who'd been digging next to the stake set his shovel down, and both men began scooping dirt with their hands. After a moment, they stopped. "Think we hit the bottom, Chief. It's all hard clay beneath here." In minutes they had cleared out all the loose dirt.

Leaving nothing but a shallow, empty grave.

Chapter Thirteen

"You think it was just a Halloween prank?" LuAnn sat at the kitchen table in their apartment. She opened her notebook and took out her favorite silver pen.

Tess chopped red pepper for the salad she was taking to Evelyn's. "I have no idea."

"It has to be more than that." Janice snatched a slice of pepper then took a chair across from LuAnn. "Someone deliberately dug right where the orange flags were." She pushed a chair out with her foot. "Hurry up with that, Tess. We want to hear this great thing you've been holding out on us."

Tess turned toward the table and smiled mysteriously. Until now, they hadn't had time without other guests around to talk openly. As she'd headed to her room to change for dinner, she'd simply said, "I have something very, very interesting to tell you two when I'm done." With exaggerated slowness, she tossed the salad then sidled over to the table. "I saw Elliott and Dr. White leave together. Any idea where they were going?" A little idle conversation just to irritate her friends.

"Out for dinner with Maybelline and Axel." LuAnn's left brow rose as she waited for Tess's reaction.

"What? Maybelline and Axel? Again? When they were here a few days ago I figured they were just making nice for Belle's sake. Wow. Is there something going on between them? Again?" It was still so hard to picture the very opinionated, often critical Maybelline in a relationship with a man who had once operated the Wayfarers Inn building as a chop shop. With his tattoos and ponytail and tall tales, Axel would never be the person an online dating service would pair with the ever-serious Maybelline. What had they been like back in the fifties when they were young and in love? Had a broken heart and an unplanned pregnancy turned Maybelline into a different person than she'd once been?

"Yep," Janice answered. "I found a not-too-nosy way to ask Belle this afternoon when she called about string practice. It sounds like they are rekindling their romance. But she didn't offer any information about why Maybelline is selling her house."

LuAnn tapped the end of her pen against her notebook. "Maybelline has shown a great deal of interest in the things that were found on the Moore land. Do you think it's just historical interest?"

Tess brought a glass of water to the table and sat down. "You're thinking her interest has something to do with Axel, aren't you?"

"It's not much of a stretch, is it?"

"No. Definitely not." The thought saddened Tess, and she could see the same look mirrored on Janice's face. Janice's husband had given up many Saturday mornings to talk to Axel and his fishing buddies. After Lawrence's death, Pastor Ben, his successor at Fellowship Community Church, had taken up the mission. They'd heard rumors that Axel's heart was softening to the things of God. Tess wanted to believe he'd turned from his former ways. She ladled cider into three mugs and carefully brought them to the table.

"So? What's this secret you've been keeping from us?" LuAnn folded her hands on her notebook. Janice mirrored her body language.

Tess's attitude about the gold had done a complete one-eighty the moment they realized there was no body buried on the Moore land. "Well, I got this call from Misty..." She told them everything she'd learned.

LuAnn's mouth froze on "Wha...?" Janice's eyes appeared about to drop right out of their sockets.

"Th...th...thirty?" LuAnn stuttered.

"P-pounds?" Janice finished.

"That's what she said. I figure that would be about half a million dollars today."

When they finally shook out of their catatonic states, her friends both nodded slowly. LuAnn clicked her pen.

"What if the legend about the buried treasure was founded on fact?" Tess ran her finger around the rim of her glass. "Maybe Jubal buried it and planned to come back for it, but he died before he could. We could come up with a ton of possible scenarios." Including Tippi's double murder idea.

Janice nodded. "If someone found the gold during the night and they got caught, could they be charged for theft?" she asked. "Technically, they stole it from the Moores, right?"

"I don't know if a charge like that would stick," Tess answered.

LuAnn wrote SUSPECTS at the top of her page. "Will the police be looking for someone?"

A platinum curl bounced on Janice's forehead as she shook her head. "They aren't going to go hunting for someone who *might* have stolen something that *might* have been buried there."

"Chief Mayfield did say they'd keep an eye on the property." A spurt of adrenaline caused Tess's pulse to do a little hop-skip-jump. "We have no idea if the gold thieves found anything last night. What if they're coming back tonight to keep searching?"

For several minutes, the only sound in the kitchen came from the ticking wall clock. "Almost full moon tonight," Tess said. No sensible gold-stealer would start digging until after most people had gone to bed, right? She could be home from Evelyn's by nine.

"Oh no you don't." Janice shot her a wary look. "You aren't going—"

The front door chime interrupted Janice. Tess set her mug down. "I'll go down." It was probably one of their guests. As she stepped onto the second-floor landing, she heard the sound of something heavy thudding to the floor. The Civil War reenactment couple stood in front of the desk. "Welcome back to Wayfarers Inn."

"Thank you." The woman smiled. "Any chance you'd have a room open for two weeks? The reenactment we were going to got canceled because of flooding."

The man grinned. "Apparently the organizers don't think their volunteers are as tough as the characters we play. If General Sherman had let flooded rivers keep his army from taking Columbia and Charleston back in 1865, the war might have had a very different ending. They were tough men back then."

"And tough women." The woman Tess assumed was his wife nudged him with her elbow, then looked at Tess. "Did you know more than four hundred women from both sides disguised themselves as men so they could fight?"

"I didn't know that." Tess opened the reservation page on the computer. "If you're staying for two weeks, you'll be here for our Heritage Tour."

"That was part of what helped us make our decision to stay here," the man said. "Marietta was the first American city established outside of the original thirteen colonies. Can't wait to learn more."

"There weren't any battles fought right here, but Camp Putnam was located along the Muskingum River, probably where our fairgrounds are located now," Tess said. "It opened in April of 1861 and two years later was used as a staging area for Union troops who were sent to stop Morgan's Raiders. They defeated him at the Battle of Buffington Island, about forty-five miles from here.

"We found a journal here in the inn that was written by a woman who was a conductor on the Underground Railroad. During that battle, she and other local women were called into service as nurses on a makeshift hospital ship. She saved the life of a Union spy and may have played a part in stopping one of the assassination attempts on President Lincoln." Tess had done so much research for the Heritage Tour, she was starting to sound like LuAnn the history teacher. She decided to save the part about the ruby decoder pin Natalie Hemmingway had attempted to steal from its hiding place beneath one of the stairs leading to the second floor. They could hear all that on the tour.

"Name?"

"Weber. Stanley and Sylvia."

Tess typed in the names and the Texas address they gave her then asked for a credit card.

"Okay if we pay with cash?" Sylvia asked.

"Of course." Tess hoped she'd hidden her surprise. It was so rare to have anyone use cash even for one night, and they were going to give her enough for two weeks? "Do you want to pay for a few days at a time?"

"We'll pay it all now."

Tess used the calculator on the keyboard to multiply then add in hotel fees and sales tax. She watched their faces as she gave them the total.

Not a twitch. Were they eccentrics who didn't trust banks… or people who didn't want to leave a paper trail?

Sylvia's charm bracelet jangled against the clasp on her purse as she pulled out a zippered pouch and counted out the money. All hundreds and a twenty. Tess started to count out their change, but Sylvia held up her hand. "I don't need coins jangling around in my purse."

Tess led them to the elevator, and they got out on the third floor. "I'll put you in Woodbine and Roses. You'll have a view of the river."

Sylvia ran her fingertips along the chair rail as they walked down the hallway. "Is this original?"

"Most of it," Tess answered. "We kept as much of the trim as possible. Wherever we had to replace some, we had it custom made to match the old." She opened the door to their room and stood back for them to enter.

"Wow." Sylvia set her bags on the floor. "I love it."

"Very authentic." Stuart touched the ball on one of the bed posts.

Tess handed them a laminated page with a list of local restaurants and churches. "WiFi password and emergency numbers are on the back. We normally lock the doors at eleven, but if you plan on being out later, just let us know." She pointed at the number that would reach the innkeeper who was "on call" and then told them about the goody basket.

Stanley stood statue still. "You have an alarm system?" His face pinched.

"Yes. State of the art."

The creases on Stanley's forehead deepened, then he shook his head and smiled. A strained smile. He stroked his chin and gave a slow, thoughtful nod. "Good. Thank you."

Odd behavior.

Tess let her gaze linger a moment on the wallpaper that reflected the name of the room. Green vines, honeysuckle trumpets in coral and yellow, purplish-blue berries, and wild pink roses. She smiled as she closed the door, remembering the laughter as they'd papered the room while Brad and LuAnn held a contest to see who could learn the words to Robert Frost's "Love and a Question." Though she hadn't been part of the competition, part of the poem was emblazoned on her brain, especially the last lines.

> *The bridegroom came forth into the porch*
> *With, 'Let us look at the sky,*
> *And question what of the night to be,*
> *Stranger, you and I.'*
> *The woodbine leaves littered the yard,*
> *The woodbine berries were blue,*
> *Autumn, yes, winter was in the wind;*
> *'Stranger, I wish I knew.'*

Encounters with strangers in the past year and a half had resulted in new friendships, shared joys and heartache, and opportunities to share her faith and offer counsel. And more than a bit of mystery.

What's on your mind, Mr. Weber? Stranger, I wish I knew.

Dinner with Evelyn and her mother was a welcome respite from the questions volleying back and forth at Wayfarers Inn. Evelyn owned a Victorian house on Center Street across from Mound Cemetery. Painted pale green with white trim and dark green shutters, the house on the cobblestone road probably looked much like it had a hundred years ago.

Tess set a green salad on the table next to the Haitian chicken dish Evelyn put on a trivet. Chicken smothered in tomatoes, garlic, onions, and seasoned with cayenne rested on a bed of multicolored rice. "I went easy on the pepper just for you," Evelyn said.

Evelyn's mother, who bore the perfectly fitting name "Lovely," laughed. "You can be ever so glad she used a light hand. One time she invited the president of the college and his wife and their dog for supper. Before he tasted it himself, the president gave a bite of chicken to the poor unsuspecting dog. You should have seen that pup running around the table howling like it'd been bit by a rattler." Her face crinkled along lines that spoke of many smiles and much laughter. Dark eyes shimmered with merriment.

"My mother does love to exaggerate," Evelyn said, resting a hand on her mother's thin shoulder.

They sat at the table, and Lovely closed her eyes and raised her hands. "Gracious God, we are ever so thankful for Your provision and protection and for new friends. Amen."

After they dished up, Evelyn turned to Tess with a look of concern. "I know it's none of my business, but…"

"Oh!" Tess's hand flew to her mouth. "I'm so sorry. It's been such a wild day, I totally forgot you were there when Amy came." She shook her head. "No body. It wasn't actually a grave."

Evelyn breathed a sigh. "Thank God. The woman, Amy, said it was on 'the property.' Was that your property, near your inn?"

"No." Tess's turn to sigh, but she kept it silent. She'd wanted this night to be an escape. But she didn't want to be rude, and she couldn't ignore the light bulb that had clicked on when Evelyn mentioned her experience on archaeological digs. It was no coincidence this new friend came into her life right now. She started at the beginning, with finding Prudence's journal, then moving on to Jerry's accident, plans for the Moore House, Elliott asking where he could use his metal detector, the tag and the watch cover, and what they knew about Cyrus and Jubal. She told her about the legend of the buried treasure and that Cyrus and Jubal could have been in possession of something valuable, but didn't mention the gold. The fewer people who knew about that, the better. It was too easy to let something slip unintentionally. "So we have ourselves a mystery. Who was digging on the Moore property, and why?"

Lovely clicked her tongue. "People will risk life and limb for treasure, won't they? When will they learn they got to be layin' up treasure in heaven instead?"

"You are so right." Tess smiled at Lovely, then looked at Evelyn for her reaction to the long and winding story that led to the hole in the ground marked RIP.

"Cyrus Tuttle." Evelyn tapped her fingers on the tablecloth. "Why is that name familiar? I'm sure I read it on something at the college. A plaque or a statue or something."

"Really?" Tess's heart rate ramped up as she leaned forward. That didn't sync with what Prudence had written. "From what we know, he was gravely ill when he arrived in Marietta, at least on his return trip. It sounds as though he died here."

"I don't know. It's just this vague feeling."

Lovely made her signature clicking noise again. "You're probably thinking of Uncle Cyrano James." To Tess she said, "My husband's great-aunt's husband. He was an aide to President McKinley when the US declared war on Spain in 1898. Uncle Cyrano won a fishing tournament when he was only fourteen and that drew the attention of a senator from Virginia who befriended him and eventually hired him as a page, which eventually led to him working for McKinley and writing that letter to William Randolph Hearst telling him to keep his opinions to himself or..."

Tess stifled a laugh as she watched Evelyn fight to keep a straight face. To her credit, she seemed amused rather than irritated at her mother's wandering tale. They spent the rest of the evening chatting about Lovely's childhood in Haiti and Evelyn's and Tess's years of teaching. As Tess hugged Evelyn and thanked her for a wonderful time, Evelyn said, "It's been bugging me all evening. In spite of how often I've heard my mother's stories of distant relatives, I know I'm not thinking of Great-Great-Uncle Cyrano James who lost his job because he blasted William Randolph Hearst in an editorial in the *New York Journal.* I remember the name Tuttle. I'm sure of it. I can see the name engraved in bronze. But where?" She tapped her salt-and-pepper curls. "I will figure this out, I promise."

"No pressure. Don't lose sleep over it. But it could be a major piece in this mysterious puzzle." *And might just be the key to finding* thirty *pounds of raw gold.*

October 17, 1858

"I wonder, if they knew the full story, if they would do anything but disdain me more and consider me unworthy of caring for even a single child." Catherine Fay poured a spoonful of sugar into her tea, using the spoon Prudence's adopted mother had given her and Jason as a wedding gift. Earlier, as Prudence had used the sugar snips to break pieces off the sugar loaf, Cyrus had watched from Prudence's rocking chair by the fire, then asked what she was doing. She had hidden her surprise well. The man had most certainly been born to privilege. When she explained, he said, "I guess there's a lot I don't know about real life."

She and Katie sat at Prudence and Jason's old, scarred kitchen table, talking in hushed tones, trying not to disturb Cyrus. He'd been awake when Katie arrived, and had shown much interest in hearing about her endeavors, but his times of alertness were growing shorter each day, and he'd soon drifted to sleep. Prudence kept one ear tuned to his labored breathing. Jason and Jubal had left earlier to hunt, so she was the one who needed to see to Cyrus.

Prudence dipped her quill in ink and put the tip to the page she'd torn from her journal. "We can leave out the part about the doctor asking thee to adopt the child, but—"

"How could anyone think me anything but cold-hearted? Could I not have stretched my hundred dollars a year to feed and clothe a two-year-old? I desperately wanted to take her in, but as a single woman hundreds of miles from any family, needing to work for my meager pay, I..." Katie pressed a handkerchief edged in blue tatting to her eyes.

This was not the first time Prudence had witnessed the wrenching guilt that fueled Katie's passion to open a home for orphans. She slid her hand over Katie's. "Let us focus on what happened after she was taken in."

"She...." Tears welled in Katie's eyes.

Prudence felt her own eyes burn. Having lost their own daughter, only minutes old, she felt she could not bear to hear the story told again. Yet part of her knew it needed to be told to stir compassion for homeless children. A young mother dies, leaving five small children. The physician who attended her, seeking to find homes for the children, approached Katie about adopting the youngest, a beautiful little girl. Though Katie's heart was tender toward the child, she did not feel she was in a position to suitably care for her. Subsequently, the child was taken in by a man and his wife who sold whiskey to the Indians. One day there was a drunken fight, and the little girl was thrown down the steps of the house and died.

The story might tug hearts and prompt people to give to Katie's home, but she could not bear the thought of her friend reading this story about her darkest hour in the *Marietta Times*, or being asked to speak about it before crowds. "No. We will not use this. We will start with the opening of thy home. We will tell the stories of the children thee cares for now." She wrote an opening line then stopped at the sound of horse hooves outside. She'd thought Jason and Jubal had left on foot. The wind blew, showering the roof with acorns. That was likely what she'd heard.

"Once people see them as individuals, get to know their hopes and dreams, they will be moved to help." An idea struck and raised gooseflesh along her arms. "We will ask them to sponsor a specific child. Does thee think—"

"I will."

The soft voice startled them. Cyrus faced them, eyes open wide and shining. "How much do you need?"

Prudence felt her tears sting once again. This man who had lost everything wanted to give. "Cyrus, that is so kind, but—"

His thin hand rose to stop her. "I was...an orphan. My uncle...took me in. Not a kind man. Had there been a place... like your home...." He closed his eyes again.

"What a dear man." Katie blotted her face. "Does he...is he able to give?" she whispered.

Prudence shook her head. "He came from wealth, but all he once had is gone." She lowered her voice even more. "He doesn't have long."

"I'm so sorry. How kind of you to—"

Heavy footsteps sounded on the porch, accompanied by voices.

"My husband," Prudence explained. "And our other guest." All she had told Katie was that Cyrus's traveling companion was hunting with Jason. She had not attempted to explain who Jubal was. Katie, a caring woman who had spent ten years on an Indian reservation, wasn't likely to be prejudiced, but one never knew. As the door opened, she stayed attentive to Katie's expression. Though she registered surprise when Jubal entered, there was no hint of discomfort. Prudence introduced the men. Jason's usual easy smile seemed forced, and Jubal's face was rigid with what she could only describe as a look of fear.

Jason took off his hat. "Nice to finally meet thee, ma'am. Prudence has told me much about thy good work. It is tender to her heart, as she was separated from her family young and in need of a good home." A shadow crossed his face, and he pulled something from his pocket. "I'm sorry to bring darkness into the middle of thy good work, but something's happened."

"What, Jason?" Fear tightened Prudence's voice. "Is thee all right?"

"Saw a man riding up to the house a bit ago. Saw him stop at Catherine's wagon and leave this." He held out a stained and ragged piece of paper. A single sentence was scrawled in childlike letters and misspelled words.

IF CYRUS T. GIVS YOU THE GOLD, NO THAT I WILL STEEL IT FROM YOU AND THE CHILDRN WILL SUFFER.

Chapter Fourteen

Church?" Tippi stared at LuAnn over the rim of her coffee cup. "Me?

It was just after ten. Dressed for church, the Inn Crowd lingered over a final cup of coffee with Tippi and Brin in the café. Brin had attended what she termed a "younger, cooler" church on Saturday night with some college friends and had offered to "woman" the front desk this morning.

"You came to some of the Bible studies in our dorm," Janice said.

"Just to harass you. Sorry, I'm not the churchy type." Tippi brushed off the invite with a wave of her hand and a laugh.

Not for the first time, both recently and back in college, Tess heard the hollowness in Tippi's laugh. "What would it hurt?" she asked.

The question seemed to surprise Tippi. "Pretty sure somebody near me would get hurt. That bolt of lightning would shatter some stained glass for sure. You don't want to be sitting near me when that happens."

"What if all that happened is you let a little truth seep in?" Tess prayed the boldness was coming from God and not her own frustration with Tippi's decades-long stubbornness.

Tippi blinked several times then gave another empty laugh. "Your truth doesn't need to be mine, girlfriend."

Janice rested her hand on Tippi's, but withdrew when Tippi glared at her. "What if we drive separately and sit near the back? You can have an end seat and be free to leave whenever you want."

"I…why? Why is it so important to you all? Do you get brownie points in heaven for every person you drag to church?"

LuAnn shook her head. "Tippi…it's nothing like that. We all remember life before we understood what Jesus sacrificed for us and how much He loves us. Life hasn't been a bed of roses for any of us, but we wouldn't go back to those days for anything. We—" She stopped talking when Elliott and Dr. White stepped out of the elevator.

"Good morning!" Elliott's large voice bounced off the tin ceiling. "How is everyone on this fine Sunday morning?"

Santa Claus. Definitely. Tess's thoughts rabbit-trailed, wondering if they could invite him back in December. That voice with a beard and a red velvet suit…

"Thought we'd take you up on your invite to church. I love visiting churches when I travel."

"Wonderful." Janice stood. "Would you like to follow us?"

"That would be great." Elliott buttoned his tweed coat. Dr. White hadn't yet said a word.

As LuAnn and Janice reached for their coats, Tess nodded, as discreetly as she could, toward Tippi. Forty years of friendship had created excellent lines of nonverbal communication. Her friends instantly started chatting with Elliott and Dr. White.

"My car is out this way," Janice said. "We'll meet you out front."

Tess turned in her chair, letting her body language show Tippi she would take all the time she needed. "No brownie points. Knowing Jesus has given us hope and purpose. Because we care about you, we want that for you. It's that simple."

Tippi banged the bottom of her cup on the table. "I was afraid it would turn into this if I came here." She stood. "I have a massage scheduled at eleven. I need to get ready." She pushed her chair back and sprinted up the stairs to her room. The forceful close of her door echoed in the upstairs hall.

"Okay then." Tess spoke to the emptiness as she picked up her coat and followed the others out to Janice's car.

Amy and Jerry were greeters at the door. Tess hugged them both. Amy whispered in her ear, "We stopped at the property on our way here. I got out and walked around the perimeter. Nothing unusual." She pulled away, crossing her arms tight across her middle.

Tess longed for some words of assurance, but nothing came to mind. If they didn't find out who'd dug the hole, and if the person had found what he or she or they were looking for, Amy would always live under the shadow of worry.

They were beginning the chorus of the second hymn when Tess felt a nudge. Not a Holy Spirit prod, this time it was a physical nudge. Tippi stood next to her, face red and scowling. She wore a skirt and sweater and clutched a notebook. Tess tapped Janice's arm, and the taps continued down to Brad. They moved down and made room in the pew. And tried to act unshocked.

Tippi stood, stiff and straight as a dried cornstalk, until the worship music ended. When they sat, it seemed to Tess that Tippi had to force her joints to comply, like folding a thick piece of cardboard. She sat with her hands gripping her notebook, her spine not touching the back of the pew. Ready to bolt.

After Pastor Ben prayed, he smiled at the congregation. "Good morning. My message today is not for everyone, so I want to give some of you the opportunity to leave right now." He paused. Ben Murphey had mastered the dramatic pause. "Those of you who have never questioned God and what He's doing with the world, you are free to head over to Jeremiah's. Coffee and donuts on me." Stepping to the edge of the platform, he pulled out his wallet and fanned a stack of bills. "Anyone?" He grinned and walked back to the music stand that held his notes. "No takers?

"Let's turn to the book of Ecclesiastes, chapter four. This is Solomon, one of the smartest guys who ever lived, talking. He says, 'Again I looked and saw all the oppression that was taking place under the sun: I saw the tears of the oppressed—and they have no comforter; power was on the side of their oppressors—and they have no comforter. And I declared that the dead, who had already died, are happier than the living, who are still alive. But better than both is the one who has never been born, who has not seen the evil that is done under the sun. And I saw that all toil and all achievement spring from one person's envy of another. This too is meaningless, a chasing after the wind...'"

Ben smiled. "And you came to church for encouragement, huh? Clearly, questioning God is not a contemporary thing. If you have doubts, and God's ways often don't make sense, you are not the first, and you are not alone."

Though she couldn't look directly at her, Tess sensed a change in Tippi. Her grip on her notebook loosened.

After reading the passage, Ben began a list. Starting with broad strokes from history—the exile of the Israelites, slavery, the Holocaust, attack on the Twin Towers, school shootings—he slowly brought it home to Marietta. "Some of you lost homes or revenue in the flooding. Where was God in all of this?" Without warning, he hopped down from the platform. "I've asked some dear friends to share their story this morning." He stepped aside, making room for Jerry and Amy.

Jerry took the microphone. He described the accident that was the result of human error—a crane operator had been talking on his phone and hadn't responded fast enough to check the imbalance in the beam he was moving. "I handled it well, didn't I?" Jerry smiled up at Amy, who rolled her eyes. "I woke up in the hospital, realized I couldn't feel my legs, and immediately told my wife and kids not to worry. God's got this,

I said. And I believed it. Absolutely, one hundred percent." He slid his hand over Amy's that rested on his chest. "For twenty-four hours."

He waited, letting the impact of his words sink in. "And then I went nuts. Anger, terror...I felt like if I didn't punch something, or someone, I was going to explode. I was so. So. Mad. At. God." He meted out each word with such force Tess could almost feel the punches he'd wanted to throw.

Tippi took a quavering breath. Movement on the other side of the church drew Tess's attention. Dr. White stood and almost ran down the center aisle. Seconds later, the heavy front door banged shut.

Janice had gone out to lunch with Stuart, Zelda, and Brin straight from church. LuAnn and Brad had offered the inn's patio as a meeting place for the young adult group led by Pastor Ben and his wife Paige. They were carrying chairs out the back door when Tess walked into the kitchen. "You're welcome to join us," LuAnn said.

"Thanks, but I think I need a little alone time before lovey time." Harper had a cold, and now Liam was sneezing, so Lizzie and Michael had stayed home from church. Tess offered to bring soup for supper so they could just concentrate on the kids. It didn't require much work, as Winnie always had gallons frozen in the café freezer. She'd taken a container of chicken noodle and set it out to thaw.

Two hours alone. It didn't happen often. She wasn't a person who needed a lot of alone time, but when she got it, she relished it. She warmed the leftovers Evelyn had sent home with her. The rich, spicy flavors were even more delicious the second day.

Now what? She washed her bowl and spoon and put them away, then stood in front of the window overlooking the garden. Sunlight glazed the oak tree just behind the inn, making the leaves look like polished bronze. "What am I doing inside?" With no idea where she was heading, she laced her hiking boots and zipped up a rust-colored fleece jacket.

The smell of popcorn wafted from the first floor. The group would be arriving soon. Good time to leave. Buttered popcorn was a weakness.

She met Elliott at the foot of the stairs. "You look like you're off on an adventure," he said, pointing to her boots.

In that moment she knew where she was going. "I want to walk around the Moore property."

"Looking for clues?"

"Just exploring." She shrugged. "Yes, I guess I'm hoping to find clues. I hate to think of Amy Moore living in fear that whoever is searching for something isn't going to leave them alone."

"Wish I could go with you. I set up a private meeting with Felicity and Maybelline Rector to look at some things in Maybelline's private collection." He stroked his beard with his thumb and index finger. "You need a metal detector."

Without waiting for her to answer, he pulled his keys from his jacket pocket and motioned for her to follow him out the front door.

"No, I couldn't. I'd be too afraid I'd wreck something."

"Well, I'm not worried, and it's my opinion that counts, right?" His laughter seemed to boom out across the river as he opened the door. "I'll give you the one that's already a bit beat up. Fell off a small cliff with it once." Again, he laughed. "Always a good idea to pay attention to your surroundings."

She followed him out and took the canvas bag he pulled from the back of his truck. He handed her a set of headphones and a pinpointer then unzipped the bag and gave her a refresher course on how to read the gauges. He pulled out the map he'd drawn of the lot. "I got to this square yesterday." He pointed to a spot in the middle of the map. "Just stick to the grid, please, and record where you search. Here." He handed her the detector. "You take this, and I'll carry a shovel to your car. If you have any problems, text me."

"Thank you. This is so kind."

"Nah. It's selfish. I'd be out there 24/7 if I never had to work. Can't wait to hear what you find."

Just before Elliott turned to walk back into the inn, Tess asked how Dr. White was doing. After she'd gotten up and left church this morning, a startled-looking Elliott had followed her. Though she wasn't in the habit of texting in church, Tess had sent him a message asking if Dr. White was okay and if they needed anything. He'd answered about ten minutes later. *Just emotional. Not sure why. God's in control.*

"I believe the Lord is convicting her of something, but I don't know what. I really don't know her well. This is only the second time we've met in person. I sense there are things from her past she needs to come to peace about. She said she wanted to take a drive alone to clear her mind." Apple cheeks rose. "I gave her a Bible. Maybe too bold, but I'm praying she fills her mind with the truth rather than clearing it."

"I'll pray too." She said goodbye to Elliott.

Tess drove to the Moores' property and parked her car in the gravel drive next to the old foundation. Armed with detector, headphones, spray bottle, pinpointer, and shovel, she strode toward the "grave." Could there be clues the police had missed? She loved that quick spurt of adrenaline that always accompanied the thought of unraveling a mystery. She stood by the mound of loose dirt. Chief Mayfield had taken the RIP stake as evidence. With it gone, it was much easier to think of it as simply a pile of dirt.

Gazing toward the river, she tried again to imagine the property when it belonged to Prudence and her husband. They now knew where the barn had been. Where would the house have been located? Was she standing on what would once have been the family cemetery? Were Cyrus and Jubal buried beneath her? Others? Mound Cemetery had been established around 1800, but were there laws in place at the time saying people had to be buried there?

The mound of dirt was only about two yards from a wooded area. Most of Jerry and Amy's property had been cleared, but what remnants of Prudence's life might remain in this tangle of undergrowth? She'd learned from Jerry that the Willards' house, which had once been part of the Campus Martius fort, moved piece by piece to this location sometime in the early nineteenth century, had burned down in the forties, and the city had claimed the land.

Pushing aside thin branches and carefully avoiding raspberry bush thorns, Tess picked her way through the underbrush. Prudence had likely walked here, picking raspberries or searching for a hen—or pet goose—that had chosen to nest away from the chicken coop. She stepped over a mossy log, then turned to look at it. Did Prudence have a favorite spot to sit and think and pray? Maybe a fallen log?

She leaned the shovel against a tree, put on the headphones, turned them on, and began making slow arcs. Sunlight fell in jagged pattern-pieces on the leaf-strewn ground, illuminating bright green moss and the muted colors of fallen leaves and rusting goldenrod. The year Jeffrey died the fall colors had seemed to whisper to her, "*Even in this season there is beauty.*"

An old hymn, one that Prudence herself may have sung, trailed through her mind, and she began to sing. "'For the beauty of the earth, for the glory of the skies. For the love—'" Her foot caught on something and she fell, landing on her hands. As soon as she was sure she was all right, she stood and brushed off her jeans. "Tess, you're a clumsy—"

The thing that had tripped her was not a rock or a buried branch, but a thick chunk of once-white marble. Roughly triangular, about ten inches wide and eight high, it appeared to be a broken corner of what might have been a two-tiered base. She dropped back to her knees and brushed dirt off the pitted surface, uncovering numbers. She found a stone and used it to scrape the dirt away, then dumped the contents of the spray bottle over it.

er 20, 1858

She'd stumbled on part of a tombstone.

Chapter Fifteen

Tess stood looking down at the grave marker. Where was the rest of it? Part of her wanted to call LuAnn and Janice to tell them what she'd found. A bigger part wanted to find the rest of the stone first. She'd slipped the headphones around her neck but put them back on. Might as well hunt for other treasures while she searched the woods for another chunk of marble.

Though she was starting to get the hang of it, she didn't have Elliott's expertise in recognizing a good, solid sound worth digging, so she took his advice and dropped to her knees whenever the meter read over fifty. She found a penny so corroded she couldn't make out the year, a canning jar ring, and a rifle shell—not old enough to fit Tippi's scenario of the demise of both Jubal and Cyrus—before getting a tone she hadn't heard before. Much louder and deeper. She zeroed in on it then made a U-shaped cut in the ground and flipped the dirt plug out of the way. The pinpointer vibrated and made a fast, high-pitched beeping sound on one side of the hole. As she placed her foot on the shovel, she wondered again what Jeffrey would say if he could see her. *"Tess, do you know how old you are?"* She laughed as she jumped onto the shovel, forcing the blade deeper into the ground, and repeated the Inn Crowd motto, the one that always made Jeffrey roll his beautiful blue eyes. "We will never be boring or bored, and we will never act our age!"

A rustle in the brush behind her made her freeze. She turned just her head and shoulders. Nothing but the slight swish of leaves swaying in the wind. She'd probably heard a squirrel or a rabbit. She turned the dirt over, shoving the clod away from the hole with her boot, and repeated the process of searching for the exact spot with the pinpointer. "There." Using her gloved hand, she pulled dirt from the hole. Her fingertips touched something, and she dug around it until she could slide one finger beneath a piece of metal and free it. A silver spoon.

"Sugar shell," she whispered. Her mother had owned one. The bowl was deep, the edges scalloped like a cockle shell. Tess stood and wiped off the handle. Was that a scratch on the end? She took off her glove and rubbed with her bare thumb, then gasped as gothic letters appeared.

JWP

Unexpected tears stung her eyes as the full impact hit. "I found your sugar spoon, Pru."

No time for more. She had to get home and get ready to go to Lizzie's. She'd hoped for a chance to talk to LuAnn, but the group was still gathered outside. Laughter floated through the screen door.

After digging around in the pantry for a few minutes, she found silver cleaner. It didn't take much rubbing for the spoon's soft silver patina to glow. The bowl was dented, and the handle pitted in spots. Holding it in her hand gave her the same sense of connection she'd had the first time she'd touched Prudence's journal on the day Brad and LuAnn found it in the hidden sub-basement room.

The café glowed orange from the lights on the branches and the leaf wreaths LuAnn had fastened around each of the wrought iron lights that hung from the ceiling. The soft tick of the clock behind the desk was the only sound. Spoon in hand, Tess stood looking out at the river. On this gorgeous day, all of their guests were gone. Elliott's red pickup, backed into the first parking spot, was the only vehicle in front of the inn. Tess positioned herself so she saw only cobblestones, trees, and water. No cars or utility poles. Nothing to clutter her thoughts of what the inn had been in the 1800s.

Had Prudence ever stood in this spot, reflecting on the beauty of a fall day, or was her time here never her own? Between working in the kitchen, changing beds upstairs, cleaning, laundry, or caring for the people she'd brought across the river and hidden in the secret room downstairs, maybe she didn't have time for reflection until she went home…and stirred a spoonful of sugar into a cup of tea. "I wish I could have joined you, Pru. I wish we could have sipped tea together and talked about our—"

A man leaped from the sidewalk along the water and strode up the grassy bank. He wore a long brown coat with a brimmed hat shoved low over his forehead. Going straight to Elliott's truck, he yanked on the driver's side door handle, then the back door. Stopping suddenly, as if he'd heard something, he looked up. He turned and ran back the way he'd come. Seconds later, another man appeared, walking a squat black-and-white bulldog. Over six feet tall and muscular, wearing black pants and a black turtleneck, sunlight glinting off a large-gage silver earring, the man looked like a bouncer. He stopped in front of the inn, stared in the direction the man in the brown coat had run, then continued walking. Tess pressed close to the window but couldn't see where the second man went.

With a shiver, she crossed her arms and almost ran to the elevator.

After changing, she stood by her fourth-floor bedroom window, staring down at Elliott's truck. She set her phone on the windowsill. Would the police think she was just some crazy lady if she called? If she hadn't seen the clearly-in-the-present man with the dog, she might have thought she was hallucinating as she stood there imagining Prudence's world. The brown coat had looked like the leather duster worn by the main character in *Man from Snowy River.* With a deep inhale for courage, she called the police station and told them someone had, once again, tried to get into Elliott's truck.

Henry's sweet face was squished against the window of the front door when she arrived. The moment she stepped onto the sidewalk, the door swung open and a four-year-old ball of energy hugged her knees, almost knocking her over. The thawing soup sloshed in its container.

"Mimi, you're here! Liam has a stuffy nose and Harper has a fever so Mommy says you and me have to play all by ourself and we can make clay and we have orange color to put in it so we can make pumpkins to put on the table for a decration. Did you know..."

Lizzie came to the door, dishcloth over her shoulder, dark circles under her eyes. "I'm sorry," she said over the chatter. "He hasn't had anyone to play with all day."

Tess hugged her daughter and hobbled in with Henry still attached to her leg. "No apologies. Why don't you go take a nap and—"

"What's in the white thing?" Henry interrupted. "Is that soup? Did Winnie make it? She makes the bestest soup ever. Does it have *noodoes*?"

Lizzie took the soup container, and Tess squatted to Henry's eye level. "It is Winnie's soup and it has lots and lots of 'noodoes,' and I have a very, very special spoon you can eat it with."

"Yay!" Henry clapped, and Tess marveled, as she had often in the past four years, how the smile of a child could chase all worries away.

"I actually think one four-year-old was harder than three." Tess leaned her elbow on the kitchen table and rested her chin in her hand. With the other hand she dunked a tea bag in and out of a cup of steaming hot water. Scents of orange, mint, and ginger wafting from the cup helped revive her. "The three of them entertain each other. Today I was at Henry's beck and call."

All in pajamas and slippers, they'd gathered at their kitchen table for a strategy session. LuAnn opened her notebook. "I actually got a nap in this afternoon after everyone left. I think we should pull an all-nighter to organize all our clues." She smirked at Tess.

"Count me out." Janice opened a can of sparkling water. "I may not have had triplets to contend with today, but that future granddaughter of mine talks enough for three."

Tess set her tea bag on the bowl of her new sugar spoon and wrapped the string around it to squeeze out every last drop. Neither of her friends had yet noticed the spoon. She got up, tossed the bag in the trash, wiped off the spoon, and set it in front of her cup as she sat. "Any hints on when Stuart's going to pop the question?"

"Not sure when, but I'm pretty sure soon. Stacy told me she saw a search for local jewelers open on his laptop at work last week. But I'm behaving. I haven't reminded Stuart even once that neither of them is getting any younger, and Zelda's biological clock is ticking faster by the minute."

LuAnn laughed. "Has it occurred to you that you could become a grandma again *and* a great-grandma in the next few years?"

"Stop! Brin doesn't even have a boyfriend. But yes, it has occurred to...me." Janice's eyes narrowed. She picked up the spoon. "Where'd you get this old—" Her eyes widened. "JWP. Is that for...Jason and Prudence? Where did you find it?"

Tess recapped her afternoon adventure. When they finished admiring the spoon and wondering if Prudence had owned an entire set of silver and if she used it every day or only for company and what kind of dishes she might have used, Tess showed them pictures of the piece of marble.

"e-r, 20, 1858." LuAnn jumped up and returned with her copy of Prudence's journal. "Were the entries about Cyrus in 1857 or '58?" She leafed through pages until she found what she was looking for. "October of 1858. So..."

"This could be a marker for Cyrus's grave," Janice finished.

"Or Jubal's." Tess blew on her tea. "Or maybe it's a marker for both. What if Tippi's scenario was right? It's not unusual for people to be buried with mementos, things that were meaningful to them. And it makes sense that the Willards couldn't afford headstones for both of them."

LuAnn shook her head. "I'm not sure they could afford even one. You're sure this is marble?"

Tess nodded. "I was on the planning board for two hotels. I know marble, and you're probably right. Prudence and Jason's headstone is sandstone. They were farmers. Of course, we're assuming Cyrus had no money."

"The journal says he was penniless." LuAnn turned a page. "'Though he has lost everything, joy shines on his face, proving treasure in heaven is of far more value.'"

"Maybe his family paid for it," Janice said.

LuAnn wrote "Cyrus's Death" in her notebook then looked up at Tess. "I'm guessing Misty knows more about it than she's letting on."

"Maybe there really was gold, and Cyrus gave some to Prudence and Jason for a proper burial."

"Then why wasn't he buried in the cemetery?" Janice strummed the tab on her can with her thumb.

"We need to start with the most important question." LuAnn clicked her pen. "Why are we doing this? We're spending a lot of time and mental energy trying to figure out who is interested in what Tess and Elliott found on the Moore property and why, but it doesn't directly affect us or the inn, so is this a good use—"

"Actually, it kind of does affect the inn. One of our guests anyway." Tess told them about the two men she'd seen outside the inn. "They weren't technically on inn property, but one of them was tampering with a guest's truck. Plus the fact that I was the one who started this whole mess, and now the Moores are involved. If word gets out that there might be gold on their lot, can you imagine? We might have a modern-day gold rush."

Janice's curls bounced as she agreed. "At the very least we need to try to find out if whoever dug what looked like a grave actually found something."

"There was no evidence of any more digging when I went out this afternoon," Tess said. "Which reminds me, Michael told me to ask Jerry if he could set up some trail cams. He has four of them and said he could borrow a few from his hunting buddies. If we aimed one at the fake grave and a few more around the property, we might catch someone shovel-handed."

"Great idea." LuAnn wrote it on their to-do list. "Okay. I think you've made a case for continuing to search. Let's start with suspects. We didn't get very far the other night. I have Elliott, which is seeming like less and less of a possibility, and Goldilocks, who could be anyone. Let's add everyone, no matter how far-fetched it seems."

"It seems like Maybelline ends up on most of our lists," Tess said, "but put her down. And Axel Barrett. I really, really want to believe the guy has changed, but his history, combined with Maybelline's interest and the time they've been spending together, makes him a possible suspect."

"What about the couple from Texas?" Janice asked. "While you were at the farmers market yesterday, they came back from the Campus Martius museum and had a ton of questions about Prudence and Jason. What are their names?"

"The Webers. Stanley and Sylvia."

LuAnn put them on the list. "If asking questions—"

"Children's books!" Tess almost jumped out of her chair. "I didn't put it together until now. Sylvia Weber collects vintage children's books."

Janice looked confused. "What does that have to do with… Oh. Like Goldilocks and the Three Bears?"

"Maybe."

LuAnn wrote the name of the fairytale next to the Webers' names. "I was going to say that if asking questions is a criterion, we need to add Felicity White. After I got up from my nap this afternoon, she was in the café fixing a cup of tea. I was hoping to get her to talk about what happened in church, so I invited her to sit by the fire. All she wanted to talk about was the history of the inn and its involvement in the Underground Railroad. It felt like she was steering the questions so I'd talk about Prudence. Maybe it's nothing. She was out at the Moore property, and I'm guessing Elliott told her everything he knows about the Willards, but her interest seemed really intense."

Tess leaned back in her chair and hugged her teacup close to her chest. "Dr. White and the Webers and Maybelline all have an interest in history, so—" Her phone rang, and she set her cup down and answered it.

"I know it's late, but"—Elliott, sounding out of breath, hadn't bothered to give his name—"did you see that post on the Marietta Buzz? Someone who calls him- or herself 'Tipper' just posted a comment saying the pocket watch belonged to a gold prospector who buried all his gold on the Moore property."

"Tipper?" Had Tippi—

"I'm out here now, and there are shop lights set up and at least four people digging holes. I called Jerry, and he's calling the police. I just"—he let out a massive sigh—"thought you should know."

"Thank you." Tess set the phone down and echoed Elliott's sigh as she looked across the table. "Well, it appears the Marietta Gold Rush has begun."

Chapter Sixteen

This is public property! You can't kick us off!" The stout woman, dressed in head-to-toe camouflage and brown rubber boots, pushed fuzzy dark bangs off her forehead with a muddy glove, leaving a streak of dirt on her face.

Officer Randy Lewis shook his head as he rubbed the back of his neck. He appeared to feel the way Tess did when all three grandkids were jumping on the furniture. "This has been private property for the past three months. Please pack up your gear and leave, or I'll be forced to charge you with trespassing."

"No one's living here yet," shouted a man in a plaid shirt and black vest. His forearms bulged as he continued to shovel dirt from a hole about three feet from the fake grave.

"Still private property, George. And what are you looking for anyway?"

"Buried treasure. The legend's true, Randy. Ain't you been reading online about the gold prospector who died here?"

"Guess the world knows," Tess said, watching from the passenger side of LuAnn's car. "We need to ask Michael to set up his trail cams tomorrow. As word spreads, there are just going to be more and more gold rushers showing up. We can't stop them, but if we can identify anyone, that will be huge."

"I'll do that right now." Tess wrote a quick text to Michael and one to Jerry, then yawned and stuck out her arm, showing the cuff of her silk pajamas underneath her coat sleeve. "Can we go home now and not pull an all-nighter?" As she rested her head against the back of the seat, her phone buzzed. A text from Evelyn.

You probably know about the men from Ohio who went to CA for the Gold Rush in 1849? The Buckeye Rovers. A professor I work with wrote a book about them. Asked him about Cyrus and Jubal, he showed me a letter in the book that was written to one of the Rovers. It was written by Cyrus Tuttle! I have a copy of the book, will bring it to the meeting tomorrow night.

Goose bumps played tag on Tess's arms as she read the text out loud.

"Whoa." Janice gripped the back of the seat. "Pardon the pun, but this could be a gold mine."

LuAnn slowed at a stop sign. "What are the chances Cyrus and Jubal went west with the Buckeye Rovers and didn't come back this way for eight years? It's possible, right? I remember a documentary about the Gold Rush that came out in the eighties. It documented the lives of six or eight men who sold everything to head west. One of them got shot, two quit, one got rich, and the others found other jobs in California and stayed. What if Cyrus and Jubal hadn't planned on coming back, but Cyrus got sick and wanted to go home to his family?"

"Very possible." Tess tapped to a reply window. "Are you two okay with me including Evelyn in on everything we know so far?"

"If you're sure you can trust her," Janice answered.

LuAnn parked next to the inn. "Maybe we should meet her first."

Tess nodded. "Everybody free tomorrow night?" When LuAnn and Janice said they had no plans, Tess typed her answer.

If you're free tomorrow night, the rest of the Unofficial Marietta Gold Rush Investigation Team would love to meet you. Bring your mom and join us for a sleuthing dinner at six. Trench coat, fedora, and sunglasses optional.

It took Evelyn only seconds to respond, accepting the invitation and adding a screenshot of a Pinterest page with "Detective Party Menu" at the top. Below it was a list including such delicacies as Clueless Chips, Detective Dogs, and Mysterious Munchies. At the end she wrote, *And here I thought retirement was going to be boring! Thanking God for you, my new friend.*

"Oh, how I've missed this." Evelyn wiped laugh tears from her cheeks. "Since"—she nodded toward Lovely who dozed in a recliner—"I haven't taken a lot of time just for fun. Thank you."

Janice took a peanut from the bowl of Hot on the Trail Mix Evelyn had brought. "I think you raised the bar on having fun tonight, Evelyn." She gestured toward the counter cluttered with the remains of their Killer Kabobs and Mashed Potato Disguise—AKA cauliflower puree.

LuAnn got up and brought her pen and notebook to the table, the sign that Evelyn had made the cut. "Let's get you caught up on what we know, and then you can show us the letter."

Tess, LuAnn, and Janice took turns, and sometimes talked on top of each other, explaining everything that had happened since they'd found the slave tag. Tess had taken the tag and the watch cover out of the safe to show Evelyn, and Janice had brought her copy of Prudence's journal. When they finished, Evelyn pulled a soft-covered book out of her purse. *Gold Rush Tales of the Buckeye Rovers.* "I haven't had time to look at anything other than the letter Dr. Martinez showed me." She handed the book to Tess.

By the second page, Tess was sure Cyrus and Jubal had not been part of the Buckeye Rovers. Twenty-two men had headed to the goldfields of California in 1849, and all were listed. She recognized a few of the surnames...Armstrong, Drake, Townsend. "No Tuttle or Hudson." She read on. "'More than three hundred thousand people flocked to California in search of gold in the mid-1800s. The easy gold quickly played out. Though each of the Rovers found gold, none struck it rich. By 1852, all of the Buckeye Rovers had returned to Ohio except the Dixon brothers, who were killed by Indians in California.

In these pages are the stories of those who lived to tell their Gold Rush tales.'"

Tess opened to the page Evelyn had marked with a sticky note. A black-and-white picture of the letter. "This was written in 1855." She turned the book so Janice and LuAnn could see it.

"Three years after all of the Buckeye Rovers had returned." Janice squinted at the grainy photograph. "Can you read it?"

"There's a transcript."

February 2, 1855

Dear Jimmy,

How are you enduring the mundane and boring life of a merchant after your adventure in the West? I imagine everything must seem lackluster in comparison.

I am well, and so is Genevieve. Uncle Vern continues to groom me to step into his shoes, but none of it interests me. All the talk of fertilizer and yield per acre makes my eyes cross. I do not believe I was born to grow cotton and tobacco. As proof, Uncle sent me to purchase two Negroes at auction last month and has not stopped berating me for my poor choices. "You know horses," he yells, "could you not have applied that knowledge to this task?" He thinks me lazy, spoiled, and inept when in fact I am merely bored to distraction. I am going on twenty-four and have yet to have an adventure worthy of sharing with my grandchildren when I am old and gray. Which is why I write, my friend.

You advised me to give careful thought before making such a rash move, and I have. I have thought and thought about nothing but the absolute lack of adventure in my life, and I am ready. Two weeks ago I told my uncle I want my inheritance from my parents, in full. It is rightfully mine, and there is nothing he can say about it. A visit to my father's attorney set the plan in motion.

I have memorized every leaflet I can get my hands on and have read and reread the letters you wrote as you prepared to leave, especially the one containing your list of provisions, and have procured most of what I need. Because my uncle is convinced I will perish on my own, he is insisting I bring one of his field hands, a giant bull of a creature twice my size, to protect me. Not to my liking, but I do see the benefit of putting his strength to work when it comes to panning, digging, and hauling our supplies.

If you are still amenable to the idea of sending me off with your blessing and the maps you spoke of, I will plan on arriving in Marietta mid-April. I assume you have room in your carriage house for the Negro.

Yours in the pursuit of adventure,
Cy

"I do believe the boy's uncle is right." The voice came from the recliner.

"Mama." Evelyn's relaxed smile tensed. "You're awake."

"And listening." Lovely rose from the recliner with slow, deliberate motions. Shaking her head, she walked toward the table. "How did we get here?"

Tess exchanged glances with the three other women. Poor Evelyn.

"We took my car. And then we took the elevator. Mama, this is Tess. And Janice. And this is—"

"LuAnn Sherrill." Lovely glared at her daughter. "I know how we got *here*. I don't know how we got *here*." She raised her hands and swiped them to the sides.

Tess wasn't sure if she was talking about Marietta or Ohio or the entire universe. She opened her mouth to ask gently for clarification, but Lovely spoke before she could.

"I know I'm a guest here, and I do hope you won't be overly offended, but I won't rest tonight if I don't speak my mind. I didn't hear all of what you read, but I heard enough to get the gist, and frankly *I'm* offended. It's bad enough people put stuff like that on the internet, but you reading out loud the whining of a spoiled young man who only wants to have fun and is so intolerant he can't even—"

"Mama!" Evelyn's face contorted in shock and embarrassment.

The room fell silent. Until Tess looked at LuAnn and then Janice, and the three burst out laughing. "Oh, Lovely." Tess put her hand on Lovely's arm. "I would never…" She sucked in a breath and managed to quell the laughter. When no words came, she handed the book to Lovely and pointed to the date.

"18…55?" Lovely's hand covered her mouth. For a moment she mirrored her daughter's mortified look. And then her shoulders began to shake. She laughed with such abandon the rest of them couldn't help but join in. "Oh my. Goes to show a person should hush up and get all the facts, doesn't it?"

Tess stood. "I think this moment calls for some Double Agent Cake." She'd tried her hand at a low-carb two-layer cake made with almond flour and frosted with lightly sweetened whipped cream. She brought it to the table and served a piece to Lovely. As she was handing a plate to Evelyn, there was a knock at the door. LuAnn got up and opened it.

Tippi walked in, shopping bags in each hand. "I just had to show you what I bought." She set the bags on the love seat and pulled out a large shoe box. "I went to the Sugar Maple Boutique on Front Street. Isn't that just the cutest name? Wait until you see these. I've spent the past ten winters in Florida, and I've got enough summery things along for Charleston, but I really, really needed a good pair of boots. Or two." She giggled as she held up a pair of rich brown leather boots decorated with an array of zippers and buckles. "Don't you love—" She stared at the group at the table. "Oh. Hi. I didn't realize you had…company."

For a fraction of a second Tess was sure Tippi had actually pouted. She forced herself to say, "Come join us." Why was it so hard to be just plain nice? *Lord, I'm trying.* A jab of conviction got her right below the breastbone. *Okay. I'm sorry. I'm really not trying very hard.* She sliced another piece of cake as LuAnn brought a folding chair and set it between Tess and Lovely. Leaning her head toward Lovely she said, "Tippi, this is—"

"Cake." Tippi sat and dipped her fork into the cake. "Hmm." She chewed slowly. "Different. But interesting. Kind of heavy, but not in a really bad way. Who made it?"

Tess kept her eyes on the task at hand. Slice, serve, repeat. "I did." She gave a piece to Janice and then LuAnn.

"Well I knew it wasn't Janice. Remember that angel food cake you made for my twenty-first birthday? I thought I'd died and gone to heaven when I tasted it. Light as a feather and just the right amount of sweet." She smiled at Janice and gave a wistful sigh.

"I'm Evelyn." Thrusting her hand across the table, Evelyn waited for Tippi to set her fork down. The two shook hands, and Tess finished the introduction she'd started a moment earlier.

"How do you all know each—" Tippi set her fork down and slid her plate to the middle of the table. Grabbing the Gold Rush book, she centered it in front of her and read silently, then looked up. "Interesting." She reached for her fork and shoved a giant piece of "heavy but not in a really bad way" cake in her mouth. Tess had the feeling she was chewing to avoid voicing the questions registering in the grooves on her forehead.

What was going on with Tippi? What did she know that she wasn't saying? Tess cut herself a sliver of cake. In the back of her mind she heard Lynette's voice. *"Food is fuel. It can be an enjoyable experience, but it should never be our primary source of comfort."*

In two days, a week and four days into her healthy eating plan, she was traveling to the land of shrimp and grits, fried green tomatoes, blue crabs with drawn butter, buttermilk biscuits, and pralines with a person who was bound to make her long for a source of comfort.

Lord, help!

October 20, 1858

"This is where thee turns back, Patience." Prudence stopped by the message tree, the twisted oak with the deep hole in its trunk. She looked up at the leaves. In the thin light of near-dawn she noticed several had begun to turn. Yellow and brown against a canvas of green. But these were not the colors she looked for. She breathed a sigh when she was sure no bit of bright cloth hung from a low branch—the cloth that would signal a message waited for her in the hole in the tree.

The messages were always coded—"Two packages arrive at midnight" or "Fragile parcel ready for pick-up before first light." God had protected their system of communication, had allowed her, for years now, to row her skiff across the river to pick up people fleeing north to freedom and shelter them at the inn, then transport them to the next station. She was grateful for the chance to help but always relieved when there were no messages. She shooed Patience toward home and continued on her walk along the sleepy river.

Pale light flickered through the windows at the back of the Riverfront House as Prudence approached the door, lifting her skirt high above the damp grass. The rest of the inn—rooms occupied with exhausted travelers and sailors sleeping off the night's revelry—was still dark. Prudence took a last glance at the calm Ohio and the streak of silver moonlight glittering on its surface. She would be too busy today to find time to linger over beauty. This glimpse of predawn calm would need to last until dusk.

Jason wasn't happy with the increase in her work hours, but it was only temporary. Elizabeth's sprained wrist had almost healed, and she would be back in the kitchen within the week. Prudence felt a twinge of guilt at how relieved she'd felt when she left the house. Cyrus's fever had returned. Jubal had wanted to sleep on a pallet on the floor in his room, but Prudence had insisted she'd check on him. She had no way of knowing if the man she'd encountered two nights ago knew Cyrus and Jubal were staying with them. If he came to the house, it wasn't likely Cyrus was in danger, but if there was a price on Jubal's head...She'd shown Jubal the cupboard under the eaves in the loft and made sure it was large enough to hide him.

Prudence had checked on Cyrus several times during the night. He slept fitfully. When she'd stepped in the room this morning before anyone else awoke, he'd motioned her closer. "Quakers...know...people." His eyes had closed again. "When I'm gone...Jubal needs to get away to Canada. They will keep hunting..." It was all he'd said, but it was enough for her to realize that he knew his time was short.

She and Jason hadn't told Cyrus and Jubal that ushering runaways north had been their mission since they'd married. She knew who to contact, where to take Jubal. She'd patted Cyrus's hand and, just as she said, "We will get him to safety." Jubal descended the ladder from the loft and stood by the door.

"Heard somethin' last night," he said. "Soon as yer up to it, we need to get on the road. Maybe travel at night, I'm thinkin'."

Cyrus had nodded and given a weak smile. "I'm ready to go home, Jubal. Ready to go home." Jubal had grinned. Prudence had wiped a tear from her chin.

As Prudence pulled the key from her apron pocket, something rustled in the tall grass behind her. She turned... and a massive hand clamped over her mouth.

Prudence kicked and tried to scream, but the arm squeezing tight around her waist and the hand pressed hard against her mouth wouldn't allow a sound to escape. His fingertips closed over her eyes. She felt herself being dragged through the grass. Sound dimmed as she was pulled into the stand of trees behind the inn.

The man cursed. "Shut up. I just want to make a deal with you."

Prudence willed her fighting instincts to still, though her heart continued to hammer against her ribs.

"All I want is the gold."

She tried to talk. Finally, the man released the hand covering her mouth. His arm remained tight around her waist. "What gold?"

"The men. I know yer hidin' 'em. Tell 'em to hand over the gold, and I'll leave you all alone. My partner's dead because of them, but I'll give up revengin' his death and forget about the reward from the Tuttles if you git me the gold. I don't want to hurt you, but I will if—"

"I don't know anything about gold."

The man laughed, low and malevolent. "Look in their packs. If they won't give it to me, you do it. I know Cyrus is sick. I know he can't fight me. If you don't get it, I'll have to—"

"I'll get it. I'll leave it right here."

"Tomorrow. This time tomorrow. I'll be here. You don't bring it, I'll come for you. No. I'll come for the orphans you been raisin' money for. Nobody will miss them. Nobody comin' after me if a few of 'em disappear." He gave a laugh that made her kick her heel at his shin with all of her strength. He swore, and his arm dropped away. "Tomorrow. Or else." He shoved her toward the inn.

Prudence stumbled, grabbed a branch, and righted herself. Her vision dimmed, stars sparked in front of her eyes. She kept her head down and forced a deep breath. *Father God. Help me.* Two more slow breaths and she was able to raise her head and turn around.

The man was gone.

Chapter Seventeen

What do you recommend?" Dr. Felicity White sat alone at a table for two by the window, staring at the board that listed the café lunch choices. Her blond hair was pulled back in a low ponytail. She looked like she hadn't slept much.

Tess hadn't seen more than glimpses of the woman since she'd rushed out of church on Sunday. Was there anything to say to get her to talk? Janice, the pastor's wife, was the expert at that, but Tess could try. "It depends on how hungry you are. The beef stew is thick and rich and delicious." She nodded toward the kitchen. "It's a requirement of my job to taste the soup every day." Most people smiled and made some comment about perks of the job when she said that. Dr. White didn't react. "Our chef's new unstuffed cabbage roll soup is chock-full of veggies, but it's a little lighter than the stew." She'd thanked Winnie profusely for this new recipe. "Isn't it nice to have something with the word *stuffed* in it that's actually healthy?"

Dr. White's expression didn't register even the faintest hint of a smile. "I'll have the unstuffed cabbage roll. And a cup of tea. And no bread, please." Dr. White massaged her forehead with her fingertips.

Pulling out a chair, Tess perched on the edge of the seat. "Are you not feeling well? I've been praying for you since you had to leave church. Anything I can do for you, Dr. White?"

Dr. White made eye contact for the first time. "Felicity, please. I don't want to be Dr. White while I'm here. And prayer is probably the only thing that will help." She heaved a loud sigh. "I recently came across something that will deeply affect the lives of several people. I don't know if God will listen, but if you could pray for wisdom, I would appreciate it."

Tess slid her hand over Felicity's. She waited for a moment, something she'd learned long ago from Janice. *Just be present.* When Felicity pulled her hand away, Tess stood. "I know God will listen." As she reached the kitchen door, Tess looked back. *Are you Goldilocks?* What was the "something" she'd just come across? Thirty pounds of gold nuggets? Where would a person hide a bag of gold? In her car? In her room?

By law, Tess had the right to search a guest's room if she suspected a person of engaging in anything illegal. They'd done it when they were pretty sure Maybelline's granddaughter Natalie had stolen the ruby decoder pin. It wasn't something any of them wanted to do without definite cause. The only thing that pointed to Felicity's involvement was a vague comment about finding something. And her blond hair.

Tess tried to push the idea aside. Hair color was not evidence. There were a lot of reasons why someone might choose to go by the name Goldilocks. As she wiped off a table, she pondered the story of the three bears. A little girl with bouncy blond curls, lost in the woods…But there was another version.

She glanced back at Felicity, then hurried toward the kitchen, whispering to LuAnn as she passed her. "Gotta ask you something."

"What's so important?" LuAnn met her next to the sink. She set a tray of bowls on the counter and looked at Tess as she washed her hands.

"Tell me the original story of Goldilocks."

"In the middle of the lunch rush you want me to tell you a fairy tale." LuAnn scrunched her nose and reached for a towel.

"There was an old lady in it, right?"

LuAnn nodded. "It's widely held that Eleanor Mure wrote the original in 1831. In hers, the bears try to burn and drown the silver-haired old lady who barges into their cottage, and finally succeed in throwing her onto the steeple of St. Paul's Cathedral and leaving her there."

"Seriously?" Tess grabbed the counter for dramatic effect. "I can't wait to read that version to my grandkids. Who in the world would write something like that for children?"

"There were a lot of versions. Joseph Cundall is credited with changing the intruder to a child. He decided to make the change because he thought there were already too many fairy tales and nursery rhymes with old ladies as villains. But Cundall's Goldilocks wasn't a sweet little thing. In his story, she's a rude, naughty kid who does everything wrong and, in the end, gets away from the angry bears and escapes through the window, never to be heard from again."

"Thanks. I'll stick to the cleaned-up version." Tess pulled a stack of hot bowls from the dishwasher.

"Why did you need to know?"

"I'll explain later." She stepped around LuAnn and handed the bowls to Winnie.

"Great cliffhanger," LuAnn said to her back. "You should write mysteries."

Winnie turned and laughed. "You ladies don't need to write mysteries. You live them."

Felicity didn't look up when Tess set a bowl of unstuffed cabbage roll soup and a cup of tea in front of her. Gaze fixed to her phone, she merely said, "Thank you."

Tess took two more orders, brought them out, and was clearing a table when the Webers descended the stairs. Tess gestured toward a table. "Good afternoon."

"And to you." Stanley pulled out a chair for Sylvia, then sat across from her. "We'll have coffee and the beef stew. We've been upstairs on our laptops smelling it all morning."

Tess wrote it down on her order pad. "You'll love the stew. Though I imagine it won't be quite the same as stew cooked over an open fire."

"And served with hard tack." Stanley laughed.

Sylvia's charm bracelet jangled as she reached for her purse. "The best stew we ever had was on a wagon train trip on the Oregon trail. Stanley shot a deer, and we cooked the meat all day. Melt in your mouth good."

"Sounds wonderful. I'll suggest to our cook that we add venison stew to our list. Not sure she's going to want to bag it herself though." Tess was laughing as she passed Felicity's table.

The woman sat staring out the window, a sad, faraway look on her face.

Tess opened the kitchen door and called to Janice. "Go use your listening skills with Dr. White, who wants us to call her Felicity. Something's really got her down."

"Okay. Is she drinking coffee?"

"Tea. And she's probably ready for some more hot water."

Janice nodded. "I'm on it."

As Tess approached the Webers, Sylvia fanned at least a dozen tourist brochures across the table. Stanley and Sylvia were deep in animated conversation, so Tess just stood there for a moment, not wanting to interrupt. The brochures were all for local attractions. Historic Harmar Village, Haunted Marietta Walking Tour, Trolley Tours, Marietta Underground Railroad Museum, Campus Martius Museum. One appeared to be handwritten, a brochure mock-up maybe. Plain paper, with words printed in block letters in ink. Above the unfinished sentence *A traveling exhibit of Ohio's*...someone had written *Red* and below the word, *Blue*. Would it be rude to ask about it? "Here you go," she said, lowering the tray to the corner of the table. Stanley, apparently startled to see Tess standing next to him, reached across the table and deftly tucked the mock-up under the rest of the brochures. Sylvia gathered them together in one scoop of her hand and deposited them swiftly into her purse.

"Yum. That looks delicious." Sylvia's smile seemed a bit wobbly. She glanced up at Tess then quickly picked up her spoon. "Thank you."

"Hope you enjoy it." Tess set the bowls and cups in front of them and hugged the tray to her chest. The Webers' body language did not invite questioning, so she headed for the kitchen. But not before witnessing a look of fear shoot from Sylvia to Stanley, answered by an angry scowl.

She smiled as she passed Felicity and Janice. Janice smiled back, but the good doctor did not look her way. As Tess entered the kitchen, she looked back at the three guests who were acting suspicious. Had one of them been digging at the Moores'? Did one of them have a massive bag of gold nuggets?

Strangers, I wish I knew.

Tess dug out the bin of summer clothes she'd stashed in her closet only two weeks earlier. With temperatures in the fifties and sixties now, it was hard to imagine eighties. She flopped her smallest suitcase onto the bed. She needed an outfit to wear for the flight, something for Wednesday night, and maybe a couple of changes for whatever they might be doing on Thursday. They'd be having breakfast with Misty on Friday morning before flying home. She could fit it all in her carry-on.

Shoving hangers along the closet pole, she reached lightweight skirts and dresses. She stopped at a lime-green dress she hadn't worn in over a year. A-line, with a scoop neck and slits along the sleeves. The last time she'd tried it on she'd hung it right back on the hanger. "Should I?" She posed the question to the dress. When it didn't say "In your wildest dreams, honey," or "Fat chance, Tess" she pulled it out. As she did, Janice knocked on her door.

"Come on in. You can have a front-row seat to my humiliation," Tess called. She motioned for Janice to have a seat and then stepped behind the door of her closet. She put the dress on, then opened the door with a flourish.

"Wow! I haven't seen you wear that in forever." Janice's smile of encouragement morphed into a squinty-eyed mock glare. "You're going to beat me, aren't you? How much have you lost?"

"Three pounds, but you know that always happens in the first week. It'll slow down, but I feel my stomach flattening just because I'm making healthier choices. Do I dare ask how you're doing? I haven't seen a cinnamon roll in your hands for days."

"About the same. And speaking of about the same, my talk with Dr. White wasn't fruitful. I told her I'd spent years talking and listening to women and said sometimes it helps to talk. She said she couldn't talk about it. She said one thing, and I'm not even sure she knew she said it out loud. As I was walking away, she said, "'Sometimes good news about one thing makes another thing worse.'"

"What did she mean by that?"

"No idea." Janice stepped back to the door. "Anyway, you look great, and I'm outta here. Going to take Larry to Whit's after school and watch him eat custard."

"What we sacrifice for this beauty, huh?"

Janice was laughing as she walked out the door.

Standing in front of the mirror a minute later, Tess grinned at herself. Maybe the dress didn't swing as loosely as it once had, but it would still be comfy. *Celebrate every little victory*, the God's Weigh manual said. She'd just decided to head out to the Shoe Dept. for a new, celebratory pair of walking shoes when she got a text from Michael. *Have five cams. Jerry's going to meet me there. Hope we catch your grave digger.*

Tess smiled. *Hope you catch him gold-handed.* Her son-in-law was accustomed to her jokes that fell flat.

She was walking down the stairs when her phone rang. Evelyn. She loved that this new friend didn't just text. "Hi there."

"Hi. Listen. I've only got a minute." Evelyn sounded out of breath, an edge of excitement surrounding her words. "Please tell me you can meet me at the Historical Society before God's Weigh tonight."

"Sure. What time? And what for?"

"Six o'clock. I can't tell you the what for because it would spoil the fun. Park in back, and I'll meet you at the back door."

"Can you give me a clue?"

"Okay. I remembered where I saw Cyrus Tuttle's name. I have a meeting with Margaret Ashworth, the director of the historical society, in two minutes to find out what it means. That's all I'm going to tell you."

Tess laughed. She thought of Winnie's comment. *You ladies don't need to write mysteries. You live them.* "Great cliff-hanger."

"I know." Evelyn laughed with a definite air of mystery. "See you at six."

Elliott was backing his truck in when Tess pulled her car around the front of the building. He opened his window and waved at her. Not a "Hi there" wave. This one definitely meant "Stop!"

As Tess got out to meet him, once again she witnessed him moving with a nimbleness that was surprising for a man who could be a Santa clone. "Find something new?"

He patted the find pouch attached to his belt. "Nothing valuable. I was out there for four hours." His expression clouded. He pulled out his phone. "I got another message from Goldilocks."

Tess leaned in to see as he pushed the button to wake his phone. The picture on his home screen made her smile. Three stairstep boys in baseball uniforms. "Grandkids?"

"Yep. My daughter's boys." He tapped on his email icon and showed her the message.

Call off your guards. The search is over. I have the gold.

Tess felt her chest tighten. So there had been something in the "grave" after all. Her hopes for the Moores…the look of joy she'd imagined on Amy's face, the relief on Jerry's as the financial weight fell from his shoulders, the specially adapted playground equipment in the backyard…turned to dust and blew away. Unless…"Maybe that's just a smoke screen."

"Could be. I'm going to keep searching that property until I've covered every inch."

Tess put a hand on Elliott's arm. "Thank you."

He smiled. "You don't really have to thank me for doing what I love to do."

They said their goodbyes. Elliott walked toward the inn, and Tess got into her car. She turned onto Second Street then stepped on the brake at the stop sign on Front Street. She eased her foot off the pedal then stopped suddenly when something that had been scratching at the back of her brain for the last few minutes popped to the front.

Three little boys. In baseball uniforms.

Chicago Bears uniforms.

Three little bears.

Chapter Eighteen

Children's Home
Washington County Children's
Home, Ohio's first, and in
1867 the nation's first sup-
ported by taxes, was founded
in 1858 by Catherine Fay
Ewing at her farm home in
Moss Run, Ohio.

Tess drove past the black historical marker with its gold lettering that stood near the road in front of the complex that now housed the historical society. Before closing its doors in the 1960s, the group of buildings had been home to hundreds of children for almost a century.

Several dormers jutted out from the roofs of the redbrick buildings. Massive chimneys hinted at rooms once heated by fireplaces. As she turned into the drive, she looked up at one of the white-trimmed dormer windows, and was sure, for only a moment, she saw movement. She didn't believe in ghosts, but LuAnn often spoke of memories floating through the hallways of old buildings. It took little imagination to picture a child standing at one of those windows, waiting and praying for a family.

Evelyn stood just inside the back door. "Margaret's waiting in the attic."

"The attic?" There was that shot of adrenaline again. After all the years she and Janice had teased LuAnn for "living in the past" because of her captivation with history, Tess was finally understanding the fascination on a visceral level.

"You are now one of the privileged few." Evelyn led Tess to a stairway. "I was home cleaning off a bookshelf and boxing some old books when it suddenly hit me where I'd seen Cyrus Tuttle's name." They walked up a flight of stairs to the second floor. Doors lined the corridor they stepped into. Tess could almost hear the distant echo of children's voices. "Last March I was here with a group of students. We were helping organize the attic. There was still stuff up there from the children's home. Our job was to catalog everything and put things in labeled plastic bins. One of my students had the job of sorting through an old cardboard box of nameplates. I remembered her holding one up and laughing at the name. She said she was going to use it for one of her future kids." Evelyn led the way to a narrow stairway.

Tess ran her hand along the banister, thinking of the people who had used these steps a hundred and fifty years earlier. Long skirts, lace-up shoes. What did they use the attic for? Just storage?

Evelyn stopped and bent toward her. "Take a look at the cage thing in the corner when you walk in. I've heard rumors they might have used it for disciplinary purposes."

"Oh my."

Margaret stood in front of a dormer window. Under five feet tall, from a distance she could be mistaken for a child. Not a specter of the past, after all. She turned, her lined face crinkling in a smile. "Tess. Good to see you. I've been hearing things about you lately." She tucked the clipboard she held in knobby, arthritic hands under one thin arm. "Guess your metal-detecting excursion really started something, huh?"

"That's a bit of an understatement. But who wants a dull life, right?"

"So right." Margaret motioned them toward a box that sat on an old scarred desk. She pulled out a board about eighteen inches long and four inches high and handed it to Tess.

Tess took the wood and turned it over. A tiny gasp escaped her lips. Cyrus Tuttle's name and the words *Dining Room* engraved on a brass plate fastened to what looked like cherry wood. "Cyrus Tuttle Dining Room?"

"It's a wall plaque."

"Why in the world would a dining room be named after Cyrus Tuttle?" The man was from South Carolina and, as far as she could tell from Prudence's journal, had only spent a matter of days, flat broke and deathly ill, in Marietta. "And why is it here?"

Margaret's shoulders straightened, and she grinned. She was in her element. "It took some searching, but we finally figured it out. I found an entry in a record book. This building was finished in 1867. They moved thirty-three orphans from Catherine Fay's home and held a ceremony to honor Cyrus Tuttle, who had made one of the largest contributions to the new facility. This plaque was hung above the door to the new dining room." She flipped through a few pages on her clipboard. "I made a copy of it. Here. 'Donor and several family members were present for the ceremony.'"

"But…" The dates didn't jive. "As far as we can tell, Cyrus died in 1858."

"On the sign out front it says that's the year Catherine Fay opened her home in Moss Run," Evelyn said. "Is it possible the record was referring to that opening?"

Margaret shook her head. "This notation is dated October 26, 1867. From everything I've read about Catherine Fay, she was always struggling to make ends meet. If someone had given her a large donation in 1858, it would have gone to fixing her leaky roof and providing basic necessities for the children. She didn't get a lot of support from the community."

So who was the donor? And were the "family members" part of Jubal's family or Cyrus's? Did this mean Jubal had escaped with the gold and then returned to Marietta to donate to the home? Or did it mean Cyrus's family had donated in his memory? Or had Cyrus lived after all?

The three women stood, staring down at the name of the man Prudence said had lost everything in California. Would they ever know what really happened?

Evelyn rode to the meeting with Tess. At first, they jabbered about their speculations. Had Cyrus given all his money to the children's home? Is that what Prudence had meant by him losing everything? That didn't make sense. Silence filled the car when they ran out of answers, and both became lost in her own thoughts.

The God's Weigh meeting was well attended. The thing that struck Tess was the laughter in the room. Each person was a testimony of Lynette's encouragement to "focus on what you *can* have, not what you can't."

Lynette opened with a simple prayer thanking God for living in a country of abundance and asking him to help them make Him, and not false satisfiers, the center of their lives. When she finished, everyone joined in with a heartfelt "Amen."

"Tonight, we're going to talk about substitutions." Lynette pointed to a chart with pictures of fruits and vegetables. "Yes, we'll cover things like making mashed cauliflower instead of mashed potatoes and using almond and coconut flour instead of wheat, but I also want to talk about substituting our go-to behaviors for healthier ones. Things like, when someone stresses you out, instead of turning to comfort foods, let's think about turning instead to praying for that person and blessing him or her with an unexpected act of kindness or some genuine caring and listening. I'm going to start by reading Romans, chapter twelve. Not a passage we normally think of to inspire weight loss, but there really is so much we can glean here." She opened her Bible. "'Therefore, I urge you, brothers and sisters, in view of God's mercy, to offer your bodies as a living sacrifice, holy and pleasing to God—this is your true and proper worship.'"

Tess tried to ignore the thought that God was using Lynette to tell her something about a certain person who often stressed her out. Someone she would be spending three days with starting tomorrow morning.

Ignoring didn't work.

"Why would Elliott stay around here if he found the gold?" Janice sat on Tess's bed watching her finish packing. As she'd folded clothes, Tess had filled her friends in on her time with Evelyn and Margaret at the historical society and her encounter with Elliott...and her theory about the three little bears.

"Maybe just to look innocent." LuAnn leaned against the doorframe, mug in hand. "If he runs, we know he's guilty."

"And why would he go through the charade of leaving comments for himself on his own blog?" Tess rubbed the back of her neck.

"I just can't imagine him being deceptive." Janice wrinkled her nose.

"He seems way too nice, right?" Tess rolled the green dress to keep it wrinkle-free. "I agree. He's so...Santa Claus-ish."

"Yes!" Janice clapped her hands. "I've been picturing him as the Burl Ives snowman in *Rudolph*."

LuAnn nudged Janice over then sat next to her on the bed. "I hate sounding jaded, but we've been fooled before by nice people."

"Too true." Tess could easily think of a few, and she knew the first one who'd popped into LuAnn's head. The man she'd fallen in love with years ago who turned out to be a complete fraud. Married. She gave LuAnn a sympathetic smile.

"We can't make any assumptions about guilt or innocence until we have some evidence either way. We still have other suspects," Janice said.

LuAnn nodded. "We still have two other possible Goldilocks. Actually, to be grammatically correct, it should be Goldilockses." She waited for her friends to roll their eyes. "And that's not counting Maybelline and Axel Barrett."

Tess nodded toward the window and the reflection of the moon, orange and bright and still low above the horizon, glistening on the river. "Full moon and clear skies. Seems like a good time to catch someone gold-handed." If the pun was good enough for Stuart, it was good enough for her friends.

LuAnn and Janice groaned in perfect harmony. LuAnn finished her tea and leaned down to set her cup on the floor in a lithe movement made possible by daily stretching into positions Tess found painful to watch. "Do you think"—LuAnn folded her arms and rested back against a pile of pillows—"we could be wrong about Cyrus dying in Marietta?"

Tess had run off a new copy of Prudence's journal and put it in a three-ring binder. She slid the binder into her carry-on, then took it out again. "I suppose..." She shoved her suitcase aside and sat on the bed. "We've combed through Pru's entries after she said she was sure Cyrus wasn't leaving the house alive, and we didn't find anything. Except..."

Janice leaned forward. "Except what?"

"I saw a Bible reference while we were searching through this for Cyrus's and Jubal's names. Pru wrote it two weeks after her last entry about Cyrus and Jubal. I assumed it had to do with the Underground Railroad." She turned two pages. "Here." She ran her finger along a line of fluid script, imagining Prudence writing with quill and ink by candle-light. "November 12, 1858. 'I have been unable to bring myself to write about what Jason and I witnessed—bravery and sacrifice on a scale that left us without words. Only tears. We have said goodbye to two dear friends, and the sense of loss has caught us both by surprise. John 15:13. 'Greater love hath no man than this, that a man lay down his life for his friends.'"

"That could mean so many things." LuAnn held out her hand for the journal. "She didn't record this on the day what-ever happened happened. So it could easily be Cyrus and Jubal. But what does 'goodbye' mean? Did they leave together? Did they die together?"

"Maybe she didn't mean it literally." Tess made a space in her suitcase for her curling iron. "Maybe Jubal was giving up his right to a life of freedom by taking Cyrus home to South Carolina."

Janice pointed to the notebook lying on the bed. "Add all this to your list of questions for Misty."

"I gather she doesn't know when Cyrus died. I think she's hoping to get that from us. I wish we had found the rest of that headstone."

"It's not too late." LuAnn arched one eyebrow, asking a question, laying out a challenge.

"You're kidding, right?" Janice hugged a pillow to her chest. "You're not seriously suggesting we go out to the Moore property at eleven o'clock at night and dig around in the woods in the dark."

Tess glanced at the clock on her bedside table. Her longing for answers, and anything that would distract her from thoughts of tomorrow, warred with the reality of her need for sleep. She had to board a plane in nine hours.

"I guess not." Reluctance coated LuAnn's concession. "Tess, how are you feeling about Charleston? You seem…hesitant. You're usually a lot more bubbly when we're planning a trip."

"Yes. When *we're*—" Tess stopped herself from finishing the sentence. Snippets of Romans 12 had been looping through her head all evening. *Honor one another above yourselves. Live in harmony with one another. Be careful to do what is right in the eyes of everyone. If it is possible, as far as it depends on you, live at peace with everyone.*

LuAnn reached out and touched her arm. "Tippi is the way she is for a reason. You've never really gotten to know her. It's no accident it worked out that only the two of you could go."

"I know. I do." Deep, deep down in some boarded-up recess of her mind, she knew. "I'll behave. I just hope we're not making a mistake including her in what—"

LuAnn's phone, in her robe pocket, rang. She pulled it out. "Speaking of…" She held the phone to her ear. "Hi, Tip." After a moment of listening, she said, "Sure, come on up." With a look part apology, part optimism, she glanced at Tess, then left the room.

As soon as LuAnn was out of earshot, Tess dropped onto the bed. “You’re going to be praying for me, right?”

“Every hour on the hour. I’ll set my alarm.” Janice picked up her phone and apparently did just that. “It sounds like Misty is going to keep you too busy to have much time just to hang out.”

“I know.” Tess lowered her voice. “There’s just something I can’t explain that makes me think Tippi’s not telling us everything. What if she’s ‘Tipper’?” It’s still too weird that she just showed up here the day after—”

“Got my suitcase sitting by the door and my clothes all laid out for the morning.” Tippi grinned as she eyed the stacks of clothes and pile of toiletries on Tess’s bed.

Call me Tess the Mess just once and I’ll— The memory of Lynette reading from Romans stifled the thought. *Bless those who persecute you; bless and do not curse.*

“Good.” It wasn’t much, but it was said without sarcasm.

“Hey.” Tippi made herself comfortable in Tess’s chair. “I wanted to tell you guys about something. I was downstairs getting some decaf a few minutes ago, and Dr. White was sitting in the corner by the library. Pretty sure she didn’t know I was there, but sound travels downstairs when it’s quiet. She was on the phone with someone, and I heard her say something like, ‘I know, this changes everything. But don’t tell her what I found until I’m sure.’”

Janice sat up straight. “Did she say anything else?”

Tippi shook her head.

"That's pretty vague." Tess closed and zipped her suitcase. She looked again at the clock. What were the chances she'd sleep with all the questions swirling through her head? She thought of one of her grandma's favorite sayings. "I'll sleep when I'm dead." How crazy would it be…"Let's do it."

"Do what?" LuAnn looked at her with hope in her eyes.

"Let's go out to the Moore property at eleven o'clock at night and dig around in the woods in the dark."

Chapter Nineteen

It was five after eleven when the four of them walked downstairs, all wearing dark clothes, gloves, and shoes they weren't afraid of getting dirty. Even Tippi. As Tess stepped onto the first floor, she was startled by the sound of rustling papers.

Laptop in front of her, Sylvia sat in a wingback chair by a dying fire. It wasn't unheard of for guests to be up this late at night, but it was a bit unusual. Tess greeted her. "Trouble sleeping?" She could imagine Sylvia needing a quiet place away from a loudly snoring husband. Tess knew firsthand the exhausting insomnia produced by window-rattling exhales. That had been her reality before Jeffrey got his C-Pap machine.

"Yes. I wanted to get some research done tonight."

LuAnn stepped closer to Sylvia. "What are you researching?"

"Oh, just business-related stuff."

Tess walked over to the fireplace and fiddled with the garland of fall leaves that wound around brass candleholders. "And here I was envious of you two. I just assumed you were retired."

"Guess you'd call us semiretired. Our nephew runs things whenever we're gone." Sylvia tucked her hair behind her ears. "Where are you ladies going this late at night?"

Tess shot a glance at LuAnn and received a barely perceptible nod. Maybe giving Sylvia a hint of what they were doing would give them a clue to her guilt or innocence. "Moonlit walk. It's almost balmy out there."

Sylvia glanced down at their feet. It wasn't hard to guess what she was thinking. Why were they all wearing boots for a moonlit walk on a balmy night? And it had to be obvious they'd all intentionally worn black. She closed her laptop and yawned. Or faked a yawn. "Well, enjoy. I'm off to bed."

Tess watched Sylvia walk up the stairs. *Are you Goldilocks?* The question was starting to make her feel a little nuts.

Tippi snickered as they walked into the kitchen. "Pretty sure she thinks we're heading out to rob a bank."

Or she knows exactly where we're going. Tess led the way to her car. Why were these Texans hanging around in Marietta for two weeks? She wasn't convinced they were here for the Heritage Tour. It just wasn't that big a deal. She couldn't voice any of her thoughts with Tippi in the car.

Mysterious shadows greeted them at the Moore property. "Jerry gave us permission," Tess said when Janice suggested, once again, that this was a really, really bad idea.

"The police said they'd be checking the place out periodically," Janice said. "What if they see us? Will they give us a chance to explain before they shoot?"

LuAnn spurted a laugh. "Janice. Chill. No one's getting shot."

Tess smiled. It wasn't like they hadn't given Janice ample opportunity to choose staying home. The fact that she'd come at all was symbolic of the fears she'd faced down since Lawrence died. "Look at you." She handed Janice a flashlight as they got out of the car. "A year ago you wouldn't have come along."

"True." Janice zipped up her black fleece jacket. "A year ago I would have been smart. And safe. You know, just because you have out-of-control anxiety doesn't mean it isn't sometimes the right response to a situation."

"But not this situation," Tess said. "We are going to have fun."

Tippi giggled. "This is what I remember most about you guys, all the spontaneous fun. Remember that Friday we came up with the crazy idea to drive nine hours to New York City to take LuAnn to Katz's Deli for her birthday lunch?"

Tess did remember. She remembered it had been her crazy idea, and Tippi had walked in on the conversation and invited herself. Again. She forced a smile. She wouldn't survive the next three days acting like a spoiled junior high girl. "Follow me." She pointed the way to the line of trees and brush just south of the spot where they'd found the slave tag. "What a gorgeous night." Though she didn't need to whisper, the atmosphere and the air of adventure invited hushed voices. It really was a balmy night. Air tinged with woodsmoke, moon so bright they could pick their way across the lumpy ground without the need of flashlights.

When they reached the trees, LuAnn put on her backpacking headlight. "Should we split up? We might—"

"No!" Janice grabbed Tess's arm. "Shh! Listen."

They stopped, barely breathing. A rustle, much like Tess had heard before. An over-active mind could imagine footsteps. One. Two. Three. Silence. "Maybe a rabbit," Tess whispered.

"I don't like this." Janice looked back at the car and then at the woods. "But if we're going to do it, let's get it over with."

"Watch out for the raspberry bushes." Tess parted branches and held them out of the way while the others ducked under. When she let the branches fall back into place, they were surrounded by trees and brush on all sides.

"This would be such a great fort for kids," LuAnn said.

Tippi kicked something tinny-sounding and bent to pick up a soda can. "Looks like it has been."

Flashlight beams crossed like light sabers as they moved slowly through the woods. Each step that brought them farther from the spot where Tess had found the chunk of what she assumed was a grave marker increased her feeling that this was a hopeless pursuit. After five minutes she stopped and held out her hand. "I can't imagine it would be this far into the woods. Maybe we should—" Her light illuminated something out of place. Bricks. She stepped closer. Had someone begun building a wall? Five bricks high, about twelve wide. No mortar held them together. And on top of the wall, a red plastic cup…filled with wilted flowers.

"Oh!" LuAnn verbalized for all of them as they looked behind the little wall. A photograph in a frame. Though water stained beneath fogged glass, the picture was easy to make out. Two children and a fluffy, droopy-eared brown dog with big, soulful eyes. A piece of paper was stuck over the bottom of the picture. Words, scrawled in a child's hand read, "Bosco. Born May 12, 2011, Died September 23, 2019. The frame was propped against a white stone. All lights converged, and a collective gasp floated through the trees. Not just a stone. A tombstone. With part of its base missing.

Without a word exchanged, the four knelt around it, silently reading the inscription.

No Greater Love…
Cyrus Vernon Tuttle
Born July 19, 1821
Reborn December 25, 1857
Died October 20, 1858

As the 767 lifted off the tarmac, Tess closed her eyes. They'd talked until well after midnight. Tess had sent Jerry and Amy an email with a picture of the gravestone. Amy had answered this morning, saying the dog wasn't actually buried on the property, and she'd had no idea what the kids had done or what they'd found.

Tess had climbed in bed around two and slept soundly until just after four when she woke from a dream that made her not want to go back to sleep. In the dream, Elliott got down on one knee and proposed to Felicity. Instead of a ring, he pulled out a Mason jar filled with melted gold. Felicity opened the jar and poured it into her hand and it coated her fingers.

Tippi laughed, and Tess screamed, "Stop! That's how Goldfinger died!" And that's when she woke in a panic.

Bizarre dream. She'd told Tippi and Janice about it on the way to the airport. Janice had responded with, "I never watched another James Bond movie after *Goldfinger.* Too creepy. But you know the actress they covered in gold paint didn't really die like everyone thought, right? You won't actually suffocate if all your skin is covered."

Tippi had laughed—a sound eerily similar to the dream.

Even now, settled on the plane, Tess couldn't shake the feeling the dream had left. Did it mean something?

She'd just leaned her head against the window and closed her eyes when Tippi said, "If Cyrus had an official burial, he would have been wearing burial clothes or funeral clothes or whatever they call what they bury you in."

"Mm-hmm. I suppose."

"And nobody in their right mind would bury a guy with thirty pounds of gold."

"I don't imagine they would," Tess answered, trying to keep her irritation out of her voice. She leaned down and pulled her headphones from her bag.

Tippi bent at the same time and took a 9×12 envelope from her bag. "I haven't been totally honest with you, Janice, and Lu."

Somehow that doesn't surprise me. Tess stayed mute and waited.

"I came to Marietta because I have an alert set on my computer for anything that comes up with the combined key words Marietta, Ohio and Cyrus Tuttle or Jubal Hudson."

Tess twisted sharply to face Tippi as well as she could with the constraint of a seatbelt and cramped quarters. "You knew something about Cyrus and Jubal before you got here, and you didn't tell us?"

"Yes."

"Wait. You got here before we found the watch cover with Cyrus's name on it. When you got to Marietta, all we'd found was the slave tag, and we had no clue who it belonged to. We still don't know for sure."

"Felicity does."

"What?" Tess's neck was starting to hurt from cranking it so tight.

"I have connections in my line of work. Dr. Felicity White is one of them."

"You and Felicity knew each other before you came to the inn?" Tess had to fight to keep her voice down.

"In a way. I read an article she had written about the Underground Railroad and messaged her several times about a year and a half ago, asking for any information she might have on slaves who went to Ontario. Jubal Hudson was on the list she sent. My client was willing to pay for any details Felicity could find. I set alerts on my computer for key words from the information she sent, including Jubal's owner and tag number."

Tess felt her eyelids stretching wide. "She said that number couldn't be found. The records had been destroyed."

"Many of the ledgers in Charleston were destroyed. Felicity has documents she obtained directly from a plantation in

South Carolina. Not the one we're visiting. Probably one that rented slaves from the Tuttles. I paid big money for the information she gave me. And for the new information she sent me a week and a half ago."

The cords at the back of Tess's neck tightened. "Did Felicity know you were here when she came?"

"No." Tippi closed her eyes for a moment and exhaled loudly through her nose. "She still doesn't." She handed the envelope to Tess. "When I dealt with her, I used a different name."

A wave of nausea swept over Tess. She didn't want to ask, but knew she had to. Was Tippi the one trying to steal the gold literally out from under the Moores? "Goldilocks? Tipper?"

"What? No. I went by my married name. Phillipa Waite."

Tess breathed a sigh. If Tippi was confessing, it didn't seem likely she'd lie about that one thing. "So Felicity has no idea she's had communication with you, Tippi Coddlesworth?"

"Not as far as I can tell."

Tess threw her headphones back in her bag. "Start from the beginning."

Tippi handed her the envelope. "Look inside."

The first page of a sheaf of papers featured a picture of a man with dark eyes and short-cropped curly hair next to his name and bio.

Dr. Reuben R. Walsh, Professor of Genealogical Studies at the University of Toronto, has spent the better part of two decades compiling stories and family trees of slaves who found freedom and opportunity in Ontario. This body of work follows forty-one men, women, and children and their descendants from their escape from plantations in the American South to the present day.

Tess turned the page over and stared at the table of contents. Forty-one names listed in alphabetical order by last name. A third of the way down the page she found Jubal Hudson.

She turned to Page 87 and felt a flutter in her stomach. A photograph of a man and a woman, maybe in their sixties, each leaning one elbow on an ornately carved pedestal. Behind them, a mural of giant cabbage roses. The woman stood at enough of an angle to show the shelf made by her bustle. A row of tiny buttons ran down the front of the striped dress, ending below the waist. Layers of soft folds draped across the skirt. The man, tall, broad shouldered, and dark-skinned, wore a three-piece suit. A watch chain hung across his vest. Below the picture was the caption *The Reverend Jubal Hudson and Mrs. Miriam Hudson, 1886.*

Jubal had lived at least twenty-eight years beyond Cyrus. Tears burned Tess's eyes. She wished she could call LuAnn and Janice to share the news. Jubal had escaped to freedom.

The next page was blank except for two words. *Jubal's Story.* The Hudson family tree began on the next page. Four sons born to Jubal and Miriam. The final entry was a great-great-something grandson born in 2018. Jonathan Jubal Hudson.

"I'm here to fill the blank pages." Tippi's voice held a kind of reverence.

Tess nodded as she stared at the list of names and occupations in Jubal's lineage. Farmers, pastors, nurses, engineers, teachers, doctors, electricians. One woman worked at NASA. Another was an aide to the prime minister.

It took a moment for the question to surface, but when it did, Tess had to concentrate on controlling her breathing. "You knew Jubal lived. You knew he made it to Canada. But you kept all of this from us. Why?" Too much force on the last word, but she couldn't help it.

Tippi stared around Tess, her gaze fixing on the clouds beyond the window. "I'm sorry. Telling you would have been breaking a promise I made to Reuben." She reached over and pulled a folded paper from the envelope. "The book is scheduled to go to print in three weeks. We know what happened to Jubal after he reached Canada, but very little before that. Reuben wants to be the first to publish the story of how he got from Charleston to Windsor. That's why he doesn't want to freely share what he knows. I wanted to tell you. He called when we were at dinner at the Buckley House, and I tried to get his permission then...Anyway, after all that's happened, he's finally given me the go-ahead to talk to you and possibly someone from the Tuttle Plantation and share this"—she pulled another envelope from her purse—"at my discretion." She took a paper from the envelope and unfolded it. "It's a copy of a letter to Jubal from Cyrus's sister." She handed it to Tess.

April 12, 1859

Dear Jubal,

Your gift arrived a week ago. You could not possibly have known how perfectly timed it was. The hope contained in Austen's writings will change the way things have always been done here. I am indebted to you for kindness you need not have shown and grateful to our Lord for seeing you to safety.

Your response from Marietta does not surprise me. I hope to meet them someday and express the depth of my gratitude. Their sacrifice of service inspires me to do what I can to end this evil.

Please continue to keep me abreast of your plans. You have my heartfelt support.

Gratefully,
Genevieve

"It's all so vague." Tippi interrupted Tess's pondering of the meaning of the letter. "I think she's saying things only Jubal would understand, don't you?"

Yes. But Tess wasn't in the mood to dissect the letter with the person who'd kept it from her this long. "Or maybe she's just thanking him for a gift. Looks like he sent her a Jane Austen novel."

"Anyway, it proves they had contact," Tippi said.

"So you're going to share what you know with Misty?"

"I hope we can have an exchange of information. Maybe together we can fill in the blanks. Reuben is more than willing to share…as long as the Tuttle Plantation agrees to give us the right to publish it first."

Tess sat back and closed her eyes. She needed sleep. And time to process.

"I'm sorry." Tippi's voice quavered. "I consider you a dear friend, Tess. I hope I haven't done irreparable damage to our friendship."

Friendship? *Dear* friend? A verse from Romans scrolled across her mind. "*If it is possible, as far as it depends on you, live at peace with everyone.*" She let out a soft sigh. "It's okay, Tip."

October 20, 1858

The trees across the river were ablaze with color. Late afternoon sun seemed to light the maples from within. Prudence ambled home, savoring the beauty, allowing it to chase the remnants of fear into the corners of her mind.

She needed to tell Jason what had happened this morning, but she dreaded telling him anything that would make him yet more aware of his limitations. He would want to ride off to find the man who had accosted her. His bad leg would make that dangerous.

As she walked up the lane to the house, she spoke Scripture aloud, trying to make the words soften her heart. "Dearly beloved, avenge not yourselves, but rather give place unto wrath: for it is written, vengeance is mine; I will repay, saith the Lord." The words of the twelfth chapter of Romans had finally, in recent years, begun to soothe her bitterness against the man who had enslaved her and her parents, and yet it had no effect on the anger raging in her soul at the man who had terrified her behind the inn. "Recompense to no man evil for evil..." She could do that only if she never saw the man's face again. "Overcome evil with—"

Movement behind the house froze her. A brown coat. She held her breath until the man stepped onto the porch and she recognized him. But why...?

"Cyrus!" She picked up her skirts and ran. He'd been almost delirious with fever when she'd left this morning. What was he doing? He didn't need to visit the privy. They'd made provisions for his comfort. She heard voices in the barn. Had Jason and Jubal checked on him at all? Was his mind so muddled by fever he didn't know where he was? "What is thee doing, Cyrus? Thee will catch thy death—" She regretted the words the moment they left her lips.

"Just getting a little fresh air." Cyrus's smile did nothing to quell her worry. In spite of the chilly air, beads of perspiration dotted his forehead. "Heading right back to bed, ma'am."

Prudence spent the next hour warming a stone for his feet, heating soup, making tea, adding wood to the fire in his room, and asking him repeatedly if he needed more quilts. Finally, he closed his eyes and slept until after the others had finished their dinner of roast pheasant and sweet potatoes. When he began to stir, they brought chairs into the little room. Prudence held a cup so he could take sips of broth while Jubal asked if he had the strength to continue their story.

Cyrus nodded, momentarily strengthened by rest and sustenance. "I wouldn't trade this"—he gestured toward the bed where he lay, head and shoulders propped on pillows—"for the life I had before.

"It all came crashing down at once on Christmas Day last year. There I was, not a cent to my name, sitting on the ground by a campfire with a bunch of smelly, ornery prospectors, and this man"—he gestured toward Jubal—"who I had once deemed ignorant and beneath me, is reciting the Christmas story by memory while he's dishing up beans for me in a tin cup. And the daft man is smiling! I'm sitting there in a sorry heap, imagining the spiced ham and yeast rolls and pecan pie I'd be eating back home, and this man who's never had a penny to his name is dishing up beans like he's the happiest man in the world."

Jubal laughed. "The Lord works in mysterious ways. This time he used beans." He wiped the dampness under his eyes. "But that ain't exactly the truth. He'd been workin' on Cyrus all along. 'Bout a year into our journey, I asked Cyrus to teach me to read. Now, it wasn't my plan at all, but you know the Lord was workin', 'cause the only thing he had to use was the Bible my mama sent with me. So here we was, porin' over the Word o' God night after night, and the Word o' God don't ever return void, you know."

Cyrus nodded. "So there I was, taking the cup of beans Jubal gave me, and two things slammed me like a load of bricks. First was, I don't want this man waiting on me anymore. It's not right. He's no less a person than I am, and..."

His voice cracked. "...and he's my friend, closer than I'd ever been to my brother. The other thing that hit me was, 'I know why he's so happy. It's because of what he's been telling me all along—Gotta give it all to Jesus.' So I did. Sitting right there with all those smelly men telling whoppin' lies about finding gold nuggets as big as a man's fist, I prayed. And life hasn't been the same ever since." He gave a weak but beautiful smile. "And wouldn't you know, just a week later we found—"

A horse whinnied. Close to the house. Jubal jumped up and parted the curtain enough to peer out. "Nothin'."

It was time. Prudence told them about the man who'd been waiting for her at the Riverfront. As expected, Jason's hands clenched.

"Who is he?" Prudence asked, aiming her question at Jubal.

"Man sent by Master Vernon, Cyrus's uncle, to bring us back. He came searchin' with another man who got shot for cheatin' at cards. Got it in his head I was the one who killed his partner, but it weren't so. I stepped in and tried to stop it, but somebody said I was the one who pulled the trigger. There's a reward for him returnin' me and maybe more for bringin' Cyrus back safe, but we're thinkin' it's revenge he's after now."

Cyrus's face had paled to match the sheets. "And the gold."

Prudence's eyes widened. "So you did find gold?"

Cyrus looked at Jubal. "There's something I have to tell you, Jubal Hudson."

"Wha's that?"

Cyrus held out his hand. "Give me that hunk of metal you got around your neck."

Jubal stared blankly until the outstretched hand began to shake. He slipped the necklace off.

"Here's what I want you to do," Cyrus said, his voice growing stronger rather than weaker. "Your take your knife and you carve 1 Corinthians 7:21 on the back. You remember that one?"

"Yes, sir. But why?"

"Sir?" Cyrus gave a weak laugh. "Don't you ever call me that again. And don't you ever put that thing back around your neck. Because you're no more a slave than I am. While we were in St. Louis, I sent my uncle money to buy your freedom. When you get to Canada, wait until you're settled and write to Genevieve and tell—"

"I'm not going to Canada." Jubal sat on a chair with a thud. "As soon as I get you home safe, Master goin' to give me my freedom, you know that. Didn't have to cost you anything."

Cyrus smiled. "It's not costing *me* anything. You're the one who did all the hard work. I'm the one with the lily-white hands, remember? And while we are speaking of money, I want you all to know, if I don't make it, I buried my half of the gold—"

A crash drew Jason and Jubal instantly to their feet. The front door, blown open by the wind.

But there was no wind.

"Where is he?" a deep voice bellowed.

Bile rose in Prudence's throat as the man who'd whispered vile threats in her ear shouted from her front room.

Jubal vaulted over the end of the bed. His gun hung from a hook near the ladder to the loft. Jubal's large hand closed around Cyrus's walking stick. Before he could raise it, the man appeared in the doorway and aimed his pistol at Jubal's head.

Chapter Twenty

Quaint, charming, steeped in history. Every adjective Tess had ever read about Charleston played out before her eyes as they passed pastel-painted three-story buildings with arched windows, some with red-tiled roofs, some topped with ornate cornices. Gabe, the man who'd picked them up in a van with the Tuttle Plantation logo on the doors, had begun their travelogue as they left Charleston International Airport, after explaining he'd been asked to "take the long way" to the island and give them a taste of downtown.

"We like to explain to visitors that our city is located where the Cooper and Ashley Rivers come together to form the Atlantic Ocean." As they drove through commercial areas lined with palm trees and streets lined with houses with balconies on each floor, he pointed out the different architectural styles that gave a time line of Charleston history. "The Georgian style was popular from 1774 to approximately 1820." He listed features common to most Georgian homes—rough-faced limestone trim, stone arches and granite pedestals flanking the front door. "Gothic Revival dominated in the last half of the nineteenth century, drawing its inspiration from the medieval era. You'll recognize these romantic buildings by their parapets, pointed arched windows, and castle-like towers." As they drove down streets that had existed for two centuries and more, Tess felt a twinge of guilt that she was here and not LuAnn, who'd always dreamed of owning a time machine.

"During the War Between the States, steeples were used as lighthouses and lookouts, and the church bells and iron gates were melted down for cannons to aid the Confederacy. Legend has it St. Michael's steeple was painted black at one time to make it difficult to see at night."

By the time they reached the sign for Wadmalaw Island, Tess's brain was beginning to feel like an overstuffed suitcase. But the crammed feeling in her mind and the irritation lingering from the flight and Tippi's revelations evaporated as Gabe turned into the drive that was even more stunning than the pictures. The words she'd reread on the plantation website on the way to the airport came alive....two-hundred-year-old moss-draped live oaks...fluted Corinthian columns... floor-to-ceiling windows...porch ceiling painted in the traditional "haint" blue...The site had not hinted at the colors of October—a riot of pinks and purples overflowing from massive clay pots. Deep red mums, pink daisies, feathery blue mist flowers, and the deep indigo of what Gabe labeled beautyberries.

This is where Cyrus lived. No surprise he'd grown up soft and spoiled. "Where would the slave quarters have been?" Tess asked as Gabe parked in the circle drive in front of the house.

Gabe opened his door, got out, and opened first Tippi's door and then Tess's. "Over there, ma'am." He pointed to a long single-story white building with at least eight doors set far behind the main house. "Those quarters were built by

Miss Genevieve. A vast improvement over the shacks her uncle provided."

Seeing the slave quarters in person, imagining a life of sunup to sundown work, owning nothing and having no power over your destiny, made the wonder of what she'd just learned about Jubal's legacy so much greater and brought home the magnitude of the miracle of a friendship between two men from such diverse backgrounds. She glanced at Tippi. *With God all things are possible.*

A woman with shoulder-length chestnut hair stood on the porch in a white linen dress belted with a floral scarf. She wore classic pearls. "Welcome." She extended her hand. "I'm Caroline Tuttle." She offered a smile that defined Southern hospitality. "Otherwise known as Misty."

"You're a Tuttle," Tess blurted as she shook the woman's hand. "I'm Tess. This is—"

Tippi nudged her shoulder and stuck out her hand. "Tippi Coddlesworth. Also known as Phillipa Waite."

Caroline's eyes widened. "You're…"

"Yes."

"Well then…this is unexpected." Caroline quickly recovered from her surprise. Her gracious smile returned. "I hope, between the three of us, we will be able to paint a more complete picture. Please come in. I'll show you to your rooms and let you get settled, and then we'll meet in the sunroom for a tour and then tea."

As they walked on the gleaming marble of the entryway, Tess shot Tippi a "what else haven't you told me?" glare.

Tippi shrugged and smiled before whispering, "I'll explain."

You'd better. Tess held her tongue, and they followed Caroline up the curved cherry stairs to a room that made them both gasp. The walls were papered in a crisscross design of mint green and peach trimmed along the high ceiling with a wide border depicting rocking horses, dolls, and toy soldiers. Peach satin curtains matched the canopy on a single bed. Furniture—dresser, bench, crib, and rocking chair—painted the palest green. "This was the nursery," Caroline said. "Tuttle children were cared for here for a century and a quarter. The first was born in 1827, the last 1954." She smiled wistfully as she touched a turned spindle on the crib. "I was the last."

Tess had studied the website while waiting at the airport. "The estate was donated to the preservation society shortly after you were born." She tried to make it sound like merely a statement of fact, but a tinge of sympathy crept in.

"Yes." Caroline may have been attempting to hide her emotions, but something came through. Resentment, bitterness, or just sadness? They left Tippi in the nursery and walked to the next room. "This was Genevieve, Cyrus's sister's, room," Caroline said. "Restored to much of what we believe it to have been in 1860. We had the wallpaper made to match the second layer we recovered."

"It's…gorgeous." White on white. Tess crossed the gleaming wide-planked floor to a four-poster bed tented in white eyelet. The same fabric formed the thick duvet cover on the bed. White pillows, white Queen Anne furniture trimmed in shimmery gold. The walls were papered in off-white covered in thin trailing vines of gold. She stepped into the private bath. White marble vanity, gold fixtures in the claw-footed tub. "Oh my." She breathed in the scent of luxury. Lavender, lemon verbena, rose.

"The books on this shelf were recently donated by one of Genevieve's descendants." Caroline rested her fingertips on a shelf in a built-in bookcase. "I haven't had a chance to look at them, but I love the idea that her hands held these." She turned her attention to a framed cross-stitch with the words *He Leadeth Me* stitched in pink. Genevieve's initials were in the bottom right corner. "She was quite the woman." Caroline walked to the door. "I'll meet you downstairs in half an hour."

"Thank you so much for inviting us. Your home is absolutely stunning."

Caroline's lips tightened into a straight line. "This is not my home."

"Oh. Of course. I'm sorry, I—"

As Tess stuttered her apology, Caroline walked out and closed the door.

Okay then. Tess let her gaze caress the room and tried to imagine Genevieve's life. *Genevieve, who were you?* She touched a fine line outlining a leaf on the wall. Gold. *Did you get any of Cyrus and Jubal's gold?* She recalled the line on the website about the plantation almost falling to ruin until Genevieve took over. Did she just have better business sense than her uncle…or did she have wealth from the goldfields of California? Would she find out in half an hour, or would sparks fly between Tippi and Caroline over their carefully guarded secrets?

Lord, please keep this exchange of information civil.

Arrived safe. Plantation is beyond words. So much to tell you. Misty is Caroline Tuttle. Learned some things about Jubal on the flight. Yup, Tippi wasn't in Marietta just for a social call. But she is not Goldilocks. I'll call tonight. Just had to give you a cliffhanger! Picturing the looks on her best friends' faces, Tess pushed SEND before walking out of the bedroom carrying a copy of Prudence's journal, the book Evelyn had loaned her, and pictures of their most recent find.

As she reached the stairs, her phone vibrated with an answer from LuAnn. *What did Tippi know about Jubal? Just plain mean to make us wait.* A second later Janice added, *Wow! And I second the mean part.* Tess replied with a laughing emoji and went down the stairs, imagining she was Genevieve Tuttle in a bustled silk dress that swished with every step.

Tippi and Caroline stood in front of an ornately carved fireplace in what Tess assumed would be called a parlor. Tippi held a framed picture, which she turned around to show Tess as she entered the room. "This is Cyrus."

As with most tintype and daguerreotype photographs, the fair-haired young man in this picture was not smiling. Exactly. His lips formed a straight line, yet his eyes shimmered with mirth, as if struggling to hold still and exercise restraint until the flashbulb popped, and he would be free to laugh again. He sat in a tapestry-upholstered chair with his feet on a matching footstool, legs crossed at the ankles. In his hand, what appeared to be a crystal drinking glass. The body language perfectly matched the tone of the letter Cyrus had written to his friend in Marietta, signing it, *Yours in the pursuit of adventure, Cy.*

"I wish I'd known him," Tippi said. "Looks like he'd be fun at a party."

"From what we know of Cyrus, that's about all he did. His uncle was very disappointed with him." Caroline swept her hand gracefully toward the painting above the fireplace. "And that's where we start our tour—with Uncle Vernon, my uncle seven generations back."

"Are you a direct descendant of Cyrus?" Had Cyrus died far from home leaving a wife and children to grieve?

Caroline shook her head. "I am descended from Cyrus's younger brother Randall. Genevieve never married, and Cyrus died…or disappeared…without offspring."

Tippi shot Tess a look. Tess gestured toward a grouping of four straight-backed chairs with curved legs and needlepoint cushions surrounding a marble-topped oval table. "Could we talk for a bit before beginning the tour? We…*I* have some information we just discovered last night."

She had no idea what Tippi intended to share. She wasn't going to put words in her mouth.

"Of course. Please, sit." Caroline took a small brass bell from the fireplace mantel and rang it. In seconds, a man in traditional butler attire entered the room and bowed. "We'll have tea now, Jefferson."

"Yes, ma'am." The uniformed man nodded, turned sharply on his heel, and left.

Tess didn't bother hiding her shock. Was this all for their benefit, or was this daily life for Caroline Tuttle?

Caroline chuckled softly as she joined them at the table. "His real name is Donny Harris. He's in training as a volunteer docent. Part of his training is learning to stay in character no matter what is going on around him."

"Oh." Tess kept her relieved sigh silent. "That would be an excellent way to train."

"We rely heavily on our volunteers. You can imagine what it costs to keep the plantation open for the public, including more than a thousand school children each year." She tapped her finger on the book Tess had set on the table. "What did you discover?" Though kind and hospitable, Caroline was clearly a woman who cut to the chase.

Tess opened her folder of loose pages and pulled out the top one. Pictures of the headstone they'd found only twelve hours earlier. Without preamble, she slid it across the table to Caroline.

Caroline picked up the paper. Her lips formed the words in silence. After a moment, she set the page on the table. "1858." She glanced up at the painting of Vernon. "It makes me sad he never knew."

Tess wondered if Tippi would share what she knew about the correspondence between Genevieve and Jubal. Surely

Genevieve would have told Vernon whatever she'd learned from Jubal. It was likely Vernon knew how and when Cyrus died, but the facts had been lost over time. She looked up at Vernon. A stern-faced man. The slight resemblance to his nephew was only in the shape of his face and the high forehead. He looked like a man who had rarely enjoyed life.

A brass plaque below the painting had been hidden by a vase of silk hibiscus blooms while they stood by the fireplace. From where she sat, Tess could read Vernon's name but not the smaller inscription below it. She got out of her chair and stepped closer.

Vernon Hansen Tuttle. 1797–1859

"He sent men to search for Cyrus and bring Jubal back in shackles."

The shackles. Tess felt her skin crawl.

"None of them returned. He never knew what happened to Cyrus." Caroline stared up at the picture. "We have some of Vernon's writings. He wasn't a man who easily showed affection, but, in his own way, he loved his brother's children as if they were his own." She stood. "I'll get my files."

Caroline left the room, and Tippi's foot began tapping the hardwood floor. "What can she possibly know if she didn't even know when Cyrus died?" she whispered.

"Wait and see. Maybe if we all put everything out on the table, literally, we'll be able to fill all of those blanks."

Tippi shrugged. "This is business, Tess. If it was only up to me, I would. Like you said, we'll wait and see."

Caroline returned with an accordion-pleated folder fastened with string. She unwound the string from the paper circles and set the folder at her feet. She started to pull out a paper, then let it slide back in and looked at Tippi. "Shall I address you as Philippa?"

"Tippi is fine."

"Shall we decide on terms before we proceed? You and I have both dealt with Dr. White, I believe. I've never thought it ethical to buy and sell information that should be freely available to the public, but I have, out of necessity, done both."

"Excuse me." Tess jumped in before Tippi had a chance to answer. She was beginning to feel like a spectator who'd just come along for the ride. "What, exactly, is Dr. White's profession, or role, in all of this?"

Caroline arched a perfectly shaped brow. "Felicity White is a historical information broker. Her practices are frowned upon but not illegal. She gathers information from various sources and makes them available to the highest bidder. Phil... *Tippi* and I became acquainted because we were recently involved in a bidding war over a letter written by Genevieve to Jubal."

All Tess could do was nod. She'd never heard of a historical information broker, but then, people found a way to turn a profit from just about anything.

Tippi rested her hands on the folder in front of her. "My client isn't interested in money. All he asks is the right to be first to publish the complete story of Jubal Hudson's escape to freedom."

Tess watched Caroline. Did it bother her that her ancestors, right here on the estate that bore her name, had bought and sold human beings and treated them as property?

Caroline's face showed no emotion. "I believe we can agree on that. I only want access to the information for display. And..." She straightened a bejeweled bracelet. "...a share of the gold."

Chapter Twenty-One

Tess crawled into bed before nine, her body tired, her brain somewhere beyond the point of exhaustion. She sent a text to LuAnn and Janice. *Call me when you're together, and put me on speaker.* Her phone rang in seconds.

"You're on speaker," Janice said. "Tell us everything. Don't leave out *anything.*"

Tess summed up what Tippi had told her on the plane, allowing them time to vent about Tippi withholding information. She described Genevieve's white-on-white room and told them about the library with its rich burgundy leather furniture and the wheeled ladders connected to tracks on the ceiling, bedrooms with tasseled velvet draperies Scarlett O'Hara would have eyed as dress material, handwoven carpets, tufted settees, coffered ceilings, and crystal chandeliers. She gave them a verbal tour of the summer house, the gardens, the slave quarters, and the school built by Genevieve after she took over running the plantation.

She saved the drama for last.

"Now, do you want to know what we've learned from Caroline that might actually help us?"

"Of course!" Their voices tumbled over each other.

"Zip. Nada. Not a thing. And you know why? Because all she's interested in is the gold. She wants a cut before she tells us anything."

"What? Did you tell her Prudence said Cyrus was flat broke?" LuAnn's irritation matched her own. "Or about the children's home? If Cyrus had any money, it looks like he gave a bunch of it to the home."

"Did you show her the picture of the tombstone?" Janice's frustrated sigh carried through the phone. "Cyrus had a proper burial. No one would have buried him with the gold. Did you tell her Jubal must have taken it all to Canada?"

"We showed her the tombstone, but that's all. I said we have every reason to believe there never was any gold, and she said she has reason to believe otherwise, and that was the end of it. She proceeded to give us a very thorough and very polite tour of the estate, and then we had a very lovely, quiet, awkward dinner and went to our separate rooms."

"Wow. What now?" Janice asked.

"I don't know. We'll see what happens in the morning. My head is too fuzzy to even think right now. I'll keep you posted."

"If anything makes you feel unsafe, you come home, okay?" LuAnn's smile was evident in her voice. Her comment was exactly what they'd said to each other before dates or parties in college.

"I will. Thanks, guys. Anything new back home?" It dawned on Tess how right the word *home* felt now. They'd moved into the inn a little over a year ago, and it had taken her a while to think of her little apartment on the fourth floor as home.

"Felicity was in her room most of the day, and the Webers got in after two this morning. They apologized all over the place for waking Janice but didn't say a word about where they'd been. And..."

Tess heard whispering but could only pick out a few words—"upset her" and "know anything."

"What's going on?"

"Well..." Janice sounded reticent. "We've both had this feeling...It's probably just crazy paranoia, but..."

"You feel like you're being watched? And followed?"

"Yes." Once again, they answered together.

"And we've seen two different men walking the same dog in front of the inn. And they were both wearing all black," Janice added.

Even though she'd talked herself into believing her senses were misfiring, Tess felt a huge sense of relief. "I've seen one of those guys, and I've had that being-watched feeling every time I've been over at the Moore property and a couple of times at the inn. I'm pretty sure we aren't all being paranoid for no reason. So if anything makes you feel unsafe, you stay home, okay?"

"Will do. See you tomorrow."

Tess said goodbye and ended the call, then rested back on the softest pillowcases she had ever felt. Before she'd become an inn owner, she never would have searched for a label. Thomaston Mills. After hours of hunting for the best linens at a price they could afford, she knew these sheets were top of the line and made in Georgia. "Bet you slept on pure cotton, Genevieve." Cotton grown and picked by people like Jubal.

As Tess reached for the lamp switch, she looked at the bookcase. Genevieve's books. Was it possible…? Throwing back the covers, she got up and flipped on the spotlights directed at the books. She scanned the titles, searching for a Jane Austen title. What had the letter to Jubal said? *The hope contained in Austen's writings will change the way things have always been done here.* It was the only sentence she'd tried to commit to memory. What hope would she have gained from reading *Pride and Prejudice* or *Sense and Sensibility*? The hope of romance?

She read the titles out loud. "*Narrative of the Life of Frederick Douglass, Moby Dick, Walden.*" And a book she'd never heard of titled *Book M: A London Widow's Life Writings.* Not a single Jane Austen book. With slow, careful movements, she took down the widow's writings. What could she learn from a woman who'd lost her husband more than a century ago? Was the grieving process the same through the ages? The leather-bound book was lighter than she would have expected. She carried it to the overstuffed chair in the corner, sat, and opened the front cover.

What jumped out at her first was the date. The original manuscript had been penned between 1664 and 1666. Her pulse skipped a beat as she read the author's name.

Katherine *Austen.* On the next page, a faded inscription.

To Genevieve Tuttle
with all our gratitude,
Jubal and Miriam Hudson
Christmas 1859

Goose bumps held a dance party on her arms. Jubal, or his wife, had written this. But why? Genevieve had never married. She ran her fingertip across the words. The page dipped beneath her touch. Now that she thought about it, the page looked strange. Sunken in the middle. She opened the book to its midpoint, and her heart nearly forgot to beat altogether.

A square, about three by three inches, was cut out. Completely hollow.

No, not completely. Something sparkled on the bottom. Glitter. She held the book under the bedside lamp. It was glitter, but clearly not the microscopic flat squares and circles of equal size the triplets managed to sprinkle everywhere during craft projects. These were three-dimensional, of varying sizes.

She was pretty sure these were real gold flecks.

Tess slept off and on, finally giving up around five. She took a long bath in the gold-fixtured soaking tub, dressed, and sat in the chair with her Bible. After reading several psalms and praying for everyone and everything she could think of, it was finally an acceptable time to go downstairs. Caroline had said they would have breakfast in a beautiful little sunroom with tall windows and bright yellow walls called, appropriately enough, the breakfast room.

She sent Tippi a text. *Bring your files. Hoping we can reach a compromise this morning.*

Though aware her emotions couldn't always be trusted when she was operating on a sleep deficit, Tess walked out of the room with a folder, Genevieve's book, a plan, and a boldness that could only come from a solid hour with the Lord.

Years ago, an older sorority sister had told Tess she was a peacemaker. "People come to Janice because she's empathetic and to LuAnn when they want logical answers. They come to you to help them navigate relationship problems because you are a peacemaker." *Lord, make that true of me today.*

Tippi was already up, standing in the dining room looking at the old portraits that lined the walls. "That's Genevieve," she said in response to Tess's "Good Morning."

"Good morning, Genevieve." Tess admired the dress with its lace-trimmed stand-up collar, fitted bodice, and voluminous sleeves. What color had it been? She stepped closer to see the detail of a cameo fastened to the collar and the long, thick banana curls clustered in front of her ears. But it was the heart-shaped face with intelligent dark eyes and just the slightest smile that captured her. Genevieve had a look of honesty about her, like someone you meet and know instantly is a person to be trusted. She must have been a remarkable woman for Jubal to have sent her gold he could have kept for himself.

Caroline entered wearing a dress very similar to the one Tess had just been examining. "We have a ladies' tea this afternoon. I have arranged for one of our docents to give you a tour of the city during that time."

Tess couldn't help but wonder if this had been part of the original agenda or if Caroline was finding ways to avoid them. She motioned for them to follow her into the breakfast room.

A woman, probably in her early twenties, wearing a duster cap and long dove-gray dress covered with an apron, set a crystal bowl filled with sliced peaches on the table, then curtsied before leaving the room. As soon as they were seated, the woman returned carrying three plates. Sliced ham, scrambled eggs, and cubed fried potatoes. After serving them, she returned with a plate of warm buttermilk biscuits and asked if they wanted coffee or tea.

Caroline didn't offer to ask a blessing. She passed the biscuits to Tippi, followed by butter and orange marmalade. In the tense silence, Tess eyed the biscuits. If ever there was a time for stress eating…She took one, broke it in half, and buttered just one piece. As discreetly as she could, she divided the potatoes in half with her fork. She would eat the eggs and half of everything else. She thought of Lynette saying, "Food is fuel. You wouldn't fill your gas tank with more than it needs. Treat your stomach the same way." Biting into the biscuit, she analyzed it for taste and texture. "This is so good." But not as good as Winnie's. She'd have to remember to pass on the compliment.

"Thank you. It's a recipe my grandmother used. I remember helping her right here in the kitchen. Of course, the kitchen didn't look like it does now." Her last few words were punctuated with what seemed like bitterness.

"It must be hard for you to see changes made to your childhood home," Tess said.

"More than you can imagine. My siblings and I have formed a corporation. We are trying…" She took a sip of heavily sugared coffee. "Ah well. I trust you both had a good night."

Tippi nodded. She hadn't said a word since they sat down at the table.

"I was a bit restless," Tess said. She wouldn't pull the book out until they'd finished eating.

"As was I." Caroline speared Tippi with a pointed look, making it clear her sleep trouble was Tippi's fault.

The meal continued in silence broken only with "Please pass…" and "Thank you." When they finished, and the gold-rimmed plates were cleared and biscuit tidbits swept off the tablecloth and onto an ornately embellished crumb tray, Tess picked up the book she'd tucked beside her on the chair. She folded her hands on top of it.

"That's one of Genevieve's, isn't it?" Thin layers of surprise and disapproval slid into Caroline's voice.

"It is." Maybe she should have apologized for touching the heirloom, but at the moment she was only focused on intervening between the two gridlocked parties at the table. "Caroline, I understand your interest in the gold. It was discovered by one of your ancestors, and I gather your family has hopes of buying back the plantation."

Caroline's chin dipped in reluctant acknowledgment.

"If there is buried gold, it's only natural that you would feel the Tuttle family is entitled to it." She turned to Tippi. "Your client only wants the right to publish Jubal's story before anyone else, correct?"

"Yes."

Tess turned back to Caroline. "I was hoping to find the gold because lack of funds are forcing the family who's building on the property that once belonged to the Willards to cut out some features that would be beneficial to the children with disabilities they will be fostering." She had no qualms about playing the sympathy card when it came to children. "We were all, for different reasons, caught up in the romance of finding buried gold. But I think that's all it was, just a fanciful hope. Caroline, if I could prove the gold was never buried in Marietta, would you be willing to share your information with Tippi's client in exchange for what we have learned?"

"I would." Caroline held her delicate china cup with white knuckles. "But you can't."

Tess blinked back her surprise. This was one tough cookie. "I believe I can." As she held out the book, she silently thanked God for preserving this evidence.

Caroline read the inscription. A divot formed above her nose.

"Open it in the middle."

Caroline drew the book closer, opened to the middle, squinted, then touched her fingertip to the bottom of the hole. She stared down at the miniscule gold chips glittering under the chandelier. After a long moment, she said, "I agree that it looks like Jubal sent her some of the gold. This does not prove that there is no gold buried in Marietta."

Caroline pushed back from the table, stood, and walked to the sideboard. She retrieved an envelope from a drawer and returned to her seat. She pulled out a piece of paper and slid the page to Tess.

A color photocopy of a letter turned yellow with age. The bold pen strokes were faded to brown.

June 8, 1860
Windsor, Ontario, Canada

Dear Genevieve,

We so appreciate your letters. I rejoice in the changes you have made and would love to be there to witness the joy on the faces of those I hold dear as they receive their pay each month. May our heavenly Father reward you greatly for the grace you have shown them.

In answer to your last question, I believe it is time to cease our hope of finding Cy's take in Marietta and let our minds rest. Jason has searched and found nothing. After almost two years, I think we must conclude that either we misunderstood Cy's last words before he left us, or someone else has uncovered it. In either case, we are not meant to find it. I have told Jason to let it be. Searching for it in the first place broke Cy in a way that drew him to Jesus, but I have seen gold fever have the opposite effect on far too many men. I cannot bear the thought of it destroying the lives of future generations. Can you join me in accepting we are not meant to find it? Can we agree to keep this between the four of us until our deaths? For all we know, it may be hidden for someone to find many years in the future, and we will hear the end of this tale in Glory.

Mama sends her love and, as always, her undying gratitude. She prays daily for you and the Willards and all of the others who helped reunite us. Though we see the storm clouds gathering, we take heart that there is still good in this world. I cling to the last two verses of the 27th Psalm: "I had fainted, unless I had believed to see the goodness of the LORD in the land of the living. Wait on the LORD: be of good courage, and he shall strengthen thine heart: wait, I say, on the LORD."

In hope,
Jubal

Tess compared the dates. This letter had been written six months after Jubal had sent the book and the gold. "Who have you shared this with?"

Caroline's shoulders straightened in what appeared to be a defensive posture. "Only Dr. White."

Of course. *And now it belongs to anyone willing to pay for it.*

Chapter Twenty-Two

What a waste of time." Tippi slid her bag under the seat in front of her for the first leg of their trip home.

"Not completely." Tess fished her phone out of the bottom of her purse and tapped on SETTINGS to switch to airplane mode. "We now know Jubal sent—" Her phone vibrated just as her finger hovered over it. Michael. She greeted her son-in-law, quickly adding, "We're on the plane, so I've only got a minute."

"This will only take a minute. I looked at the trail cam feed from last night. We got something. A very weird something."

Tess leaned toward the window. "Really?" She kept her voice low but couldn't disguise her excitement.

"There is one person in the frame at first. He starts waving a metal detector over the ground for like a minute then starts digging. Not even a foot down, he pulls out a cloth bag tied with a rope. He opens it, sticks his hand in, and pulls out what I assume is the gold, but then he puts the bag back in the hole, and another guy steps in and kicks all the dirt back in the hole, Then the first person picks up the detector and does the exact same thing all over again. A retake, I think. I'm guessing someone was videoing."

"Very weird. Also strange that a cloth bag that close to the surface would still be intact after more than a hundred and fifty years. Can you see any details that would help identify the person? Body type?" Elliott's ample physique couldn't be missed. She hoped it wasn't him.

"He, or she, I guess, was wearing a stocking cap. You can see a profile for a few seconds. I'll try to get pictures of the best frame. Not sure the quality is good enough to identify anyone."

"Ladies and gentlemen," the pilot announced. "Welcome onboard Flight 1422 with service from Charleston to Atlanta. We are next in line, so please—"

"I heard that," Michael said. "I'll talk to you when you get back. And thanks for letting me get in on this. It's kind of exciting."

Tess put her phone away and pulled out her headphones. A little soothing music…

"Who was that?"

She should be used to Tippi's abruptness by now, but she wasn't. "My son-in-law."

"You're so lucky. Such a beautiful family. You always were lucky."

Leave it alone or engage? *You picked up right where you left off forty years ago…pointing out every one of my shortcomings, and now you're calling me lucky?* Tess decided to skip the part about not believing in luck. "What do you mean?"

"You've always led a charmed life. Good grades, confidence, a ton of friends in college. Everything came easy for you. I used to sit back and watch the three of you. The In Crowd. You had so much fun. I just wanted…to be part of that.

And you were the funny one. People gravitate to you. I wanted to be like you, but..."

Tippi sniffled and pulled a tissue from her pocket. "I know you're alone now, but you had years of a happy marriage. I've chased two men away. I'm forced to sell the beach house in the settlement, and here you are living in that gorgeous old building. And on top of it all you've got triplet grandkids."

"Tippi, you've got the wrong—"

"Remember that night four guys called to ask you out? And that time Mr. Connor asked you to sing a solo in the Easter cantata without giving any of the rest of us a chance to audition?"

Tess massaged her forehead with her thumb and index finger. "I actually remember both of those things. The boys called because of a bet. I was humiliated. And I sang that solo in the cantata because it was also the song I'd picked for the solo and ensemble competition."

Tess closed her eyes, took a deep breath, and shifted her body to face Tippi. "I worked hard for the grades I got. I finished with a 3.2 average. Nothing to brag about. And I didn't have my first real date until I was a senior in college. I *have* been blessed with good friends and a wonderful family, but please don't think for a minute my life has been easy or that I'm in any way, shape, or form perfect. I struggle daily with being critical of others and impatient. I eat too much, exercise too little, and many days since my husband died I wake up in the morning with no clue what my purpose in li—" She stopped talking when Tippi began to cry. "What's wrong?"

"I know I've been a terrible friend. I just always wanted to be like you, to belong like you do, but people don't like me the way they like you." Tippi sniffled and wiped tears from her chin.

Lord, what do I say? How do you tell a grown-up it takes a friend to be a friend? "Tip, can I be very, very honest?"

"Sure. I deserve it."

"I think you've wasted energy being jealous of the me you created in your head. I have been very blessed, but I haven't led a charmed life. I'm as imperfect as they come, but I do have something you don't."

Tippie rolled her eyes. "You're going to say Jesus."

Tess gave a soft laugh. "Yes, I'm going to say Jesus. But I'm not going to give you the speech about peace and joy and all the Christian clichés you've already heard. Let me just tell you about one moment that changed my life.

"Years ago, back in junior high, we moved, and I had to transfer to a new school. I didn't know anyone, and I was miserable. Back home, my friends were kids I'd known all my life. Here I was, twelve years old, and in a cliquey school where no one cared who I was. I had no idea how to fit in. One night I prayed, and then I opened my Bible. I was reading through the book of Luke, and as soon as I opened to where I'd left off, I saw Jesus's words, 'Do onto others as you would have them do unto you.'"

"The golden rule."

"Yes. Simple words, but it was like a floodlight illuminated them. I realized it was up to me. If I wanted friends, I needed to put those words into practice. The next day I started complimenting people, asking them questions, showing an interest. The following week I was invited to two sleepovers. Not because I'm some amazing person, but because I started to actually care more about other people than myself."

"Ouch." Tippi wiped a hand across her cheek. "I've never been good at that."

No, you haven't. "It's never too late."

Tippi nodded and closed her eyes. Tess decided to give her some time to think. She settled into her seat.

"See, I told you."

Tess was sure she heard a smile in Tippi's voice. She turned and confirmed it.

"You always do everything right. You just did it again. You nailed me. I needed that. Most people are afraid of me."

"Maybe they won't be from now on."

"Yeah. Maybe not. Tess?"

"Yes?"

"Maybe we'll end up friends after all. Like Cyrus and Jubal."

Tess smiled as she watched the cars and houses below them shrink. "I think that's very possible, Tip."

It felt good to wake up in her own bed. Maybe it wasn't a four-poster with the most expensive sheets. And maybe her room was half the size of Genevieve's. But it was home.

Tess looked out over the brooding river. A leaden sky threatened to open up and douse the world. She checked her phone. As of 6:30 a.m., the farmers market was still on. She showered and pulled out long underwear and wool socks, then piled layers on the bed. Turtleneck sweater, quilted vest, rain jacket. Something about this damp cold bothered her more than a snowy twenty-degree day. Today, she would be prepared.

She read a chapter in Hebrews and a page in her daily devotional but spent less time than usual praying. She'd have time between customers this morning. Probably a lot of time. It would be a quiet morning, and she was fine with that. And after she returned from the market, there'd be time for a luxurious nap. Lizzie and Michael and the kids were coming for supper. Jeff Jr. was joining them too. A rare opportunity to have her whole family together. And to watch the feed from the trail cam.

Before going downstairs, she picked up the notebook she'd used to journal everything they'd learned in Charleston. Tippi's "waste of time" comment wasn't completely wrong. They'd come home with just as many questions as when they'd left. Was there buried gold? Could they find it before someone else, or could they put an end to the rumors to give the Moores peace of mind? And who was the someone else they were racing against?

The front door opened as she reached the bottom of the staircase. Their early arrivals. A mother and daughter here for a wedding. To save money, they'd booked a red-eye flight that landed in Columbus at 4:00 a.m. Janice had taken the reservation. When they'd asked for a "no frills" room, Janice booked them in Moonlight and Snowflakes. Smaller than some of the others, but the Wedgewood-blue walls, silver and white accessories, and sleigh bed covered with a snowy white quilt never failed to evoke oohs and ahhs.

Tess checked them in then unlocked the drawer where they kept the keys. The old drawer stuck, and she gave it a yank. Something rolled to the front. The tiny corked bottle filled with gold flakes.

Gold.

She showed the women to their room, waited a polite couple of minutes while they gushed about the silver snowflakes surrounding the oval mirror and the sparkly throw pillows on the bed, then tried not to rush through her usual spiel. She took the elevator downstairs. LuAnn was in the café, putting a "Come See Us at the Farmers Market" card on each table.

Tess didn't bother with a greeting. "Lu"—she held up the tiny bottle—"did you write down everyone who was here the day we found this?"

"I couldn't. I didn't have a clue who all was here. Why?"

"Because…it's gold. Strange coincidence, isn't it?"

LuAnn nodded. "It could be. So who have we seen wearing something this could have been attached…" She pointed to the lobby window. "Elliott's talking to one of the dog walkers."

Tess stepped around the end of the desk and went to the window for a closer look. Elliott was talking with his hands. Animated gestures, first pointing at his truck, then the inn, and then the bag in his hand. Finally he calmed, shook the man's hand, and walked toward the front door.

Elliott came in, the backpack that held his metal-detecting gear in hand. He stared at LuAnn, eyes narrowing, not saying a word.

"Good morning," Tess said. Elliott didn't answer. "Elliott? Everything okay?"

"No. Not okay at all."

"What did that man say? Do you know who he is? We've seen him before, and I'm about ready to call the police on him. I think he's stalking us."

"Stalking?" Elliott blinked as if suddenly realizing where he was. "No." He shook his head. "I'm sorry. I had no intention of scaring you."

"Scaring us?" LuAnn said. "*You're* not scaring us. The man, those men are..."

"I hired those men. I've had private security on the inn and the Moore property since the first threat from Goldilocks. It's my fault all this started."

"What?" Tess was the one who blinked now. "Was that what you meant when you said you would 'fix it'?"

Elliott nodded.

How much did it cost to hire people to do that? "Elliott, you didn't have to do that."

He waved her comment away. "They're on my payroll anyway. I just gave them some new scenery."

"Payroll?" Had Elliott ever said what he did for a living?

He ran a hand through his hair and sighed. "I own MacIntosh International Realty."

Tess's mouth slacked open. Jeffrey had sold a golf course through MacIntosh…in a week…to a buyer who had just bought a course in Scotland through MacIntosh. The New York City hotel she'd interned at in her first year out of college had bought a second location through MacIntosh. Big company, *very* big company. Fortune 500 company. "You…*own*…MacIntosh? The whole company, not just a franchise?"

Elliott laughed. "Started it in 1976."

"Oh…" Tess knew she was gaping like a tween fan girl.

Again, Elliott stared at LuAnn. At her head. In a way that was clearly making her uncomfortable. Tess cleared her throat. "You said something was wrong."

"Yes." He lumbered to the desk, set the pack on it, and carefully pulled out his headphones. "I must have forgotten to lock the back of my truck." He shook his head. "I never forget. It may have been open since Thursday." He pointed just above the right earpiece. "Look."

Strands of long blond hair, five or six of them, caught in the hinge.

Elliott looked again at LuAnn, and it was easy to see what he was thinking. LuAnn pushed her silvery hair away from her face. "Not me."

"I'm sorry. No, your hair is lighter. I didn't mean to accuse you. I'm just upset. So this narrows it down to…" Elliott glanced toward the ceiling. No other words were needed.

There were two women with long blond hair staying at Wayfarers Inn.

October 20, 1858

The gun didn't waver. This was a man who'd killed before.

"I've got orders to bring you both back to Charleston." He pulled back his coat to reveal a pair of iron shackles hooked to his belt. "But I ain't gonna do that. I'm just gonna take yer gold off yer hands, nice 'n easy like. Unless you try to stop me, and then I'm gonna kill you both and then take yer gold. And if either of these nice people try to stop me, I'll put an end to them too. So hand it over."

"Mine's in my coat," Jubal said, motioning with his head toward the front room.

"Sure it is." The man swung the gun at Cyrus. "You wouldn't give no gold to this—"

"Stop." Cyrus held up a weak hand. "The gold is buried."

"Where?"

"Somewhere you're never going to find it."

The man laughed, deep and throaty. "Sure shootin' I'm not goin' to find it. You are. Get up. I don't care if yer—"

Jubal made a dash for the door, knocking into the man as he dove for his holster. The man pivoted, raised the gun again, and a shot rang out. Jubal lurched back. Prudence screamed, eyes riveted on Jubal's wide, stunned eyes.

But it was the stranger who fell to the floor.

Prudence whirled around to see Cyrus holding a silver pistol.

The stranger rose on one arm. Jason and Jubal lunged at him. But a second shot shattered the silence.

Cyrus collapsed against the pillows, a crimson stain spreading across the front of his nightshirt.

Chapter Twenty-Three

The breakfast crowd was light. Tess was about to leave early for the farmers market when four men walked in. Work boots, canvas gloves. She sat them near the front window and asked what they wanted to drink.

"Coffee all around. Black," one man said. "But…before you go, I need to talk to one of the owners if possible."

"Very possible." She held out her hand and introduced herself. "How can I help you?"

One shoulder shrugged. He fingered the brim of the stained hat in his hand. "I owe you an apology. We found the dirt mound out on the Moore site. Figured it was just more treasure hunters, but it looked so much like a grave…I put the Rest In Peace sign on it. Just foolin' around. I should have fessed up right away, but I've had some dealings with Chief Mayfield and…anyway, I didn't think anyone would…"

Tess laughed. "I have a son. I understand. Thank you for clearing that up."

One more puzzle piece. She told Janice and LuAnn as she filled a basket with fresh-baked goodies then drove to the market.

After Brin left, Tess began adding fresh cinnamon rolls to their display of mini pumpkin bread loaves, snickerdoodles, and cranberry orange muffins. The clouds were receding, leaving patches of blue. Shafts of sunlight shone through, hinting at an unexpectedly glorious day to come, but Tess's thoughts were more suited to a dark day.

Felicity or Sylvia? They'd narrowed it down to two suspects. Now what? Had one of them found the gold? If so, why were they still here? If they hadn't found it, they weren't guilty of anything other than trespassing. If they had, could they actually be charged with stealing? Could they be forced to give it to the Moores if they were caught?

She was so deep in imagining possible motives and scenarios, she startled when Maybelline, her two granddaughters, and three great-grandchildren stopped in front of the table. Maybelline was smiling.

"Good morning." Tess included all six of them in her greeting as she stepped from behind the table to hug Belle and then Natalie and said hi to the kids. She offered a smile to Maybelline, who had never seemed fond of hugs.

"Morning, Tess. Looks like it's going to be a beautiful day after all, doesn't it?"

Who was this cheery woman, and what had she done with Maybelline? "Sure does."

"I've had some interesting talks with the Webers."

Now that was the old Maybelline. Direct and to the point. Was that the reason for the smile? Softening her up to get information? Tess's phone vibrated, but she ignored it. "Have they been over to see you at the museum?"

"Several times. Fascinating people. I'm—"

"Speaking of the museum"—Tess had a question she had to get in—"the shackles you used to have hanging in a shadow box…where were they found?"

"Those?" Maybelline was clearly stalling. "I think someone from the college found those years ago."

"Where?"

Maybelline tilted her head to one side. "Actually, now that I think about it, it had to have been very close to where you found the tag."

"What do you know about them?"

"Nothing really. There are some letters stamped on them."

Tess nodded. "CR. Do you know if that stands for Camellia River?"

"Hmm. Could be. I'll have to research that. Back to the Webers…I'm going to hire them to cover for me while I go on my…" She stopped, her face flushing. "I'm going to Cancun in January, and they offered to run the museum."

"They're staying that long?" Tess tried to divide her thoughts between the Webers and the shackles. If the shackles were found on the Moores' land, that meant the men sent by Vernon had made it here. Before or after Cyrus died and Jubal escaped? Had there been a confrontation?

"Apparently the Webers are rather nomadic in their retirement. They don't own a home. They generally spend their winters in Texas and the rest of the year traveling or here in Ohio where their nephew runs their—"

"Tess!" Brin ran up to her. A déjà vu moment. "Janice just called. She needs you back at the inn. I can stay here."

"What happened?" Tess lowered her voice as Maybelline sidled closer. There was no way to signal Brin to be discreet.

"One of your guests is creating some kind of a scene."

Who? And what kind of a scene? "Okay." She tried to sound calm and professional, but it wasn't easy with Maybelline straining to hear everything. "Thanks." She grabbed her purse, gave Brin a quick hug, and waved to Maybelline and gang.

She prayed as she drove the few blocks back to the inn. Prayed and tried to picture any of their guests pitching a fit or creating any kind of a scene. Of course, she didn't know the people who'd checked in this morning. Maybe a mother-daughter spat. And then it hit her—Elliott must have confronted Sylvia or Dr. White. Or both. A sinking dread settled in her gut as she parked next to the building and went in through the kitchen.

Janice looked wild-eyed as she rushed in with a tray of plates. "Thank goodness you're here. We got a busload of women, and we were just barely keeping up, and then somebody started yelling upstairs. LuAnn ran up, but she's got three tables that need to be served. Can you go up?"

"What kind of yelling?" Tess was already half sprinting to the door leading to the café, taking her jacket off as she went.

"Two women. I don't know if it's the mom and daughter or Felicity and Sylvia."

Tess wound her way through the tables, smiling at everyone. A hand grabbed her. Evelyn. "Everything all right?"

"I'm about to find out." She glanced at the stairs. She could hear muffled but loud voices. "Did you hear anything?"

"Someone screamed, 'None of this is true!' and the other person said, 'That's none of your business! Give it back.' After that it was all kind of garbled."

"Okay. Thanks." Tess ran up the steps. The voices were coming from the third floor. LuAnn stood in the hallway between Felicity and Sylvia, holding her hands out like a boxing referee. Tess zeroed in on their hair. Felicity's was shorter and lighter. Her gaze traveled down…to the fresh mud caked on Felicity's boots. "What's going on?"

Sylvia pointed at Felicity with a finger aimed at the hand in which Felicity clutched a rolled-up paper. Sylvia's bracelet jangled as her arm trembled. Tess was close enough to see a link, a small loop of metal, with nothing attached to it. Next to the space was a miniature gold pickax. "I dropped something on my way out, and she picked it up and won't give it back," Sylvia yelled.

Tess changed her impression of LuAnn's role. Not a ref, a playground attendant. "I'll take over, Lu."

LuAnn gave her an uncertain look before putting her hands to her side and sprinting down the stairs. Tess pulled her keys out of her coat pocket. "Let's go up to the fourth floor and talk this through."

Both women hesitated, and Tess tried another approach. "Much easier to come to an agreement over coffee."

"There's nothing to agree to." Sylvia's laser gaze threatened to burn holes in Felicity's face.

"Please." Tess gestured to the stairs leading to the fourth-floor apartment. "You're upsetting our guests."

Finally, Felicity agreed.

"No." Sylvia darted around Tess and ran after Felicity, catching her on the third step and ripping the paper out of her hand. It tore, and a piece fluttered to the floor.

Tess picked it up. Red and blue. Thick, shiny paper. The cover of a brochure.

Ohio Gold
A traveling exhibit of Ohio's gold history—
from the Buckeye Rovers in 1849
to present-day prospectors in the Clear Fork River

She scanned the page until she came to "*The company began its trip in April, joining thousands who traveled the overland route to California, enduring numerous hardships and the seemingly constant threat of attacks from hostile Indians. On reaching their destination, the Ohioans discovered that rich deposits of gold were extremely rare and that except for a few lucky fortune-seekers, mining required intense labor and yielded few rewards.*" If she ripped a triangle off the bottom corner, the fractions of words left in her hand would perfectly match the piece of paper they'd found when Chief Mayfield's men were digging.

She turned the paper over. Small text. One word jumped out at her: Marietta. She read the sentence out loud. "'Watch the video of the discovery of thirty pounds of gold nuggets buried along the Muskingum River in Marietta in the 1850s by two men who killed each other in their greed.'" At the very bottom were the words, "Curated by Stanley and Sylvia Weber."

Sylvia sank against the wall.

"So you're Goldilocks." Tess stated it.

Sylvia's blond ponytail brushed the wall as she shook her head. "Stanley is. It was his nickname back in his hippie days. He likes…theatrics."

Tess pushed aside the image of hippie Stanley. "You found the gold."

"No." Tears brimmed in Sylvia's eyes. "We found a piece of a grave marker. It said 1858 on it. That gave Stanley the idea of making a video for our museum. We own the Buckeye Rovers Gold Museum upstate. We…have a letter…written to James Armstrong by Genevieve Tuttle saying they never found the gold Cyrus had buried. We've had it for years. We had no idea where he'd buried it, but then we saw Elliott's post…I told my nephew to keep it quiet, but he knows someone here in Marietta, and that's how it got on the Marietta Buzz,"

Sylvia started to cry. "I'm sorry. Stanley t-took Mr. MacIntosh's metal detector, and I helped…I'm sorry. We didn't want this to turn into such a big deal. Stanley sent the message saying we'd found the gold to throw you off so you wouldn't find it before us. But I promise we didn't find—"

"We did."

"What?" Tess and Sylvia spoke over each other as they stared at Felicity.

The stairs creaked behind them. Tess turned to see Elliott trudging up to meet them.

"We just found it this morning." He held out his phone. A picture of a brown-glazed stoneware crock stamped with

Cowden & Wilcox. It lay on its side, and out of it spilled gold nuggets.

A second picture showed the contents spread on a white towel. Two nuggets were as large as the palm of Tess's hand. There was a quarter on the towel for reference. The rest ranged from quarter-sized to smaller than a dime.

"Felicity called me early this morning. She wanted to go to the Moores' with me. We focused our search on the barn area. We found the crock underground, stuck between two stone blocks in the foundation." He pointed at the picture. "There are at least ten pounds there."

"Wh-what did you do with it?" Tess looked from Elliott to Felicity and back again. Elliott didn't look triumphant, he looked angry. *And why did you come back here?* A smart thief would have run.

"Elliott took it to the Moores." Felicity shot a look at Sylvia. "I walked past the Webers' room as Sylvia was walking out last night. I heard Stanley say they knew where the gold was now and they—"

"That wasn't real!" Sylvia pulled herself away from the wall. "He was recording a video. It wasn't real. It—"

Felicity dismissed her with a wave of her hand. "I couldn't stand the thought of them using Cyrus Tuttle and Jubal Hudson's hard-earned treasure for selfish gain."

Sylvia's face deepened to scarlet. "We were not going to keep it. We only wanted to find it so we could use the video in our exhibit. We're touring Ohio with it next year, and we're competing with other exhibits for the largest museums, so we needed something new and amazing and…when we couldn't find it, Stanley decided to stage it. I didn't want to, but…"

Sylvia closed her eyes and sighed. "We had a child…cerebral palsy…he died when he was eleven. I would never, ever take anything from those children." She covered her face. "Stanley dug a hole right by where we found the piece of tombstone, and it looked so much like a grave and…A police car drove by, so Stanley quit filming and said we'd come back another time, but I had to fill in the hole because the Moores have children, and I couldn't stand the thought of one of them…"

As Tess took a step toward Sylvia, her phone rang. Thinking it might be Janice or LuAnn, she took it out of her pocket. Amy Moore. "Hi Amy."

"Tess, did you hear? Elliott found the gold and gave it to us and—" Her voice broke, and she began to cry.

LuAnn ran up the stairs followed by Janice. "Everything okay up here?"

Tess nodded. "Everything's crazy, but more than okay." She nodded to Elliott, and he motioned for LuAnn to step down the hall with him as he began to explain. Tess turned her attention back to the women. Felicity mirrored Sylvia's pose, sitting on the second step, face in hand, shoulders shaking.

Janice went to Sylvia. Tess sat next to Felicity and waited for her to calm. After a few minutes Felicity looked up, wiped her face, and gave a weak smile. "I'm okay. Really. It's just been an emotional week. My sister thought her husband was embezzling from her business, and I found out it was actually her business partner, her best friend."

Fragments of Felicity's comments and phone conversation came into focus. *This changes everything. Don't tell her what I found until I'm sure. Sometimes good news about one thing makes another thing worse.* Tess smiled as Lovely's words came back to her. *Goes to show a person should hush up and get all the facts, doesn't it?* She thought of all the people that applied to…Felicity, Elliott, Caroline, Cyrus, Jubal, Tippi…and herself.

By two o'clock on the day of the Heritage Tour the thermometer read sixty-two degrees. The river reflected a cloudless azure sky. While Brin, her mom, and Winnie finished serving their lunch patrons, the Inn Crowd hurried upstairs to change. Tess had something to do before she got dressed. On her knees in her bedroom, she slid a large oblong box out from under her bed. Tucking it under her arm, she hurried down to Lily and Lace. She knocked twice, and Tippi opened the door.

"Aren't you supposed to be getting ready?" Tippi asked.

"Aren't you?" She held out the box.

"What's this?"

"Open it."

Tippi carried it to the bed and eased the cover off the box. And gasped. "Tess. I…It's beautiful. But why?"

"Because you're an honorary member of the Inn Crowd."

Tippi's eyes filled with tears. "After all I've done to you." She pulled out a nineteenth-century style dress and fingered a pearl button. "Thank you."

"You're welcome." Tess stepped into the hallway.

"Tess?"

"Yes?"

"I've had some questions since…God made me go to church with you. That's the only way I can explain it. I didn't want to but…I couldn't not go."

Tess laughed. "That's the Holy Spirit. I call those feelings nudges, but sometimes they're more like shoves."

Tippi nodded. "Definitely a shove. Anyway, after the tour… could we have a Jesus talk? If it's not too late."

"Never too late for that talk."

Tess's long dress hung on the closet door. This time, she wasn't afraid to try it on. The scale showed a drop of six pounds. She'd just slipped into it when Janice knocked once and stepped inside, wearing her blue and green plaid dress. Tess smiled. "You look stunning."

"I think LuAnn would label that hyperbole, but thank you." Janice motioned for Tess to turn around so she could button her dress. "Look at you. I can button this with ease."

"We did good." Tess sat on her vanity stool and held out a dish of hairpins as Janice pinned on her hairpiece for her. "Let's reward ourselves with a tour of the town."

LuAnn met them in the hall wearing a pale blue dress trimmed in lace. "You two are beautiful." They walked down the steps together, laughing like college girls which, Tess realized, they still were deep inside.

Brad stood at the bottom of the stairs, snapping pictures.

"Let's wait for Tippi and get a few with her," Tess said.

LuAnn and Janice gaped at her.

Tess laughed at their shock. "I'll explain later." *After the Jesus talk.*

Elliott and Felicity sat by the fire in the lobby, deep in a hushed conversation. Felicity had declared on Monday that she was retiring. She was tired of trying to coerce people to pay for information that should be free. Elliott hadn't done a good job of hiding his happiness at her announcement. The next day he'd order a top-of-the-line metal detector for her. There was more going on between them than a mutual love of history.

The Webers came down next, dressed in Civil War attire. Stanley, in the long brown coat and hat Tess had seen once before, still seemed to have trouble making eye contact. He hadn't yet apologized or even spoken of their intentions to break into Elliott's truck or to deceive everyone around them. Tess was surprised they'd decided to stay, but it seemed Sylvia, for once, was making her wishes known. The Inn Crowd had some good talks with her in the past week, and Sylvia had apologized so often the women, and the Moores, had begged her to stop. "I don't understand how you can forgive what we did," she'd said once, opening a door for Janice to have a "Jesus talk" with her.

They all turned when Tippi came down the stairs, looking radiant in pink. Was it just a reflection from the vintage dress that lit her face? The change in Tippi had been subtle but undeniable. Tess had laughed several times when Tippi had caught herself in the middle of a snarky remark and, as she called it, "pressed rewind."

After pictures, Tippi told the women she had a surprise for them at the end of the tour. She refused to give hints.

The crowd began to gather. Tess fingered the script in her pocket and walked up to the fourth step of the stairway. She was on first. Before beginning, she smiled at familiar faces. Evelyn and Lovely, Maybelline and Axel who, to the shock of the entire town, had announced their engagement, and Margaret Ashworth from the historical society. Each of them had played a part in the recent unfolding drama.

"Ladies and gentlemen," Tess began. "Welcome to Wayfarers Inn. I'm going to give you a brief history of the inn along with a tour of our secret rooms and passageways, and then we'll get on the trolley and take a drive through Marietta, the first settlement in the Northwest Territory, with stops at the Castle House, the Marietta Underground Railroad Museum, and Historic Harmar Village. Our last stop will be at the location of the Moore House, where you can see the progress of the home you are helping to build. After that, we invite you all to join us for a heritage meal of soups and biscuits originally served in this building in the 1850s."

That was her segue into the history of the inn. "Wayfarers Inn was originally called the Riverfront House. Built in 1851, the inn has played many roles in Marietta history. Hotel, warehouse, antique store, and even a chop shop in the 1950s. A hundred years before that, a woman named Prudence Willard brought men, women, and children fleeing to freedom in the North through the secret tunnel we will show you in a moment, and sheltered them in the hidden room below us. A year and a half ago we found Prudence's journal, which is now on display..."

The tour of the inn took forty-five minutes. They boarded the trolley, and it was LuAnn's turn to narrate the history of the town founded by the Ohio Company of Associates in 1788. By five o'clock, with the sun low on the horizon, they gathered beside the framed-out house. Jerry and Amy and their children stood in stunned silence as the crowd grew to include many who hadn't been on the trolley tour.

The two-gallon glass jar Tess had set on a makeshift table made from a sheet of plywood across two sawhorses filled until Janice had to take the cover off so they could pack the money down to make more space. Amy Moore fought a losing battle with her tears as she thanked the crowd. One hand on Jerry's shoulder, she ended with, "When your trust is in the Author of Life, nothing can touch you that is not for His glory. What we originally saw as tragedy has turned, in His hands and with the help of your generosity, into our greatest blessing."

It was Janice's turn to share what they knew of Cyrus and Jubal's story. When she finished and was about to tell the tour members to get back on the trolley, Tippi appeared from the back of the crowd. She introduced herself. "I work for a company that creates family trees. Our genealogical research takes us all over the world. This time, it led me to some dear old friends right here in Marietta to uncover the story of Jubal Hudson's escape to freedom. I'd like to introduce one of my clients."

A dark-skinned man walked out of the crowd. "Good afternoon."

Tippi introduced Dr. Reuben R. Walsh who said, "Recently, with the invaluable help of a descendant of Cyrus Tuttle's brother..." He gestured toward the crowd and, to Tess's astonishment, Caroline Tuttle stepped out. Though Caroline had finally agreed to enter into a free exchange of information, this was a surprise. "...we now have a fairly detailed picture of Jubal's journey and Cyrus's heroic death as he took a bullet to save the life of a man who had once been his slave but became his brother.

"Jubal's story did not end with his escape to freedom. Exactly one hundred and fifty-two years ago, on October 26, 1867, Jubal Hudson, his wife Miriam, and Cyrus Tuttle's sister, Genevieve, met here in Marietta to honor Cyrus. They began by donating a portion of the gold Jubal took with him to Canada to the Marietta Children's Home, a cause near to the heart of Prudence Willard. They then came here and, along with the Willards, erected a headstone on Cyrus's grave, on which Jubal hung the slave tag he no longer wore because of Cyrus.

"We don't know the exact location of the grave, but today we join Jubal and Genevieve in honoring Cyrus." He gestured toward a construction truck, and it slowly backed away. Behind it stood a marble platform that supported the repaired tombstone.

When the clapping died down, a woman Tess had never met stepped forward with Evelyn right behind her. The woman introduced herself as Patricia Harken. "I represent a group of people who once lived at the Marietta Children's Home. In the past few years, thanks to the internet, many of us have reconnected. When we heard the story of Jubal Hudson donating a large portion of his find from the gold fields of California to the children's home back in 1867 in honor of his dear friend Cyrus Tuttle, we all remembered the name." Evelyn held up the plaque. The woman turned to face Jerry and Amy and slipped a folded check into the overstuffed glass jar. "We would be honored if you would accept this gift from all of us and hang this plaque in your new dining room in honor of the man who sacrificed right here, for his friend."

Arms around each other, Tess, LuAnn, Janice, and Tippi stood shoulder to shoulder, grinning through joyful tears. Tess leaned toward Tippi. "I can't believe Caroline's here."

Tippi grinned. "Turns out she's actually a pretty nice person."

"Huh. Who knew?" Tess winked at Tippi. *Goes to show a person should hush up and get all the facts, doesn't it?*

Over the backdrop of clapping, LuAnn looked from Tess to Janice and whispered, "Hey, who won the friendly competition?"

Janice patted her waistline. "We both did." She pulled a check out of her pocket and slipped it into the jar.

Tess added her money to the overstuffed jar and then reached out to include Tippi in a group hug.

It was, after all, what friends do.

Dear Reader,

This is the third book I've written for the Secrets of Wayfarers Inn series, and I'm starting to think of the Inn Crowd as close friends.

Research for this series was so much fun, beginning with a trip to Marietta while I wrote *Family Secrets.* For *Hushed October,* I couldn't let my Ohio sisters have all the metal-detecting fun—I had to try it myself! My son Aaron instructed me, and we spent a fun day digging up a (very forgiving!) friend's yard. We found a few wheat pennies, an old hinge, and a spoon that inspired me to include Prudence's sugar spoon as a find. The most interesting thing we found was a small metal art deco-motif lipstick tube from the forties or fifties. When we first pulled it out of the ground, I assumed it was a bullet shell. I'm so glad we took the time to rub the dirt off instead of casting it aside.

As Tess discovered, the same thing applies to people. I've been guilty of distancing myself from someone because they rubbed me the wrong way when what I really needed to do was dig a little deeper and try to really get to know that person. Sometimes, as with Cyrus and Jubal, that's all it takes to begin transforming a difficult relationship into a lasting friendship. As Lovely would say, "Goes to show a person should hush up and get all the facts, doesn't it?"

I hope you've enjoyed your time with Tess, Janice, LuAnn, and Prudence as much as I have, and I hope you've been challenged, as I have, to consider what it takes to be the kind of friend that Christ calls us to be…the kind that lives out “no greater love…”

Blessings,
Becky Melby

About the Author

Wisconsin author Becky Melby and her husband have four married sons and fifteen grandchildren. When not writing, reading, or spoiling grandkids, Becky may be found plotting and brainstorming on the back of their Honda Gold Wing or traveling the country with their camper. Connect with Becky at: beckymelby.com or on her Facebook Author Page at: facebook.com/Becky-Melby-Author-Page-147542291976020

Catherine Fay and the Washington County Children's Home

Prudence is, of course, fictional, but Catherine Fay isn't. In 1838, at the age of sixteen, Catherine Fay attended Marietta College and became a teacher. After teaching in Marietta for a short time, she traveled west to Oklahoma to teach at a mission school for Choctaw Indians. For board and an annual salary of $100.00, she remained at that position for ten years.

In the fall of 1853, while serving as a missionary among the Choctaw Indians, a physician asked her to visit a poor family. The mother had died leaving five small children, and the doctor wished for Catherine to adopt a beautiful two-year-old girl. Catherine would have loved nothing more but felt it would be very impractical for a single woman on her salary to attempt raising a child. The little girl was taken in by a couple who sold whiskey to the Indians. One day there was a drunken fight, and the child was thrown down the steps of the house and killed. This tragedy affected Catherine so deeply that she determined to secure a home of her own where she could care for homeless children. From that time on, she saved every dollar she could.

Catherine returned to Marietta in 1857, where she purchased twelve acres of land at Moss Run, about ten miles east of Marietta. On April 1, 1858, she moved with nine orphaned children, all of them under ten years of age, into a small two-room house on the land. The first few weeks were very difficult. When she took five of her children to the district school, sixteen men barred their entry. They told her she could not send her "little paupers" to school with their children. Catherine promptly went to Marietta where she petitioned the Washington County Court to gain legal guardianship of the children. She won the lawsuit and obtained permission to send the children to school, but still the children were taunted and treated poorly.

With an unexpected inheritance and credit extended by a contractor, Catherine built a twenty-room structure at a cost of $2000.00. Then, in 1867, a 100-acre farm near Marietta was purchased for $18,000 by the Washington County Commissioners. The Washington County Children's Home operated through the 1960s, and Catherine's radical ideas became the blueprint for establishing children's homes all around Ohio. The Ohio Children's Home Law became the model that was eventually enacted throughout the United States. Today, the Washington County Complex that houses the historical society stands at the site of Catherine's children's home.

When I think of the character traits needed to accomplish what Catherine Fay achieved, I can't help but believe that if our Prudence lived in reality and not just in our imaginations, she would have had the courage and tenacity to join forces with her. Though Catherine met with much opposition, I think Prudence would have been one of her champions…a true friend.

Something Delicious from our Wayfarers Inn Friends

Winnie's Unstuffed Cabbage Roll Soup

Servings: 6 2-cup servings
Calories: 242 per serving

Ingredients

- 1 pound extra lean ground beef
- 1 medium yellow onion, chopped
- 3 garlic cloves, minced
- 5 cups chopped green cabbage
- 4 cups beef broth
- 3 cups tomato sauce
- 1 cup shredded carrots
- ½ cup uncooked white or brown long grain rice
- 2 dried bay leaves
- 3 tablespoons packed brown sugar
- 1 teaspoon salt
- ½ teaspoon dried oregano leaves
- ½ teaspoon ground black pepper
- 1½ teaspoon lemon juice

Instructions

1. Put beef in large soup pot and place over medium-high heat. Break beef apart with a wooden spoon. Add onion. Cook about 8 minutes until beef is brown, stirring occasionally.

2. Add garlic. Stir and cook 1 minute.
3. Add cabbage, beef broth, tomato sauce, carrots, rice, bay leaves, brown sugar, salt, oregano, and pepper.
4. Bring to boil. Reduce heat to simmer and cover. Cook until rice is tender (25 minutes for white rice and 45 minutes for brown rice).
5. Remove from heat. Stir in lemon juice. Remove bay leaves and allow to rest for 10 minutes before serving.

Read on for a sneak peek of another exciting book in the Secrets of Wayfarers Inn series!

BEFORE IT'S TOO LATE

by Kathleen Y'Barbo

Forget December. November was by far the busiest month of the year.

Janice Eastman absolutely adored the holidays. From the first hint of fall in the air until the last bell was rung at midnight on New Year's Day, she loved every minute of it.

When her husband was living, she would make sure that everything in their home, a lovely parsonage adjacent to the church where he was senior pastor, was decorated just so. That careful attention to detail also made its way into the church where she either hung decorations or supervised their hanging in every nook and cranny of the building.

Thanksgiving decorations ranged from beautiful pumpkins and horns of plenty filled with fall foliage to a quilted banner she sewed herself and hung in the entryway of the parsonage. Close on the heels of the annual city-wide Thanksgiving festivities came the Christmas season, which generally meant clearing out the fall decorations while the leftover pumpkin pie still languished in the fridge to make way for the celebration of Christ's birth.

From beautiful red poinsettias in every room to fragrant greenery draped wherever she could find a place for it, she never failed to create a festive atmosphere. Now that she was a widow, and a lovely young couple had taken up residence in the parsonage along with their little one, Janice translated that affinity for the holidays to other outlets—and other beneficiaries, namely her best friends Tess Wallace and LuAnn Sherrill.

Though the trio had only owned Wayfarers Inn for a short time, Janice found it difficult to recall most of what life was like prior to moving to the inn's top floor. Some of it she couldn't help but recall. Losing her husband and finding a void that had been impossible to fill was the one memory that would never fade. Moving in with her daughter and searching for what God wanted as she faced widowhood was another.

Oh, but God had blessed her so wonderfully with friends and a purpose, even though that void where her husband used to be would never be filled completely. Last year her grief had been too fresh, but this year she determined to at least begin a very special banner to honor the holidays. Made from her husband's Christmas ties, the quilted banner would not only brighten up the inn's lobby, but it would also bring a little of the past into the present.

But first she had to get through Thanksgiving.

She lifted her attention from the ancient Betty Crocker cookbook on the counter in front of her to watch Winnie Washington, the inn's cook, effortlessly stirring the three simmering pots in front of her. Standing in front of Big Red, the inn's massive antique red stove, Winnie looked like a conductor directing an orchestra. First the saucepan, then the soup pot, then back to the frying pan she went, her strong arms never pausing.

"Janice, you're woolgathering again," Winnie said before turning to face her. "What's the matter?"

The question flustered her. "Nothing and everything," she finally admitted.

Winnie swiveled to adjust the knobs on the stove and then moved over to pour two cups of coffee. She perched on a stool opposite Janice and slid one of the mugs toward her.

"All right," she told Janice. "Spill, and I don't mean the coffee."

Janice smiled in spite of herself. "How is it you always know such things, Winnie?"

Her friend shrugged and took a sip of coffee. "You're stalling. Something wrong?"

"I'm just tired," she said. "Busy. Maybe a little overwhelmed."

Winnie just sat quietly and sipped her coffee while the delicious scents from the stove swirled around them. Janice gathered her thoughts and then picked up her mug.

"What happened to the days when we had Thanksgiving before Christmas?" she mused. "I love celebrating Christmas as much as the next person, but the decorating committee had us out hanging tinsel and lights in downtown Marietta before the end of October this year. And the Christmas parade is two days after Thanksgiving. We won't even be rid of the leftover turkey by then."

"I agree," Winnie said, her voice soft and silky against the quiet of the morning. "They do tend to rush things nowadays, but that's not limited to the holidays." She paused. "Is that all that's bothering you today?"

Janice glanced one more time at the cookbook, now open to a pumpkin pie recipe that she could recite by heart after more than forty years of making it. She closed the book and traced the ragged edge of the red-checked cover with her index finger.

"Can't we just slow down?" Janice met Winnie's comforting look. "I know we can't, not really, but what's the harm in trying?"

"No harm at all," she said. "Unless you happen to own an inn that is fully booked for the entire month and has a waiting list the week of Thanksgiving. And don't forget we are also contributing to the city-wide meal."

"And entering a float in the Christmas parade two days after Thanksgiving," Janice quipped. At the sight of Winnie's wide eyes and open mouth, she hurried to amend her statement. "I guess I hadn't mentioned that part, had I?"

"No," Winnie said. "I would've remembered if you had."

"It'll be a simple float just like we did for the Fourth of July parade before the inn opened. Since Jeff Jr.'s truck is red, it'll be the perfect parade float. I'll drape the Christmas quilt we usually hang on the upstairs railing over the tailgate, and we'll put a big wreath with a red bow on the front of the truck. No fuss, and it will be adorable."

The kitchen door burst open, and Tess hurried inside. LuAnn followed on her heels. Both went straight for the coffeepot.

"What will be adorable?" Tess asked as she set two mugs on the counter and then stepped back to allow LuAnn to pour.

"Oh, we're just talking about the inn's float in the Marietta Christmas parade," Winnie said with a grin.

"We are entering a float in the parade?" LuAnn said. "I had no idea."

"Nor did I," Tess said, "but it sounds like fun."

"I'm sorry," Janice said as her best friends joined them at the table. "It all happened while we were working on the decorations for downtown. I told you I couldn't be trusted to attend a Christmas event so early in the season. I get way too enthusiastic."

LuAnn reached over to pat Janice on the arm. "There is nothing wrong with enthusiasm. Exactly what have you—or rather we—committed to?"

"Just a float in the parade," she said. "I thought we could keep it simple and do something similar to last year's Fourth of July parade only swap the red, white, and blue quilt for a red and green one. Put a wreath on the front, and Jeff Jr.'s red truck is a parade float."

"With one big difference. Instead of melting into a puddle in the July heat, the three of us will be freezing in the back," Tess said.

"That's true," Janice said. "I don't suppose it's too late to pull out."

"No," LuAnn and Tess said in unison.

"It will be great," Tess added. "Weather permitting, we can have the grandkids ride too. Maybe have candy or trinkets they could toss out to the spectators. They will love that."

Janice smiled. "You're right. Larry would love that."

"Then it's settled," LuAnn said as she opened her ever-present notebook and reached for her pen. "We'll do the parade. And if it's too cold, we will just dress up in something warm enough to get us all the way down Main Street without turning into popsicles."

"Oh, we'll all be popsicles when we're done, I guarantee," Tess said, "but it will still be fun. I wouldn't miss it for the world."

"Well, you all can count me out," Winnie said. "I will be far too busy back here at the inn keeping the soup and wassail warm so my popsicles can come back and thaw out."

"So when is the parade exactly?" LuAnn said, her pen poised to write the information on her calendar.

"The Saturday morning after Thanksgiving," Janice told them.

"What?" Tess said. "So soon? It won't even be December. What's the rush?"

Janice shrugged. "Exactly what Winnie and I were just talking about. Next thing you know we'll go straight from Fourth of July to trim-the-tree without blinking."

"Well, I don't like it," Tess declared.

"But what can you do about it?" Winnie said.

Janice grinned as a thought occurred. "I know what I'm going to do about it. I am going to declare this month a Thanksgiving-only month." She shrugged. "Okay, except for what we absolutely have to do to get ready for the parade, which is really to just make sure Jeff Jr. has the old truck running and that we can find a nice wreath for the front."

"And the Christmas decorations for the inn," LuAnn reminded her. "Our guests will expect it."

"Our guests can wait until the first day of December," Tess said. "I think Janice is onto something here. We rush through a season of giving thanks in order to get to a season where we wear ourselves out giving gifts. I think we need to be intentional about doing something different this year."

"Like what?" LuAnn said.

Both women looked to Janice as if she had the answer. Her phone rang, giving Janice a brief reprieve. She pulled her phone from her pocket and saw her son's name.

"It's Stuart. I should get this." She shook her head as she fumbled with her car keys. "Stuart, it's the middle of the morning. You should be at work."

"Mom," he said slowly. "Are you sitting down?"

A Note from the Editors

We hope you enjoy Secrets of Wayfarers Inn, created by the Books and Inspirational Media Division of Guideposts, a nonprofit organization that touches millions of lives every day through products and services that inspire, encourage, help you grow in your faith, and celebrate God's love in every aspect of your daily life.

Thank you for making a difference with your purchase of this book, which helps fund our many outreach programs to military personnel, prisons, hospitals, nursing homes, and educational institutions. To learn more, visit Guideposts Foundation.org.

We also maintain many useful and uplifting online resources. Visit Guideposts.org to read true stories of hope and inspiration, access OurPrayer network, sign up for free newsletters, download free e-books, join our Facebook community, and follow our stimulating blogs.

To learn about other Guideposts publications, including the best-selling devotional *Daily Guideposts,* go to ShopGuideposts .org, call (800) 932-2145, or write to Guideposts, PO Box 5815, Harlan, Iowa 51593.